Berkley Prime Crime titles by Mary Stanton

DEFENDING ANGELS
ANGEL'S ADVOCATE
AVENGING ANGELS
ANGEL'S VERDICT

Titles by Mary Stanton writing as Claudia Bishop

Hemlock Falls Mysteries

A TASTE FOR MURDER
A DASH OF DEATH
A PINCH OF POISON
MURDER WELL-DONE
DEATH DINES OUT
A TOUCH OF THE GRAPE
A STEAK IN MURDER
MARINADE FOR MURDER
JUST DESSERTS
FRIED BY JURY
A PUREE OF POISON
BURIED BY BREAKFAST
A DINNER TO DIE FOR
GROUND TO A HALT
A CAROL FOR A CORPSE
TOAST MORTEM

The Casebooks of Dr. McKenzie Mysteries

THE CASE OF THE ROASTED ONION
THE CASE OF THE TOUGH-TALKING TURKEY
THE CASE OF THE ILL-GOTTEN GOAT

Anthologies

A PLATEFUL OF MURDER
DEATH IN TWO COURSES

ANGEL'S
Verdict

Mary Stanton

BERKLEY PRIME CRIME, NEW YORK

THE BERKLEY PUBLISHING GROUP
Published by the Penguin Group
Penguin Group (USA) Inc.
375 Hudson Street, New York, New York 10014, USA

Penguin Group (Canada), 90 Eglinton Avenue East, Suite 700, Toronto, Ontario M4P 2Y3, Canada
(a division of Pearson Penguin Canada Inc.)
Penguin Books Ltd., 80 Strand, London WC2R 0RL, England
Penguin Group Ireland, 25 St. Stephen's Green, Dublin 2, Ireland (a division of Penguin Books Ltd.)
Penguin Group (Australia), 250 Camberwell Road, Camberwell, Victoria 3124, Australia
(a division of Pearson Australia Group Pty. Ltd.)
Penguin Books India Pvt. Ltd., 11 Community Centre, Panchsheel Park, New Delhi—110 017, India
Penguin Group (NZ), 67 Apollo Drive, Rosedale, North Shore 0632, New Zealand
(a division of Pearson New Zealand Ltd.)
Penguin Books (South Africa) (Pty.) Ltd., 24 Sturdee Avenue, Rosebank, Johannesburg 2196,
South Africa

Penguin Books Ltd., Registered Offices: 80 Strand, London WC2R 0RL, England

This is a work of fiction. Names, characters, places, and incidents either are the product of the author's imagination or are used fictitiously, and any resemblance to actual persons, living or dead, business establishments, events, or locales is entirely coincidental. The publisher does not have any control over and does not assume any responsibility for author or third-party websites or their content.

ANGEL'S VERDICT

A Berkley Prime Crime Book / published by arrangement with the author

PRINTING HISTORY
Berkley Prime Crime mass-market edition / February 2011

Copyright © 2011 by Mary Stanton.
Cover illustration by Kimberly Schamber.
Cover design by Rita Frangie.
Interior text design by Laura K. Corless.

ISBN: 978-0-425-23987-2

BERKLEY® PRIME CRIME
Berkley Prime Crime Books are published by The Berkley Publishing Group,
a division of Penguin Group (USA) Inc.,
375 Hudson Street, New York, New York 10014.
BERKLEY® PRIME CRIME and the PRIME CRIME logo are trademarks of Penguin Group (USA) Inc.

PRINTED IN THE UNITED STATES OF AMERICA

10 9 8 7 6 5 4 3 2 1

For Sally, Bud, and Phoebe

Author's Note

I have taken liberties with the geography of that most beautiful of cities, Savannah, Georgia, for the purpose of this novel. My apologies to her citizens.

Neither the characters nor situations in this novel are based on actual events.

Cast of Characters

The Winston-Beauforts

Brianna "Bree" Winston-Beaufort . . . appeals attorney for dead souls

Antonia Winston-Beaufort . . . Bree's sister, an aspiring actress

Royal Winston-Beaufort . . . Bree's adoptive father

Francesca Winston-Beaufort . . . Bree's adoptive mother

Cecilia "Cissy" Carmichael . . . Francesca's sister, Bree and Antonia's aunt

Franklin Winston-Beaufort . . . deceased, Royal's uncle

The Company of Angels
(Angelus Street Office)

Lavinia Mather . . . Bree's landlady

Ronald Parchese . . .Bree's secretary

Petru Lucheta . . .Bree's paralegal

Armand Cianquino . . . director, retired law professor

Gabriel . . . the enforcer

Sasha . . . a guard dog

Cast of Characters

Some Citizens of Savannah (1952)

Haydee Quinn . . . a dancer at the Tropicana Tide nightclub

William "Bagger Bill" Norris . . . gangster-owner, Tropicana Tide nightclub

Alexander Bulloch II . . . son of Alexander and Consuelo Bulloch

Consuelo Bulloch . . . matriarch of the Bulloch family

Lt. Edward O'Malley . . . homicide detective

Sgt. Robert E. Lee Kowalski . . . homicide detective

And others

Some Citizens of Savannah (present day)

John Stubblefield . . . law partner, Stubblefield, Marwick

Payton McAllister . . . associate lawyer, Stubblefield, Marwick

Emerald "EB" Billingsley . . . secretary, Bree's Bay Street office

Sam Hunter . . . lieutenant, Chatham County Sheriff's Department, homicide division

Cordelia Eastburn . . . Chatham County District Attorney

Sgt. Robert E. Lee Kowalski (ret.) . . . a resident of Sweet Briar Adult Care Facility

Samantha Rose Waterman, nee Bulloch . . . granddaughter of Consuelo Bulloch

Marian Lee Cicerone, nee Bulloch . . . granddaughter of Consuelo Bulloch

Alexandra "Dixie" Bulloch . . . granddaughter of Consuelo Bulloch

Megan Lowry, MD . . . a pathologist

Cast of Characters

Eric Causton, MD . . . an orthopedist
And others

Some Members of the Celestial Courts

Goldstein . . . a recording angel
Beazley . . . attorney for the Opposition
Caldecott . . . attorney for the Opposition
Some Employees of Sundowner Productions, Inc.

On the set of the movie *Bitter Tide*

Vincent Victor White . . . a producer
Phillip Mercury . . . director
Tyra Steele . . . actress in the role of Haydee Quinn
George Adderly . . . actor in the role of Bagger Bill
  Norris
Hatch Lewis . . . actor in the role of Alex Bulloch
Justine Coville . . . actress in the role of Consuelo
  Bulloch
Craig Oliver . . . actor in the role of Lt. Edward
  O'Malley
Florida "Flurry" Smith . . . scriptwriter
William Dent . . . driver for hire

Prologue

Fireworks on the Savannah River: a starburst of vermillion, gold, and blue cascaded through the inky night, the colors drifting to oblivion on the breeze that came off the midnight water. The crowd gathered on the cobblestone walk along the banks sighed, and sighed again as three more rockets went off in quick succession, showering glitter with careless exuberance. Here and there along the cobblestone street, a scatter of bonfires thrust a fierce orange glow against the shadows.

One of the fires was moving.

Lt. Edward O'Malley, shoulders resting against the warehouse wall, hands shoved into his trouser pockets, pushed his hat a little further back on his head and narrowed his eyes. He was off duty, after a sleepless twenty-four-hour stretch on the Haydee Quinn murder. So what he was seeing wasn't real. It was a fragment of nightmare, borne of fatigue. A hallucination. There was a pint

1

of rye in the inside pocket of his suit coat; as he reached for it, the screams started: just one, at first, the startled shriek of a horrified woman; then a shout; then the confused clamor of a terrified horde of people.

The blazing fire moved on. The flames billowed up from the handcart; some part of O'Malley's mind registered it as a baler wagon, maybe from the Cotton Exchange up on Bay Street. And he knew the man who pushed it. The cart bumped awkwardly along the cobbled street, the wheels groaning over the uneven bricks. The youngster behind it cried out a long, continuous mourning keen, a wail of grief, his head thrown back, and his mouth wide open to the dark sky above. Alexander Bulloch. Haydee's lover. A briefly considered suspect in Haydee's death, until Bagger Bill Norris confessed and the case was done.

The stench from the cart was overwhelming: a roasted stink of flesh corrupted by flame. The iron wheels groaned, skidded, and the cart tipped over, throwing flaming logs across the stones. A blackened human form hung halfway from the cart. The flames hadn't yet consumed the hair, which stirred in the wind as if lifted by a loving hand. Black as a crow's wing, black as a starless night, no longer scented with gardenias, but the scent of burning. Haydee's hair. Haydee herself hung from the cart, the violet eyes now sockets in her grinning skull, the creamy skin now flaked into ash.

O'Malley turned and ran up the iron steps, as if pursued by the corpse itself.

One

My age is as a lusty winter, frosty, but kindly.
—*As You Like It*, William Shakespeare

"Alexander Bulloch was insane with grief," Justine Coville said. "I was a mere child at the time, of course, but the murder made all the newspapers. I'd always been exceptionally sensitive to the adult world, even then. I remember the headlines as clearly as I see this law office where I'm sitting right now. Alexander snatched the body from the funeral home. Said her ghost had come to him and demanded the purification by flame. So he set her body afire." She closed her eyes dramatically, with a faraway expression, as if looking back sixty years ago. "And all that remained of the body was her long black hair, black as a crow's wing, black as a starless night." She sat back in the visitor's chair. "What do you think of that, Miss Winston-Beaufort?"

There was only one visitor's chair. Bree and her secretary Emerald Billingsley didn't have much of a furniture budget. Bree's desk, a small bookshelf, and the client's chair were set behind the rattan screen that partitioned the small office into two separate spaces. Bree had the window. EB's desk faced the office door, which was the old-fashioned type, with frosted glass on the upper half.

"It's a terrible story!" Bree said. She knew that on the other side of the screen, EB was listening just as hard as she was. Justine Coville's acting career stretched back more than fifty-five years, and the old lady knew how to hold an audience. She was a . . . Bree searched her mind for a tactful adjective—remarkable-looking woman. She favored bright red lipstick and startling blue eye shadow, and patronized an overenthusiastic plastic surgeon. The effect would have been a little ghoulish if it weren't for the intelligence in her faded blue eyes. "What happened to Alexander, then? And Haydee's body? Was it completely burned up?"

Justine shook her head. "There was enough to bury, certainly. She's over in Belle Glade with a tasteless memorial. A huge marble angel. Of all the beings who may be watching over Haydee Quinn, an angel is the least likely. Of course, since this is Savannah, the most haunted city in the nation, there were those who believed Alexander Bulloch about the visitations from her spirit. There was enough talk about Haydee's witchy charms when she was alive, so everyone was more than ready to believe she would come back from the dead and tell Alexander what to do. All those men in her life, my dear! In those days, she made quite a scandal. Folks didn't think it was natural. So it stood to reason, so the

Savannah gossip went, if anyone could come back from the dead, it would be she."

"Which meant the powers that be didn't come down too hard on Alexander about stealing Haydee's body and giving it a Viking sort of funeral," Bree guessed.

"I doubt they would have in any event," Justine said candidly. "Alex was a Bulloch, after all. The family doesn't mean much nowadays, of course. Alexander senior, Alex's father, didn't have a lick of sense about agribusiness. Switched from hogs to tobacco in 1961 just before the surgeon general's report. It was all downhill from there. But back in the '50s, the family had money, and money means clout. He told Judge Franklin—your great-uncle, of course, who is the man who brought you and me together after all—that she appeared to him three times, begging him to consign her bones to the fire."

Bree doodled pensively on her yellow pad. She didn't know if her own last three clients had been ghosts or not, but they definitely had been dead. She knew better than most that Haydee could have visited her grieving lover from beyond the grave. As for Franklin himself . . . "Surely not *Judge* Franklin then," Bree said mildly. "He wouldn't have been more than thirty years old. He wasn't named to the bench until the late '70s."

"I believe the family retained him to represent Alex at the commitment hearing."

"Alexander claimed an insanity defense?" Bree sat up. Franklin's other law practice, the hidden one, specialized in handling appeals for dead souls condemned to Hell. She knew that to her cost. She'd inherited his practice after he died. She'd inherited this one, too, with its office on Bay Street for the convenience of his mortal caseload.

"That the boy was mad—temporarily at least—was the only possible interpretation of his bizarre behavior. The family had better sense than to claim he was actually visited by a ghost," Justine continued cheerily. "They wanted to send the poor young man away to the booby hatch in lieu of a prison sentence. A private sanatorium. I suppose it would be called rehab these days. Either way, it'd be nothing so non-PC as booby hatch, would it?" Her crimson lips stretched in an over-collagened smile. "He got out after a year or two and eventually married one of the Bulloch cousins. Maria? Madeline? Something like that. She was from Charleston, I believe. They had the three daughters, Samantha Rose Bulloch, who is a Waterman now; Alexandria Charles Bulloch, who never married; and Marian Lee Cicerone. Some dago name like that."

Bree winced at the slur.

The old lady continued merrily on. "Yes, Marian Lee married down, as they say. Alexander had a pretty successful career as a mortgage broker in the family bank. That part isn't in Phillip's script, of course. Too *ordinaire* for the movies."

Behind the bamboo divider that separated her corner of the Bay Street office from her assistant's, Bree heard Mrs. Emerald Billingsley start to type on her computer keyboard again. Then, because the body in the handcart seemed a weird conclusion to an equally weird story, (and because she was sure EB was dying to know, too) she asked, "Did he ever say why Haydee asked him to burn her body?"

"Purification," said EB from behind the screen. "Stands to reason. Isn't that what that Alex said?"

"Poor deluded boy," Justine said with a dismissive air. "If there was ever a sane reason, I didn't hear of it myself. Phillip's script has some hoodoo explanation that makes very little sense at all." Then, "Do come around that screen and see me, young woman. I'm not fond of spectral voices at the best of times."

There was a sound of a chair being hastily shoved back, and in a moment, EB's face appeared around the edge of the screen. She smiled. "Been a long time since anyone's called me a young woman, Ms. Coville. Thank you. And I do beg your pardon, Ms. Beaufort. And yours, Ms. Coville. Couldn't help but listen in." She wore an old but neatly ironed beige suit and a carefully starched white shirt with a handmade ribbon collar. Her Afro was combed in a perfect neat puff around her head. "It's your voice. Just like listening to music. Don't know anyone doesn't like to listen to music. And you have a way of telling a story, Ms. Coville. You surely do." Her eyes, brown and shamelessly guileless, met Bree's green and skeptical ones. "Was your voice something you had as a baby? Or did it come on a bit later, like? I remember you on that cop series on TV. I wondered about that beautiful voice of yours then, and I wonder about it now."

"Years of stage training, Mrs. Billingsley. I began on the stage, you know."

"That is something," EB said. She edged a little further into the area. "Really something. On the stage, you say? Now, how'd you get from the stage to this TV movie they're making down on the river?"

Justine waved an arthritic hand toward the corner. "Perhaps you'd like to bring a chair and hear a little bit about it? If you don't mind, Miss Winston-Beaufort."

Bree didn't mind. Clearly, EB didn't, either. Usually EB had firm views about being professional—and gossip rated high on her list of what was unprofessional—but she was as interested in the activities of Sundowner Productions as anyone else in Savannah. They wouldn't charge the old lady for time spent listening to reminiscing. It wasn't as if mortal, paying clients were beating down the door to the Bay Street office anyway. Bree's alternate office at 666 Angelus, which was just around the corner, had another set of problems altogether. There was no shortage of souls wanting to reverse their sentences to Hell; but those cases didn't pay the bills.

Something else nagged at Bree; Justine Coville didn't behave like a client who had accomplished what she'd come in for. There was something else on the elderly actress's mind. Whatever it was, Bree hoped she'd get around to it soon.

EB stretched out one hefty arm, pulled her desk chair into sight, and sank into it with a grateful sigh (which meant, Bree knew, that her feet were bothering her again).

Justine smiled at her audience. "My initial training, of course, was for the theater. Of course you are aware that in the current climate . . ." She paused, one eyebrow raised. "But surely you don't want to hear about all this."

EB quirked her own eyebrows encouragingly. "I surely would."

"Well, the current theater has this maniacal emphasis on youth. Any actress over forty will tell you how hard it is to get decent parts these days. It doesn't seem quite fair. My early days were hard enough, and then to end them with a small but telling role in a made-for-TV movie . . ." She let a shadow come and go over her face. EB murmured in sympathy. "I'm sure you know what I mean, Mrs. Billingsley. It was hard for your people, too. In a different way, naturally. But both of us, you and I, having to take jobs we weren't suited for. Jobs that were quite beneath us, just to make ends meet."

Bree bridled a little at the term "your people," but if EB wasn't going to call Justine on it, neither would she.

EB said, "Isn't it the truth."

"Of course, you can't get anywhere without a bit of talent, too," Justine said modestly.

"And hard work," EB said.

"*Very* hard work. Now for women? Women in the acting profession, there's a prejudice even harder to combat than color, Mrs. Billingsley. Especially for actresses who'll admit to being a little over sixty." She paused.

"Sixty? Never!" EB said, right on cue. She caught Bree's eye and winked. "You don't look a day over forty. Not a day."

Bree murmured, "A-hum!" in spurious, but kindly, agreement. She sneaked a look at her watch. Almost noon. EB had scheduled an hour's appointment beginning at eleven. Bree had to meet her sister, Antonia, at home for a quick lunch and then get on to the Angelus office.

Justine patted her artfully streaked hair. "One has to work at it."

Justine was one of the first of Franklin's former clients to make an appointment. She'd called in response to the letters EB had sent out announcing Bree's assumption of the Bay Street practice. Like Bree, the judge had two case loads, one mortal, one not. Franklin's files on his mortal clients were scrupulously accurate: Justine's stated purpose was to come in and make changes to her will. The changes were minor. Bree had wondered at first if the old lady was merely bored and looking for a way to spend some time. This was fine with Bree. Justine's birth date was January 1930, which made her exactly eighty this month. She was a gallant old lady—her attempts at looking young with the outlandish makeup and too much plastic surgery were brave stands against the erosions of time. Regardless of what she said about her difficulties in the business, Justine was pleased with her part in the movie being made about the 1952 murder of Haydee Quinn the B-girl. She reported to the set every day, despite the severe arthritis that gnarled her wrists, hands, and ankles. She deserved a little slack.

Besides, there was that nagging sense that something

else was on her mind. Bree sat back and prepared to listen.

"There's no getting around the fact that I'm older than the current kingpins would like. Fortunately, people like Phillip Mercury are not ageists. Phillip Mercury is interested in talent and talent alone."

"I heard that," EB said disingenuously. "Sundowner Productions is his company, isn't it?"

"His and the bank's," Justine answered cynically. "Although there are a couple of backers, I believe. At any rate, dear Phillip absolutely refused to have anyone else play Consuelo Bulloch." Justine patted the pearls at her throat with an air of mild complacence. " 'It's not just that you're Savannah-born and bred,' he said to me. 'It's that aristocratic air.' "

"This Consuelo was that boy Alexander's mamma," EB said. "And you say she hated that poor Haydee like poison?"

"Worse than poison," Justine said with relish. "There were no tears from *her* when the poor girl's body was found floating in the Savannah River. One of the finest scenes in the script is when that policeman O'Malley shows up at the door of Bulloch House to tell Consuelo and her son that Haydee's been stabbed. The camera comes in for a close-up." She spread her hands on either side of her face and opened her eyes wide. Her collagen-filled lips formed an "O" of dismay. "Closer, closer, closer . . . and I'm to gaze into the distance with a purr of triumphant satisfaction. That's what the script calls for." She closed her eyes slowly and opened them again. "Like that."

Bree and EB exchanged doubtful looks. EB clapped her hands together and said, "Isn't that something? Did you catch that, Ms. Beaufort?"

"I did," Bree said. "It was great."

"Wonderful. Wonderful," EB said with kindly emphasis.

"Of course," Justine added, "*Bitter Tide* is only television, after all. Not what you would call the legitimate theater."

"I watch television," EB said. "I watch it all the time. So does Ms. Beaufort. Tell you what. Point of being a famous actress is to get your face on out there, isn't it? And how many people know you on account of that TV role you had, I mean—as that cop's mamma."

Justine sighed theatrically. "Dear old *Bristol Blues*. It will be how I'm remembered. Not for my Lady Bracknell! Not for my Medea! But for that cheesy cop series."

Bree had loved *Bristol Blues*. It'd gotten a slew of Emmys. "Craig Oliver was great in that. I had a huge crush on him when I was sixteen. He's here in town, too, isn't he?"

"Dear Craig," Justine purred. "We go way back. Charming man. He was the one who brought my suitability for the role of Consuelo to Phillip's attention. He's playing O'Malley. The police lieutenant who cracked the Haydee Quinn case. A fine actor, of course. Very fine. But never quite achieved the fame he felt he deserved after *Bristol Blues* ended." She glanced obliquely at Bree, curved her hand as if holding a glass, and tipped it toward her mouth. "And there's the liquor, of course."

"Drink," EB said. "Takes some of the finest, drink does. What a shame."

"Not nearly as disastrous as drugs." Justine shook her head. "I could tell you stories . . ."

Bree and EB maintained a hopeful (if slightly guilty) silence.

"Tyra Steele," Justine said flatly. "And Hatch Lewis, of course."

"Huh." EB let her breath out. "There's been more than a few stories about that. Is she really holding up the movie, like the papers say? And having it on with Hatch Lewis? That boy is about the best-looking thing I've seen in a long while."

"The only love affair Hatch Lewis has is with himself," Justine said dismissively. "As for Tyra. Well! Drugs took down Marilyn, took down Judy, and very nearly did for Liz." Justine settled back in her chair with a judicial air. "Tyra's not in their league, of course. I've seen high school cheerleaders with better talent, and if you think that body's a gift of God, I can give you the names of her plastic surgeons. But there's no denying she's captured the public imagination." Justine paused, crossly, and took another sip of tea. "As for casting her as Haydee . . . Phillip must have been out of his mind. According to the script, Haydee is magical. Alluring. Tyra's just tacky. As for her other behavior . . ." Justine trailed off, a grim look on her face.

"But very beautiful," Bree prompted.

Justine seemed to give herself a mental shake. "Vincent White certainly seems to think so." Justine glanced from Bree to EB. "Vincent White's one of the producers. The man has a great deal of money and very little sense. Quite insistent about casting Tyra in the part, if you understand what I'm saying."

EB chuckled. "Not much changes about this old world, does it?"

Justine's faded eyes narrowed. "Truer words were never said, Mrs. Billingsley." Her twisted hand trembled as she set her teacup down on Bree's desk. She clasped her wrist with her other hand to steady it, pretending to look at her watch. "Heavens! Is that the time?" She fumbled at the thin gold band. "Phillip will have my head on a plate if I'm not on set in two minutes. I must leave you now, I'm afraid."

Bree gave Justine a gentle assist out of her chair. "As far as your legal business is concerned, we'll get right on those revisions to your will, Mrs. Coville."

"Justine, please."

"Of course. Justine. It shouldn't take too long to update your assets. And you're sure about the changes in your beneficiaries?"

"Quite sure," she said firmly. "Dixie Bulloch has been marvelous to me. Any director will tell you that I'm an absolute fiend about research, and when I wrote to the family asking for information about Consuelo, she responded immediately. It's only right I leave her a little something. She lent me a brooch that used to belong to Consuelo. When I play real characters, I always like to have something that helps me connect to the essence of the character. Dixie said her grandmother simply cherished it. Wore it all the time and had it on when she died. They even considered burying her with it, but thank heavens they thought the better of that! I make quite a ceremony of pinning it on when I'm dressing for the part. I feel her spirit right here." She pressed her open palm against the lapels of her dark blue linen jacket.

EB handed the actress her navy clutch, her lace-trimmed handkerchief, and a neatly folded umbrella. "Are you going over to the set right now, Ms. Coville? Would you like me to call you a taxi?"

"The hire car should be waiting downstairs," Justine said. "And I'd be pleased if you'd call me Justine, Mrs. Billingsley. So many great performers can be identified that way. Sarah. Cher. Liza. Marilyn."

"Haydee," Bree pointed out with a slight smile.

Justine blinked. "Oh dear. And look what happened to the poor thing. I hadn't thought of that." She patted Bree's arm. "That's quite a good point. I find myself quite pleased that you've taken over Judge Beaufort's practice." She worked her lips for a moment. "Do you specialize in estates, my dear? I mean to say, do you handle other kinds of law?"

"We handle it all," EB said.

"Is there something else you'd like to discuss with us?" Bree asked.

"If there is, you just come right out with it," EB said. "You got a problem, we can help you with it." She walked the few feet to the office door and opened it. "Now that we've got the Bay Street office up and running, we're ready to handle a few select cases of any kind, Ms. Coville. Be sure and tell your friends about us."

"I surely will. Thank you both for your assistance. And, oh!" She lifted her chin. "I'd appreciate it if you'd bring the paperwork directly to the set."

"I'll make sure to send it by courier," EB said. "In case Ms. Beaufort's in court, or with another client. This is a growing practice, and you just never know what the day will bring."

"That's just it." Justine stood still, trembling a little, her gaze on the floor. "I never know what the next day will bring." She brought her head up and seemed to have come to a decision. "May I sit down again? I haven't been entirely candid with you about the extent of my concerns."

"Oh my," EB said. "One thing you have to be is honest with your lawyer."

Bree waited a moment and then said gently, "We'd be happy to help if we can."

"It's an ugly story." Justine brushed her hand lightly over her forehead and perched on the edge of the chair. "Those changes to my will aren't at all essential, as I'm sure you realized. I could have phoned them in to you. As busy as I am, I probably should have. But I may need some help."

She took a deep breath. "I'm being cowardly about this. And of all the things I've been in my life, I've never been a coward. No. I do need some help. I wanted to meet you. See if you were . . . sympathetic. Not the I'm-so-sorry-for-your-loss sort of sympathetic. The we-understand-you kind. Do you see what I mean?" Her gaze was unexpectedly sharp. "There's a lot of steel underneath you. Don't think I don't see it. You would have made an excellent Eleanor of Aquitaine. Except for your hair. Hers was reputedly red, not silver-blonde. It's *The Lion in Winter* I'm speaking of. One of my finer roles."

Justine wasn't dithering, Bree realized. She was trying to avoid addressing something painful. "Thank you for the vote of confidence." She made a conscious effort not to look at her watch. Antonia might spit tacks if this appointment took too much longer, but there was a lot she could occupy herself with at home. Walk Bree's dog, Sasha, for instance. And it was Antonia's turn to do the laundry. "Shall we all sit down again, and you tell us what's troubling you?"

Justine stood up. "What's the matter with me? I can't sit down. I must get going. It doesn't do to stay away from the set for long. But I will tell you this. Someone on that set is trying to kill me"

"Kill you?" EB gasped. "Lord, Lord."

Justine blinked away tears. "Professionally, I mean. Someone is dropping poison in Phillip Mercury's ear about my performance. He's threatened to void my contract. There's more. Strange things have been happening to me on the set. A rug rolled up so that I'll trip on it. A chair moved out of position so that I'll fall." She dabbed at the tears with the back of her hand. "There's a concentrated malevolence there. Violence. Aimed at me. Aimed directly at me.

"I want to know who is behind it.

And I want to know why."

Two

From ghoulies and ghosties and long leggity beasties
that go bump in the night, Good Lord deliver us.

—Old Saying

"Someone's trying to physically harm you? Of course I'll come by the set," Bree said, alarmed. "I'll come with you now if you like."

"You sit right down here," EB ordered, planting the visitor's chair next to her own desk. "Shall I get my steno pad, Ms. Beaufort? Shall I take notes?"

"'Alarms and excursions,'" Justine murmured. Then, loudly, "No notes, Mrs. Billingsley. I don't want to say anything more right now, Bree. And before you ask, no, I don't want to call the police." She suddenly looked her full age, and exhausted as anyone Bree had ever seen. "If I may be frank, I need this part. You're how old . . . twenty-five? Thirty?"

"Twenty-eight," Bree said.

"So you haven't a clue. About how the world looks at you when you have a few years on you. Actually it's

19

Mary Stanton

how the world *doesn't* look at you when you're old. They raise their voices, as if you were deaf. Their gazes slide right past you in a crowd. You're treated like a child, or a mental defective. But I'm not losing it, as you young people say. My powers of observation are as great as they've ever been." Her lower lip trembled. "The whole production seems to be in trouble. Things disappear. Equipment gets damaged. The cost overruns are horrendous. Something is very wrong on the set of *Bitter Tide*. And they are trying to blame it on me." Justine breathed in and out slowly, visibly willing herself calm. "I beg your pardon. I'm a bit frightened. I'm not used to living in fear."

"Blaming it on you?" Bree said. "How can they blame cost overruns on you? Or damaged equipment?"

"Phillip is an artist. He insists on multiple takes and that costs money. He can be a bit of a bully. Most great directors are, of course. Erich von Stroheim used to walk around with a riding crop in his hand. And he used it. So it's no wonder I get a bit flustered and forget my lines. Anyone would. It's impossible to be at one's best under those circumstances. But as far as replacing me with Allison Buckley. T'uh!"

"Allison Buckley?" EB said. "She was in that TV show *The Silver Sneakers*, Bree. You know, the one about the lady detectives in the nursing home." She patted Justine's shoulder "That Buckley's not half the actress you are, Ms. Coville."

"She certainly is not."

Bree leaned back against the desk and folded her arms. "Mercury wants to void your contract and put someone else in the role. Is that it? Because he doesn't feel you're up to the job?"

"He says I'm too old."

The word seemed to hang in the air like a curse. Bree felt swamped with pity.

Justine held up her hand. "Listen to me, please. These incidents Phil blames on me could be viewed as the imaginings of a dotty old lady. I want you to come to the set because I want you to see for yourself. "

"All right," Bree said.

"You appear to me to be both forthright and honest. If you think Phillip's right, you will tell me."

"I will."

Justine held her head up with spirit. "But if what I think is correct—that someone is out to get me—I expect you to take all appropriate action."

Bree suppressed a smile. "You bet," she said.

"Then if Mrs. Billingsley can make those few—admittedly minor—updates to my last will and testament as quickly as I believe she can, I will expect you on the set tomorrow afternoon. About three o'clock." She lifted her chin, looked slowly from Bree to EB and back again, and walked out of the office, closing the door firmly behind her.

"Hm," EB said after a long, startled moment.

"That was quite an exit." Bree sank down in the visitor's chair. "Good grief."

EB tugged the yellow pad with the amendments to Justine's will out of Bree's hand and sat down at her desk.

"You don't think we should see her down the elevator?" Bree asked. "Make sure that the hire car's waiting? That she's safe?"

EB looked at Bree over her reading glasses. "That's one old lady who can take care of herself. You heard her. Wants help on her own terms, and my goodness if she didn't dictate those terms like Joe Stalin bossing FDR at Yalta."

Bree blinked.

"The teacher's up to World War II in my night school class." EB tapped at her keyboard with a self-satisfied air. "You better get yourself on home for lunch while I finish this will up. Antonia e-mailed me twice wondering where you are. Sooner I get this done, the sooner we can go get a gander at what's happening on that movie." She shook herself. "Lord! What a great place to work this is! Go on, now, Bree. Get some food in you. You're getting thinner than a fence post."

"Lunch," Payton McAllister said as he pushed the door open and stepped inside the office. "Precisely why I dropped by. Can't have you assuming fence-post proportions, Bree."

Bree stared coldly at him. "If it isn't Payton the Rat."

The second floor of the Bay Street building was given over to a satellite office of Payton's law firm, Stubblefield, Marwick. Bree didn't know which she despised more: Payton, with his gym-toned body and his insolent attitude, or his sleazy boss John Stubblefield. Payton himself was lithe, well dressed, smart, and very good-looking in a Hugh Jackman kind of way. One of the biggest regrets of her not particularly active love life was that she'd fallen for the outside of the man before she'd realized the snakiness of the inside. The affair had been short, painful, and an embarrassment to remember. "I take it you were listening outside the door?"

"No lawyer worth his salt should pass up a good entrance line. Timing is all." Payton crossed the carpeted floor, lifted the blind, and looked out the window. "I see the hire car's already picked her up. I didn't know you were advertising for has-been actresses as clients."

Bree picked up her briefcase and slung her tote strap over her shoulder. "Bye, Payton."

"Aw. Leaving so soon? Thought we might drop by Huey's for a quick bite."

Since he wasn't going to leave, Bree decided to pretend he wasn't there. "Call me if anything important comes up, EB. I'll be at the Angelus office later this afternoon."

Payton rattled the blinds. "Ah. Here comes the Chatham County patrol car. At last! I told them they'd miss her if they didn't get a move on, and damned if they didn't. Miss her, I mean. That's our county Mounties for you . . . a day late and a dollar short." He dropped the blinds against the window pane with a clatter. "I suppose they can always arrest her on the set. More fuss that way, and there's always the possibility that Phil will have a real excuse to kick her off the movie. He's been looking for a way out of that contract for a couple of weeks now."

Bree's temper stirred, which was not a good thing. She dropped the briefcase to the floor in case the temptation to clock Payton over the head proved irresistible. "All right. You've got my attention. What's up?"

"Your new client is what's up."

Bree shrugged. "You've lost me."

Payton linked his hands behind his back, strolled over to EB's desk, and looked over her shoulder. She covered her computer screen with one large hand and said with majestic calm, "Don't even think about it, white boy."

"Ooh," Payton said. "Scary."

"These client files are confidential."

"So the ABA tells me."

EB scowled.

Bree flattered herself she was keeping calm. She said, evenly, "You've got two options, Payton. Option A is to beat it. Option B is to beat it faster than that."

"Option C would be to let you in on the real skinny about the old broad that just left your office?"

Then he smirked.

Bree considered that smirk. Payton was arrogant and conceited and thought ethics were for losers. But he wasn't stupid and he was very good at manipulation. "So you're pissing me off for a reason," she said aloud. "Hm. My first thought is you're scared. That's my second thought, too. What do you suppose would scare Payton McAllister, Esquire, EB?"

"My cousin Titus," EB said promptly. "And there's

no supposing about it." She pursed her lips and looked Payton over. "Goin' balder might scare him, too."

"Balder?" Payton said involuntarily. He put his hand on the back of his head.

"Going balder, definitely. What about our client? You think Justine Coville scares him, EB?"

EB chuckled richly. "That brave old lady? Nah. But we do."

Payton shrugged. "Fine. Have it your way. I came down here with the intention of offering a little professional courtesy in the matter of Waterman v. Coville, but what the hell. You want to see your client end up in jail, that's fine with me. And even finer with my client Mrs. Waterman."

"Waterman?"

"Mrs. Henry Newton Waterman. Nee Samantha Rose Bulloch."

Payton was the only person Bree knew who'd actually pronounce the word "nee" aloud.

"Sammi-Rose Waterman," EB said, after a look at her steno pad. "One of Alexander Bulloch's daughters."

Payton sneered. He had a good line in sneers. "More importantly, one of Consuelo Bulloch's granddaughters. Most importantly, the owner of a valuable piece of jewelry now in your client's possession. Illegally. Mrs. Waterman would like nothing better than to see the surgically enhanced Justine in the slammer." He tapped his fingers against his lip. "Hmmm. Can you call it surgically enhanced when the result's a freaking disaster? Maybe not."

Bree snorted. "In jail for what?"

"Let's try grand theft, for a start. Of a sapphire and diamond brooch, designed in the shape of a peacock by none other than the little worker-bee elves at Louis Comfort Tiffany and belonging to—"

EB snapped the steno pad shut. "The matriarch. We got that. But Consuelo's dead. How can a dead person own a piece of jewelry?"

"Very well," Payton said with an air of humoring small children. "The estate of the late Mrs. Consuelo Bulloch, if you want me to be precise."

EB shook her head. "Uh-huh. According to Justine, Mrs. Bulloch left her estate equally to her three granddaughters . . ."

Bree gave Payton a delighted smile. "Mrs. Billingsley takes terrific notes."

". . . so how come only one of them is thinking about suing Ms. Coville? Because," EB continued with the inexorability of a John Deere bulldozer, "unless this here brooch was left to Sammi-Rose in a separate . . ." She rolled her eyes at Bree.

"Codicil," Bree supplied. "There'd have to be a specific codicil."

"Codicil. Right." EB made a note on her steno pad. "Wouldn't all three grandkids have to be bringing suit? Not just this Mrs. Waterman?"

Bree nodded. "Of course they would. The plaintiffs would be something like Bulloch, Waterman, et al. What was the name of the third granddaughter? The one who lent Mrs. Coville the brooch? Cicerone. No, wait.

26

It was Ms. Dixie Bulloch that lent our client her jewelry. It's pretty obvious Payton's going for intimidation rather than facts, Mrs. Billingsley." She eyed him coldly. "Harassment. Clear and simple." She'd had some doubts about Justine's claims of career sabotage. The doubts were disappearing.

"Because she's an elderly lady with no kin to help her. I got that." EB fixed Payton with an intimidating glare of her own. "What's next? Roasting puppies for Easter dinner? You know, Ms. Beaufort, I don't think that patrol car out there was after Ms. Coville at all. He's not only trying to intimidate old ladies. He's trying to intimidate us. You ought to be ashamed of yourself, Mr. McAllister."

"I believe you're right, EB. He's lying like a rug. Typical. So we're back to options A and B," Bree said cheerily. "Beat it. Sooner rather than later."

"You have no idea what you're messing with here." Payton's face was pale. Two bright red splotches burned on his cheeks. He was furious. "You two bitches are going to hear from us."

EB frowned at him. "Language, language, Mr. McAllister. What would your mamma have to say about you talking like that?"

There was only one other gender-related insult that made Bree angrier than "bitch," and it was the next word out of Payton's mouth.

EB couldn't suppress an offended gasp.

Payton showed his teeth in a grin.

Bree lost her temper.

Air eddied in the far corner of the office, stirring the covers of the files on EB's desk. Bree felt the wind rising and the presence of strong silver light. Time seemed to stop, and in that brief, suspended moment, Bree looked Payton over.

Stubblefield, Marwick insisted its associates adhere to a dress code long dead to all but the most conservative members of Savannah society. Which meant Payton wore a tie, in addition to an extremely well-cut gray pinstriped suit. A rather garish tie, if truth were told.

Bree sprang forward and grabbed Payton by the tie with her right hand. The wind roared about her head and shoulders. She jerked him off the floor, spun him around, backed up, and opened the office door with her left hand. She slung Payton into the hall like a Frisbee.

He landed hard on his right knee, hands sprawled in front of him. Which spared him a broken nose at least, she supposed. Not that she gave a hoot in hell.

She slammed the door shut, cutting off his yelps of pain.

The wind died away.

The brilliant light faded.

EB stared at her, speechless.

"Mercy," she said finally.

Then, "He all right?"

Bree shrugged. She took a deep breath and tucked her hair behind her ears. Then she cracked the office door and peered out. "He's halfway down the hall," she reported. "And he's only limping a little bit."

"I'm thinking maybe you overreacted," EB said. She

looked around the office in a puzzled way. "Goodness knows where that wind comes from. And the light?" She rubbed her forehead as if it hurt, then looked up at the ceiling fixture. "Maybe we ought to change that fluorescent overhead for something reliable. Look! The window's open. See what that breeze done to my files. Did to my files," she corrected herself absently. "Hm." She got up and began to collect the papers scattered over the floor.

Bree wasn't sure where her fits of abnormal strength came from; they didn't happen often, and only since she'd taken on the cases representing the souls of the damned. The only thing she was certain of was that EB wouldn't remember anything unusual about her attack on Payton the Rat after a little more time had passed.

Then the usual physical reaction set in. She sat down in the visitor's chair before her legs gave way. "I shouldn't have done that."

"Shoved that little turkey outside like that? Don't see why not. That man has a mouth on him, that's for sure." EB tapped the papers into a neat pile and looked at her employer. "Maybe you should go on home and get some food in your belly, though. You know what? I bet you had a drop in your sugar. That gives most folks a bit of a temper. Get yourself some good sweet tea. Put your feet up."

"I'll be all right." Bree, suddenly, was close to tears. This was part of the reaction, too. She pinched her leg hard, to distract herself. "I think I'd better get on over to the set of *Bitter Tide*, though. Just to check on Justine.

Do you suppose this Mrs. Waterman really swore out a warrant for her arrest?"

"I wouldn't bet a flat nickel on that boy telling you the truth. On the other hand, a visit might be a good idea. I'll key in those will changes and print it on out. Then you have a genuine reason to go poking around. It'll be about half an hour, if that's okay."

"Of course," Bree said.

"You'll have enough time to walk on home and have some sweet tea with your sister."

Bree clapped her hand to her mouth. "Oh my Lord. I forgot all about Antonia."

The office door bounced open, and Antonia herself stood there, her cheeks pink with annoyance. "There you are!" She put her hands on her hips and tapped her foot. "I thought you were coming home for lunch? I went and used the last of this week's paycheck to buy that shrimp salad from the Park Avenue market you love so much? And did I have to eat practically all of it myself because it, like, totally sucks if it sits around in the open air? The answer is yes." She pulled a paper bag out of the tote hanging from one shoulder and tossed it to Bree. "Here's the rest of it. I made it into a sandwich. Two itty-bitty sandwiches, in fact. One for you and one for Mrs. Billingsley. Hi, Mrs. Billingsley. Have you decided to quit working for my scatterbrained sister and get a job working for a prompt and timely person yet?"

"Not yet," EB said placidly. "How are you, child?"

"Fine. Haven't seen you since before the holidays." Antonia looked around for a spare chair, didn't find one, and plunked herself onto the floor. "I'm back working as a tech manager for the Savannah Rep Theater, you know. Which is why I don't have enough money to buy more than enough shrimp salad for an anorexic." She dug back into her tote. "I forgot. Potato chips." She tossed the bag to Bree, who regarded it doubtfully and gave it to EB.

EB looked at the two of them in turn. "I swear if I didn't know better, I'd never guess you two were kin. It's not the looks so much as the attitude."

They were, in fact, first cousins, although neither EB nor Antonia knew it. Royal and Francesca Winston-Beaufort had adopted Bree on the death of Leah, her mother. Royal's uncle, Franklin Winston-Beaufort, was her birth father. Bree knew a little bit about him. She knew almost nothing about Leah.

"We've got the same nose," Antonia offered. "And my hair's the same color as Mamma's."

"Mamma's is lighter," Bree said. "More of a reddish gold. You're frankly auburn."

"And Mamma's eyes are blue, like mine. And she's short, like me. You're tall, like Daddy and Uncle Franklin. As far as that seaweed color of your eyes . . ."

"My eyes aren't seaweed colored," Bree said a little indignantly. "They're green."

"Algae, then. Or mold. Anyhow, I don't know where Bree's moldy eye color comes from, Mrs. Billingsley. Nobody on the Beaufort or Carmichael side has 'em except her."

Bree, exasperated, took a bite of her sandwich. "I'm sorry I didn't get home for lunch."

"I'll live."

"Did you walk Sasha?"

"I walked Sasha. Although I swear that dog is perfectly capable of walking himself. If it weren't for the leash laws, you could just let him out on his own. He'd be just fine. He's a real angel."

This was truer than either Antonia or EB knew. Like her employees at the Angelus Street office, Sasha's antecedents were rooted in other times and spaces. Sasha; Petru Lucheta, her paralegal; Ron Parchese, her secretary; and Lavinia Mather, her landlady, were all angels and members of Beaufort & Company.

Bree tucked the remains of her sandwich back into the bag. "Thank you for the food. I'm not sure what time I'm getting home tonight, so if you could see your way clear to taking Sasha out again after supper, I'd appreciate it."

"I thought we'd planned on hitting the movies tonight," Antonia said. "It's Monday."

"Antonia's theater is dark on Monday," Bree said to EB. "It's her night off."

"My only night off," Antonia said. "So how come your nose is to the grindstone and your shoulder's to the wheel?"

"I've got some work stacked up at the Angelus office."

"And she's got to get over to the *Bitter Tide* movie shoot," EB said. "We've got ourselves a nice new client, Antonia. Ms. Justine Coville, the famous actress. I'm working on her file right now. And then we're going to take the papers over to the set. I expect we'll run into all sorts of famous folks. Hatch Lewis. Tyra Steele. Craig Oliver."

Antonia's mouth dropped open. "Hatch Lewis!"

Bree winced. She'd forgotten to warn EB about Antonia's passionate desire to get into that movie.

"Just when," Antonia asked, after a long, dangerous silence, "were you planning on letting that little item of news drop?"

"Hm," Bree said feebly.

"You've got an invitation to that set?! No! No! Even better than that. An actual cast member is your client?" She leaned forward and hissed, "And you were planning on going over there without me?"

"I'm sure Justine wouldn't mind if you took your baby sister along," EB said comfortably.

Antonia leaped to her feet and began pacing around the room—which was far too small for this energetic activity. "I worked myself to the bone in the theater for years!"

Bree figured it would be counterproductive to point out that Antonia was only twenty-two.

"Years! Waiting for a break. Longing for a break. Dying for a break. And when one of the hottest TV productions in years! Years! Comes along to Savannah, the first person you should have thought of was me!"

"Maybe I should rethink that business about Justine not minding your baby sister," EB muttered.

"No kidding," Bree said.

"So how's about it, Sis? I can carry your briefcase or something. Drive your car. I've got it! I'll be your consultant! I mean, you've spent most of the productive years of your life with your nose stuck in a law book. How much does a lawyer know about film, anyway?"

EB smacked her hand flat on her desk. "That's enough."

Antonia stopped midstride.

"You just sit yourself down and think about your behavior, young lady. Your sister and I are in the middle of building one of the finest law firms in this city."

"You are?"

"We are. This is not all about you, Miss Actress of the Year."

"It's not," Antonia admitted, her voice considerably smaller.

"This is about an important client with an important problem."

"What is her problem?"

"That is confidential," EB said sternly.

"Sorry. Of course. Sorry."

"But it has to do with threats to the poor woman's life."

"Oh dear." Antonia thought about this for a minute. "What sort of role is she playing? I'll bet it's something I could do. If anything should happen, God forbid."

"Mrs. Coville is eighty years old, child. And I cannot believe I heard what you just said!"

"You don't know actors," Bree muttered.

Antonia's face fell. "Sorry, sorry, sorry. It's not that I want anything to happen to her. Eighty years old? Jeez!"

"So you mind yourself, now. I think an apology is

due." She snorted. "Imagine. Busting in on that poor old lady like you wanted to do."

Antonia pulled at her lower lip. "Mrs. Billingsley's right. I'm a jerk," she said to Bree. "It's just so hard. I audition and audition and audition, and I never seem to get anywhere."

"It's a horrible life, the actor's life," Bree said. "I'm sorry myself." Then, because she couldn't stand the desperate look in her sister's eyes, "Okay. So I probably do need a consultant. A very well-behaved one, though."

"You do?"

"And a well-behaved assistant," EB said with authority. "We all have to go along. I read about it. It's called having a posse. But you"—she shook her finger at Antonia—"no shenanigans."

"A posse?" Bree said. "You want me to show up on the set with a posse?"

"Oh, c'mon," Antonia said excitedly. "Mrs. Billingsley's right. Everybody who's anybody has an entourage. We'll be your entourage. Except we have to be a better-dressed entourage."

"We look just fine," Bree said repressively.

"The money I do have goes to night school tuition," EB said. "I'm not hauling out of here to buy anything else."

"Okay, so you guys look fine. Boring but fine." Antonia waved her hand dismissively. "You don't expect me to show up in sweats, do you?" She bounced to the door. "Give me twenty minutes. That's it. It'll take you that amount of time to run and get the car."

"If you make it thirty, I'll have Justine's will ready for her to sign," EB said. "If nobody believes Bree's worth a posse, we'll say we have to be there as witnesses so Justine can legally sign her will. The State of Georgia requires two."

"Hey!" Bree said. "What do you mean I'm not worth a posse?"

"Oh my goodness," EB said, chagrined. "I didn't mean that the way it sounded. I do believe I'm flustered."

Antonia clapped her hands with excitement. "Who wouldn't be? It's perfect, Mrs. Billingsley! I'm out of here. I'll meet you two outside the townhouse, okay?"

"Stop!" Bree said, more loudly than she meant to.

Antonia deflated like a balloon stuck with a pin. "You mean we can't go?"

"Will the two of you keep cool? You're behaving like crazy people. I'm not sure we should hare off down there to begin with." Her cell phone chimed. "Lord, Lord. Hang on a minute. I'm getting a text message." Bree kept her business dress simple; she alternated between three elegantly cut pantsuits and a series of silk tees. All of the suit jackets had inside pockets where she could keep her cell phone, a credit card, and a fifty-dollar bill. She dug her cell phone out:

CAR WTG DWNSTRS

The sender was Armand Cianquino.

Her former law school professor and director of Beaufort & Company, the firm specializing in celestial law based on Angelus Street. *Her* firm, since she was the only advocate.

"Lord," Bree said again. She clicked on Reply and tapped in "?"

The reply was GET TO BITTER TIDE SET SOONEST.

Suddenly, Justine's fears for her safety seemed very real.

"Okay," Bree said. "I'm headed out."

"I've got to change!" Antonia wailed.

"I can't take you with me, Tonia."

"You have to!"

Bree hesitated. "You promise not to pitch a fit, right?"

"Right."

"We'll see." She picked up her briefcase. "I'm not making any promises. Not yet."

"But . . . !"

Bree shook her head. It all depended on who was driving the car.

Three

**All the world's a stage, and the men and women merely
players.**

—*As You Like It*, William Shakespeare

The hire car was a black Lincoln Continental with a discreet bumper sticker that read, SAVANNAH DRIVES.

Savannah Drives had been around for ages. In the years when Royal and Francesca had spent part of the summer at the family townhouse on Factor's Walk, she remembered her mother and father using them to send home the odd dinner guest who'd had too much to drink. The driver was male, white, middle-aged, and perhaps the most exhausted person Bree had ever seen.

He also claimed he'd never heard of Professor Cianquino.

"Don't know any Cee-anquo, miss," he said. He resettled his cap on his head. What hair he had left was ginger colored. He was bulky without being fat, although at second glance, Bree noticed that his stomach edged over a belt that was on the last hole. He might have been an athlete when he was younger. His eyes were gray, the sclera edged with yellow-pink veins. And he had a pale, indoor look that wasn't common in a Southern state like Georgia. He stank of cigarette smoke.

"Cianquino," she said, peering through the open driver's window. "Professor Cianquino."

"Nope."

"Who did ask you to pick me up, then? I told you, I received a text message."

"Text message!"

This was a man who scorned technology. She could see that right off.

He eased his shoulders against the back of the driver's seat. The Lincoln was double-parked, and although Bay Street in January was relatively free of tourists, Bree was concerned about stalling traffic. Antonia and EB stood aside on the sidewalk. Antonia shifted impatiently from one foot to the other. EB clutched a hastily assembled file containing Justine Coville's last will and testament.

"Our company provides transportation for Sundowner Productions on an as-needed basis. My shift begins at noon. I just go where they tell me, lady."

"Mr. . . ." Bree took a quick glance at the name tag pinned to the driver's black wool jacket. "Mr. Dent. William. Somebody told you to come here. I just want some confirmation about the order before I get into the car." Bree wasn't concerned about herself particularly. By and large, she went where her job as a celestial advocate took her, and she had a terrific backup team. But involving her sister and assistant was another kettle of fish altogether. Especially since Mr. Dent had never heard of Professor Cianquino.

William Dent sighed, an oddly grudging sound. "Okay, it's like this. Nobody sent me. I came on my own. I was just about ready to come up and get you when you three showed up down here. Thing is, Mrs. Coville's not getting the right deal with those punks filming that damn movie. I thought you could help her out."

"Justine?" Bree said in quick concern. "Is there anything wrong? Has something else happened? Is she all right?"

"Mrs. Coville," Dent said with reproving emphasis, "could use a helping hand, is all. She doesn't have any family left here in Savannah, and God knows she doesn't have any friends on the set. I picked her up this morning after her appointment with you and took her right back to that hellhole. Seemed to think you had the goods."

"The goods," Bree repeated. "Thank you. I guess. So what brought you here at this particular moment?"

"She fell on the set. No, no, she's okay. Bruised up some, but that's one tough old bird. Thing is, I think she was pushed. She won't talk to me about it. Figure she might talk to her lawyer." His glance flicked Bree up and down in an oddly impersonal way. "Didn't know you were a skirt until I saw you."

"Didn't know I was a what?"

"A skirt," he said impatiently. "You know, female. What, they're making women lawyers now?"

"Yes," Bree said. "They've been making women law-yers for quite a long time now."

"You look butch enough to take care of yourself. So maybe you can be of some help after all. Hop in. What? You okay? You got something caught in your throat or something?"

"I am," Bree said evenly, "trying to control myself." *And it's working*, she said to herself. *It's working.* She counted backwards from ten, very slowly, until her temper was under control. "Okay, Mr. Dent. I'm not going to pull your ears down around your socks. I'll hop in. But I want to get something straight about your attitude."

"What do you mean, attitude? What's wrong with my attitude?"

Bree gestured to EB and Antonia that it was okay to come with her, let herself into the Lincoln's rear seat, and then tapped William Dent firmly on the shoulder. He slouched around in the seat to face her. "What's wrong with your attitude? Where shall I start? Your sexism, for one. Your demeaning language for another. Your absolute lack of respect for a third."

He flushed beet red, then turned around and faced the windshield. She settled her briefcase at her feet and then looked challengingly at the back of his head. She could see his eyes in the rearview mirror.

He looked hurt.

"To sum up—I'd appreciate it if you'd keep a more civil tongue in your head," she said in a milder tone. "There's no need to be offensive." Then, slightly ruining the stern-professional act, she added, "Thank you."

Antonia scrambled into the car from the opposite side and announced her intention to sit in the middle. "With my feet on the hump."

"Noble and self-sacrificing sister that you are," Bree commented. Once EB was settled on the other side of Antonia, Bree faced front again and said, "Okay, William, we're ready." Then, since she'd been pretty hard on him, she asked in a friendlier tone, "Or is it Bill?"

"It's Dent," he said shortly. "I'm William to my friends and family."

"Fine," Bree said.

"Fine," Dent said.

"What the hey?" Antonia shook her head, shrugged at EB, who murmured, "whatever," and then began rummaging in her tote for her makeup. "Where are they shooting today, Dent? How much time have I got?"

"Mercury's shooting interiors all this week. They tore out most of the guts of the old Rattigan plantation. It's about ten miles upriver. Should be about forty minutes."

"It shouldn't take that long," Bree said. "There's an exit for Toller Road off of Highway 153. You've got about twenty minutes to slap some makeup on, sis."

"The new highway?" Dent said.

"Not all that new," Bree said crisply. "Let's get going, Dent."

"No need to put anything at all on that pretty face," Dent said with that same slightly reproving air. He signaled and pulled onto Bay, heading east. "Most men prefer the natural look."

Antonia cut her eyes at Bree. Then she said, "There

is no possible response to that comment, Dent. So I am going to ignore it."

The back of Dent's neck turned red. Bree tried not to think of the significance of this and failed. Then a possible reason for Dent's pallor, his unease with women, and his general churlishness hit her, and she felt her own neck turn red.

An ex-con, maybe?

Or was she imagining things?

Would Professor Cianquino get her mixed up with an ex-con? Of course he would, if he thought it would serve some angelic purpose. But her sister and her friend were with her this time, and if Cianquino had put them into any kind of danger, he was going to hear about it.

Bree had an excellent memory, and she rapidly reviewed her brief glimpse of Dent's arms and hands. No tattoos, but that didn't mean much. She'd have to call in a few favors at the Chatham County Sheriff's Department, see if they knew anything about a William Dent who mistrusted female lawyers and called women "skirts."

Dent was an obnoxious throwback, and maybe even an ex-con, but he drove well, with an easy authority. Bree spent the drive time checking the revisions EB had made to Justine's will. She had left the bulk of her estate to a home for retired actors in New York City. The only individual named in the will was Dixie Bulloch, who had been left the sum of one hundred dollars in "thanks for her support of my art." The addendum requiring her list of assets was blank. She'd listed Franklin Winston-Beaufort or his assignees as executors.

No family left in Savannah, Dent had said, and she couldn't count any friends on the crew of *Bitter Tide*, except Dent himself. On the other hand, Bree didn't have any independent verification of Justine's claims about being harassed. But Payton had let something drop about Phillip Mercury's attitude toward Justine before she'd tossed him out of the office. She put her hand on the passenger-side headrest and leaned forward. "Dent. Talk to me about Sundowner Productions. Why should Justine be at risk from anyone there?"

"You want background, talk to Mrs. Coville."

"But I'm talking to you," Bree said pleasantly.

Dent either wasn't going to answer or was taking his time about it. He executed a smooth right-hand turn onto 153. It was a one-lane highway, the shoulders thick with trees and brush that hid the river on their left from sight. This was the Low Country, and shallow pools of brackish water appeared among the foliage.

"Dent?" Bree said, more firmly this time. "I can't help Justine if I don't know what's going on. When I spoke with her this morning, she said Phillip Mercury had a high regard for her acting abilities."

"Mercury," Dent said in disgust. "That little asshole. He'd paint his mother and sell her to the Arabs if he thought it'd get him somewhere."

EB tsked at the language. Bree shook her head at the racial slur and said, "Dent, Dent, Dent."

The traffic was light in both directions. Dent slowed up as they approached the turnoff for the Rattigan plantation; he turned left onto a gravel road and pulled over. He put one hand on the steering wheel and scanned the heavy brush on each side. "Okay," he said rudely. "I'll talk. And I'll try not to offend your sensibilities, although it's a new one on me when a lady lawyer in pants gets huffy over a little straight talk." He blew air through his nose. "This is most of what you need to know. First, you're dealing with a bunch of bozos. There's not one straight shooter in the whole sloppy crowd. For one thing, they're all stuck on themselves. What do you call it? Egomania. Mrs. Coville's no different. She's a demanding old biddy with a lot of airs and she's the best of them."

So Dent didn't think a lot of his employers or even the poor old lady he was trying to help. Which wasn't a big surprise. He didn't seem to think a lot of anybody. "My information is that someone's trying to get her off the set, one way or another," Bree said cautiously.

"Everybody is. Mercury, the writers, even the other actors. They think she's a joke. I mean, yeah, she's maybe overdone it a bit with the plastic surgery." He glanced at Antonia. "She's got a heavy hand with the lipstick and rouge, no question. But she's a movie star. One of the great ones. And her style of acting is the old way, you know? It's big. Big and grand. It doesn't fit this kind of movie, with all the close-ups and two-shots and whatnot. What I think is, Hollywood gone all to Hell." He bared his teeth in what he must have thought was a smile. "Pardon my language, ladies."

"They think she's a ham," Antonia said. "That's my guess. They probably think she's too wrinkly, too."

"Antonia!" Bree protested.

"Just telling it like it is," Antonia said matter-of-factly. "Movies aren't like the stage. All those tight head shots mean you have to be perfect. Perfect skin, perfect teeth, perfect body."

"Not natural," EB observed.

Dent looked into the rearview mirror at Antonia and scowled.

"I'm not being critical, Dent. Acting styles change over the years. I mean, just take a look at Sir Laurence Olivier. He was the greatest actor of his generation according to this history of film class I took when I was in school, and when we look at him now, that's all we think. Ham. Porker. That he chows down the scenery. But there's a whole theater named after him in England."

"Yeah, well. So you say."

"I do say," Antonia said. "Poor old Justine. It's a shame."

Dent snarled a little at Antonia, then said, "There's another reason they're trying to dump her. It's probably on account of this lawsuit."

Bree hadn't been much interested in the disquisition about current demands for movie stardom. But she was interested in a potential lawsuit. So Payton may not have been lying after all—or perhaps not lying as much as usual. "Which lawsuit would that be? Over the brooch?"

"What brooch? Oh, that peacock thing? No. This one's a big sucker. The Bullochs aren't crazy about this movie being made. They tried to get an injunction to stop the shoot, and that didn't work, and now they're suing that asshole . . . sorry, ladies. . . . that crumb-bum Mercury, personally. Mercury and his backer, Vince White. Defamation of character, blah, blah, blah." He looked into the rearview mirror. "Thing is, Mrs. Coville is real tight with one of the Bulloch sisters. Not all of 'em—the two nasty ones are trying to sue Mrs. Coville over that bird brooch you just mentioned. But Dixie likes Mrs. C. and hates her sisters, so she's pretty tight with Mrs. C."

"Dixie," EB said. "Alexandra 'Dixie' Charles Bulloch. Daughter of Alexander junior, and granddaughter of Consuelo."

"Right. And Mercury figures Mrs. Coville is feeding the broadie the inside dope."

Antonia's lips formed the word "broadie." She rolled her eyes.

"What inside dope specifically?" Bree asked.

Dent shrugged his meaty shoulders. "Who's smoking what? Who's sleeping with whom? Cost overruns. Budget issues. Mrs. Coville's a gossipy old broad. What old broad isn't? She doesn't realize that sort of crap can get the investors fighting each other." He put the car in gear and drove back onto the gravel. "Word is the movie's having more trouble than most getting made."

"All those movie stars get up to shenanigans," EB said. "Why would that make any difference to a lawsuit?"

"Depends on the cause of action, I suppose," Bree said absently. "You never know what information might be useful to a plaintiff. Dent, Mrs. Coville has a contract, right? Has Phillip Mercury made any effort to buy her out?"

"Does your grandmother suck eggs? Sure he's waved some coin at her. Wants this Allison Buckley to take over the part, or so the scuttlebutt goes. I don't know much about actresses, or actors, either, but I haven't seen one that'd take a paycheck over a part."

"Very true," Antonia murmured. "If I'd wanted money, I would have gone into banking."

"Tonia," Bree said, "there are so many things wrong with that statement I don't know where to start."

Antonia gave Bree a pinch. "Hush up. We're almost there."

"Don't pinch me, Tonia."

"Then don't lecture me, Bree."

The narrow road snaked to the right, then to the left, and finally debouched into a vast green lawn thick with cars, trucks, vans, generators, and trailers. The Rattigan house—three stories high, with wide verandahs wrapping around each level—sprawled on a slight rise at the end of the green space. The front of the house looked splendid; the black shutters were freshly painted; wisteria and ivy curled around the white clapboard; out-of-season roses bloomed underneath the stone balustrade of the front porch. The brick steps to the front porch had been recently pointed. The front was in stark contrast to the north side of the house, which was visible from Bree's vantage point. The battered shutters hung askew, and at least one of the mullioned windows was broken. Dirty white paint bubbled under the eaves of the slate roof.

"Welcome to the anthill," Dent said.

"It certainly is busy." EB pushed the button to roll down her window and peered out, wide-eyed. The whole area was alive with people, most of them dressed in jeans, T-shirts, and flip-flops, despite the forty-degree temperature.

EB surveyed the chaos. "How are we going to find Justine in this big old mess?"

Dent drew the Lincoln under a large live oak hung with Spanish moss, killed the motor, and took a small clipboard from the glove compartment. "I have a general idea of where they might be. They issue a shooting schedule every morning, but they never stick to it. What time is it, one thirty?"

"One thirty-five exactly." Antonia jumped out of the car, eyes glowing, cheeks flushed with excitement. She drew a deep breath. "Just smell this air, Mrs. Billingsley!"

EB sniffed obligingly. "Roses in January," she said. "And somebody's cooking chili."

"It's the movies!"

Bree followed Antonia out of the car, ready to rein in her sister if need be.

"Haydee was murdered the first of July," Dent said as he, too, exited the car. "They're trying to fake the time of year. Make good sense if they waited for summer and saved the cost of the rosebushes. But this place isn't swamped with common sense." He tossed the clipboard onto the driver's seat. "I can't make head or tail of this schedule." He put his hand on Bree's shoulder. "You see that colored girl over there?"

"I see two African-American women," Bree said pointedly. "I don't see any colored girls."

"Right, sorry. I keep screwing that up. Anyhow, the pretty one in the gray cardigan. That's Florida Smith. She's the head writer. She usually knows what's going on." He put two fingers to his mouth and gave a sharp whistle. "Hey! Flurry!"

A slim woman in a gray hoodie and tattered jeans glanced their way. Dent waved at her, pointed at Bree, and then pushed Bree forward a little. "Right. You go ask her about where to find Mrs. Coville."

Flurry Smith met them halfway across the lawn. "Where have you been, Willy? Did you turn your cell phone off again? Phil's been looking for you."

"Had to make a run back into Savannah to fetch these folks."

"I'm afraid you'll have to head right back there again. Phil wants a couple of beignets from Huey's."

Dent made a noise between a grunt and a cough.

"Yeah, yeah. I know it's beneath your dignity, but you better step on it." She grabbed at his sleeve as he moved away. "Hang on a minute. Who are these people?"

"They have business with Mrs. Coville." He jerked his thumb over his shoulder at Bree. "She's a lawyer."

"Is that so?" Flurry cocked her head. Her smile never left her face, but she was clearly wary. "Okay, then. I'll take care of them. You'd better get a move on, Willy. Try to make it back by three, okay? He's shooting now, but I've scheduled him for a script revision. He's promised faithfully, absolutely to be there, which makes it a real possibility."

Dent turned and began to trudge back to the car.

"And turn your cell phone on!"

"Go soak yourself."

"Go soak myself?" Flurry marveled. "Can you beat that guy?" She chuckled.

"That man's a few puppies shy of a litter," EB said with more than a touch of indignation.

Flurry rounded on EB in sudden delight. "He's what? Two puppies shy of a . . . hang on a sec." She pulled a small spiral notebook from a back pocket and scribbled in it. "I love it. I'm stealing it. And no, you don't get a writing credit." She tucked the notebook back where it came from. "Willy's not so bad. If you can get past the attitude. He's working on it. Now, what's up with the three of you?"

Bree stepped forward. "I'm a lawyer from Savannah . . ."

Flurry's smooth face tightened, but the smile didn't waver. "Look, if this is about that insane Bulloch lawsuit . . ."

"This is about Justine Coville. She's retained my firm to update her will. She asked us to bring the amended version to the set. It's ready for her signature." Bree held up the file folder.

Flurry relaxed a little. "Oh. That'll be okay, I guess. Phil's in the middle of an interior shot right now, but she'll be free in a bit. Follow me to the food wagon. We can probably find a cup of coffee for a lawyer who isn't in the middle of suing us. As opposed to the ones that are. I'm Florida Smith, by the way. Call me Flurry."

"Brianna Winston-Beaufort. This is my associate, Emerald Bil—"

Flurry stopped and turned her delighted grin on Bree. "Get out! Any relation to Franklin Winston-Beaufort? The lawyer who represented Alex at the insanity hearing? How cool is this? I haven't been able to dig up much on him at all!"

"We're his nieces," Antonia said. She elbowed her way in front of Bree, the better to face the scriptwriter. "We both are. Bree's his older niece, and I'm the younger one. Antonia Winston-Beaufort." She grabbed Flurry's unresisting hand and shook it. "I'm temporarily with the Savannah Rep. We're staging a revival of *The Winslow Boy* at the moment. I'd be happy to comp you if you're free some night this week."

Flurry's smile disappeared. "So *you're* not a lawyer. You're an actor. And you're here because . . ."

"You need background info on my uncle Franklin," Antonia said promptly.

"Not because you're an aspiring actor who is willing to do anything for a role in a TV movie?" Flurry's tone was light, but the message was clear. "Ah-huh. Tell you what. I'm sure not going to be the person that keeps Justine from seeing her lawyer. So it's okay for your sister to be here. But maybe you'd better ride back to town with Willie."

Bree decided it was time to intervene. "My sister's curious about the whole process here, Flurry. But she's harmless. She won't be any trouble at all."

Antonia blinked innocently.

"We have a professional reputation to maintain," EB said with an admonitory look in Antonia's direction. "I can guarantee nobody's going to be up to any shenanigans."

"You can, huh? You'll pardon my skepticism, though. There's nothing peskier than an actor in search of a job. No offense meant, Antonia."

"None taken, Flurry."

EB took a firm grasp of Antonia's upper arm. "I'll keep hold of her all the while we're here."

Flurry's lips quirked upward. "You look like you can handle her, sister."

She smiled graciously. "I'm Emerald Billingsley, Ms. Smith. Delighted to meet you. And you have my permission to use the puppy thing."

"And you've got my permission to pump me about Uncle Franklin," Antonia said with shameless opportunism. "Bree, too."

One of the chief aggravations of Bree's current professional life—the otherworldly part at least—was that she didn't know much more about Franklin than Antonia did. He'd behaved as a fond, if distant, great uncle to them both. She saw him four or five times a year while she was growing up, usually at family functions. When she was younger, she was always in the company of her adoptive mother, Francesca, when Franklin visited.

After she graduated from Duke Law School, she'd taken a probationary job at her father's law firm in Raleigh, and she'd seen more of the professional side of her uncle. When she looked back, she realized Royal had always been with them when they met. No, she didn't know much more than anyone else about Franklin Winston-Beaufort. She hadn't learned about her true parentage until after Franklin died and left his law firm to her and her alone.

"So is it okay if I stay here with Bree, Flurry? Or I could sit down with you right now and do a data dump about Uncle Frank."

Bree moved her sister gently aside. "What is it you need to know, exactly? *Bitter Tide* is about the murder of Haydee Quinn, isn't it? The script's finished, or you wouldn't be shooting."

Flurry laughed cynically. "No script is ever finished. Even on a Phillip Mercury movie."

Phillip Mercury must run a tight ship. "Okay, so you revise a bit as you go along. But Franklin only had a tangential relationship to the case. He represented Alexander Bulloch at the sanity hearing, but he certainly wasn't involved before that."

"I'm writing a book."

Antonia gave a delighted gasp. "About the Winston-Beauforts?"

"Why would I write about the Winston-Beauforts? I'm writing a book about who really killed Haydee Quinn. It's going to be big. As big as . . ."

"Don't say it," Bree muttered.

"... *Midnight in the Garden of Good and Evil* ... It's going to put Savannah on the map."

Savannah was already on the map, but Bree decided not to point this out. As far as another book about yet another notorious Savannah-based murder ... the word "phooey" came to mind.

Flurry spread her arms wide. "The working title is *Death of a Doxy: Who Killed Haydee Quinn?*"

Bree raised her eyebrows. "I thought they executed her pimp for the crime."

"Bagger Bill Norris did it," EB said. "That's what *we* were told."

"They sent an innocent man to the chair," Flurry said with assurance. "It's all coming out in the book."

Antonia beamed. "A true-crime novel. Righting injustice! That is, like, so fabulous. Any information you need, anything at all, you can count on me."

"Great. That's just great." Flurry's words were addressed to Antonia, but her eyes were on Bree. "Hang on, folks. I'm vibrating." Flurry pulled her cell phone off her belt. "Yeah, Phillip. You're kidding me. Shit. Shit, shit, shit. Okay. I'm on it. I've got her lawyer with me right now." She glanced at Bree. "I'll ask, but I doubt it. We're not liable anyhow, are we? We'll be right there." She snapped her phone shut and slipped it into her pocket. "That was Phil. I told him you were here. He's over the moon, of course. Can't wait to sit down and talk with you."

Bree's acquaintance with Flurry Smith was short,

but she was already beginning to mistrust her persistent good humor.

"I told him you were here. He'd like to meet you right now." The insincere smile broadened to include Antonia and EB. "And you two are going to have a chance to see a real production in operation. Pretty cool, huh?"

"Actually, it's Justine that we're here to see, not Mr. Mercury," Bree said. "I heard that she had a fall on the set today. I'd like to see that she's all right."

"Justine's fall? Where'd you hear that? Don't tell me. Willy. Willy's got a bee in his bonnet about Justine. Yeah, she fell. More of a tumble, really. But that's the least of the worries around here. If you stick around long enough, you'll see what I mean. It's the other, weirder—" She cut herself off. "Never mind. Come on. They're on the interior set. We're supposed to be shooting the scene where Consuelo confronts Haydee for the first time and orders her to leave her son alone. It didn't actually happen, but what the hey. It's great theater. Follow me." She turned and began to wind her way through the crowd of people, equipment, and vehicles. She looked back over her shoulder. "Y'all coming right along? Good. Anyhow, it's a damn good scene. I spent a lot of time working that scene, and we should have wrapped it an hour ago."

"But there's a problem?" Bree prompted.

They'd reached the house. Flurry paused for a moment at the top of the brick steps until they'd all caught up with her, and then walked through the open front door. "When hasn't there been a problem? This whole shoot has been a problem. Props gone missing, more than the usual number of injuries, financing issues. The problem today seems to be that 'Consuelo' doesn't want to read the lines the way I wrote them. The *continuing* problem—yesterday, today, and for as far as I can see into the freakin' future—is that archfiend"—she stopped at the open foyer to a large room and lowered her voice—"Tyra Steele."

The first thing Bree noticed was a rhythmic smashing, as if someone was methodically throwing china against a wall.

The second thing was what a hodgepodge the place was.

Bree didn't find the source of the sound at first; instead, she faced a bewilderment of activity. This must have been the ballroom in the days when the plantation was up and running; the space ran the entire length of the house. The back wall faced south and was built almost entirely of French doors, so that the view fell away to the Savannah River. The west wall held a huge fireplace. The mantel was made of marble, and it was supported by marble cherubs with gilded wings. A large oil painting of a blandly smiling woman in a ball gown hung over the mantel. Two bland blonde children leaned at her side. That half of the room was furnished with damask-covered settees, elaborately carved tables, and masses of fresh flowers: lilies, roses, lavender, and an abundance of freesia. A richly colored Oriental carpet covered the old oak floors.

The other half of the ballroom was a messy collection

of big lights on tall stands, monitors, large cameras on wheels, trolleys, carts, wheelie bins, portable tables, and canvas-backed folding chairs.

Bree had expected a crowd of people, like the anthill outside.

There were only four.

Justine sat regally on a divan to the left of the fire-place. She wore a vintage Chanel suit, a large strand of pearls, and matching shoes, of the kind Francesca Beaufort always referred to as pumps. A jeweled peacock was pinned on the jacket's lapel.

A muscular man with orange hair slouched against the east wall. It took Bree a moment to register this was the director, Phillip Mercury. The man's peculiar orange hair, impressive biceps, and surly expression were known worldwide, thanks to the pervasiveness of Facebook and YouTube. What wasn't as commonly known was how short he was. Not much taller than Antonia, who was five-four to Bree's five-nine.

As Bree recognized the third person on the set, she felt a slight jolt in her midsection. Craig Oliver. She and Antonia had been nuts about him as the *Bristol Blues* leading character, Stone Cavendish. His eyes were a pale, almost transparent blue. His gaze was calm and direct. Bree half expected him to bark the famous catch-phrase, "Hit it!"

"He's let his hair get gray," Antonia hissed. "But he's still gorgeous."

The fourth person was the source of the smashing china. Tyra Steele. She was grabbing ceramic coffee mugs from the coffee service and smacking them onto the oak floor with the rhythmic, regulated grace of a tennis player lobbing practice balls.

She was improbably beautiful, even in the middle of an impressive rage. She had thick, glossy hair, the color of dark oak, flawless olive skin, and eyes exactly the color of the Caribbean Sea.

"Just a couple more mugs to smash," Flurry said. "Then we can go in."

The last mug crashed against the floor. Tyra thrust her fists into the air. Then she covered her face with her hands and bent forward at the waist. Her hair rippled to the ground. She wailed, quietly at first, and then more and more loudly until Bree wanted to clap her hands over her ears. The wail cut off suddenly.

Tyra collapsed dramatically into a broken heap and went silent.

Nobody moved. Phillip Mercury scratched his jaw. Justine glared steadily at the girl's motionless body. After a long moment, Craig Oliver unfolded his arms and walked over to her. "Need a hand up?"

"She's . . . she's . . . gone." Tyra's voice was a mere whisper, but it was a lush resonant whisper. "For now, anyway. It's Haydee, of course. She just won't leave me alone."

"She believes she's possessed?" Bree asked Flurry quietly.

Flurry nodded. Her face was noncommittal.

"Possessed! Good grief. That's the worst acting job

I've ever seen. Can you say ham bone?" Antonia muttered under her breath.

"Diva," Flurry muttered back. "Her, not you." The two of them grinned at each other.

Tyra accepted Oliver's outstretched hand and got lithely to her feet. She didn't glance over at Bree and the other three women clustered in the archway, but Bree knew the actress was aware of them.

"All better now, darling?" Phillip Mercury shoved himself away from the wall and sauntered to a canvas chair with his name emblazoned on the back.

Tyra drew the back of her hand across her perfect forehead. "All better, Phillip. But maybe . . . could I have a glass of water?"

"If Haydee hasn't broken 'em all, sure. Craig? Would you mind? As a matter of fact, why don't you give Tyra a hand back to her trailer? Your fridge is full of Evian, Tyra, and I know how you feel about tap water. I sent the crew on break the minute Haydee showed up. We'll get back to the scene after I have a quick story conference with Flurry. So take an hour. No more than that. Okay?"

Tyra nodded and said "okay" in a childish little voice.

Craig Oliver cast a rueful glance at Justine, who raised her hand in weary resignation. Then he supported Tyra out of the room.

Phillip Mercury waited a moment, then snapped his fingers at Flurry and called, "Come! And bring whichever one's the lawyer with you. Boot the other two."

"Mrs. Billingsley and I will wait outside," Antonia said nervously. Then, "Nice to meet you, Mr. Mercury!" She whispered in Bree's ear, "I'll just take a look around."

"Good idea." Bree patted her sister on the back. "Don't go too far."

"I'm waiting here!" Phillip Mercury called petulantly.

Bree nodded pleasantly in his direction and raised her voice a little. "I'll speak with my client first, Mr. Mercury."

"Is that so?" He regarded her steadily for a moment. He sucked his teeth. "Okay. So you two want to talk, no reason you can't talk in front of me. Justine, you get over here, too."

The elderly actress rose from the sofa with difficulty. Bree moved quickly across the set to help her up.

"I'm fine." Justine steadied herself with one hand on the sofa. "No, I don't need to lean on you. I sat there so long my muscles stiffened up."

Bree put her hand under Justine's elbow in a companionable way. "You had an accident on the set this morning?"

Justine snorted. "If you call being throttled by that lunatic girl an accident." She sank back onto the couch.

"I thought you fell," Bree said with concern.

"I fell this morning before I came to see you. That little hellcat tried to strangle me just minutes ago."

Although Bree had her back to him, she knew Mercury had gotten out of his chair, moved noiselessly across the set, and stationed himself behind her.

"A little mishap with the rug?" Phillip Mercury said

in her ear. "Not bloody likely. She fell over her own two feet."

Bree straightened up in seeming surprise. "Mr. Mercury? How interesting to meet you at last." He was too close to her. She tapped him lightly on the chest, and he took an instinctive step backwards. "Brianna Winston-Beaufort, attorney-at-law. I represent Mrs. Coville's interests. You say there was a mishap?"

"I was shoved," Justine said. "And it wasn't any ghostly presence. That was Tyra, too."

Bree sat down next to Justine. "Tyra shoved you over this morning and tried to strangle you this afternoon?"

"Yes!"

Mercury stuck his hands in his jeans pockets and rocked back on his heels. "Tyra didn't shove you, Justine. You got tangled up in your own feet and fell down."

"Is that right, Phillip? And I suppose Tyra didn't do this." She lifted the pearls encircling her throat to show them the faint bruises there. "You have it on tape, for God's sake!"

"Yeah, well, she got a little carried away with the role. When Haydee takes over, there's not too much the poor girl can do, is there? Besides, people your age bruise at the drop of a beer mug, Justine. It's a known fact. Makes you a liability to have around."

"Is this harassment intentional, Mr. Mercury? Or is your rudeness to my client the norm for you?"

His eyebrows rose. "Harassment. What are you talking about?"

"Your language, for a start. These accidents, too, if that's what they actually are."

He didn't say anything for a moment but stood looking at her with his head tilted to one side. His eyes were small, dark brown, and definitely unfriendly. He snapped his fingers. "Flurry! Get me a chair. Bring one for yourself."

Flurry grabbed two canvas chairs by the backs and dragged them over. Mercury positioned them directly in front of the couch. Then he sat down, his clasped hands between his knees, and leaned forward. "What I want to know," he said in a low voice, "is how the heck you do that?"

Bree raised an eyebrow.

"You know. That I'm-going-to-kick-your-ass-from-here-to-Topeka look. As far as I can tell, you didn't move a muscle. But you are the scariest beautiful woman I've ever met, and I've gone head-to-head with Angelina. And that silver hair." He reached forward. Bree grabbed him by the wrist before he could touch her. "Ouch! Okay! Lemme go! I'm backing off." He grinned cockily at her. "I give, okay?" He rubbed his wrist. "Quite a grip you've got, darlin'. Why don't you tell me what I can do for you?"

Bree smiled back. "All I need is a moment with my client."

"That's it?"

"That's it."

"You got it, then." He got to his feet with a grunt of effort.

"There is just one more thing," Bree said.

"I'm too young to have worked on *Columbo*, but I'll fall for it anyway. What is it?"

"Your star, Tyra Steele. She thinks she's possessed by the spirit of Haydee Quinn?"

"She *is* possessed by the spirit of Haydee Quinn. You haven't kept up your *National Enquirer* subscription or you wouldn't have to ask."

Bree searched his face. His tone was jocular, but there was a definite unease at the back of his eyes. "You believe that?"

"You saw for yourself."

"I saw a temper tantrum. I'm not sure I saw a case of possession."

"Hey. Gotta believe in my star."

Bree couldn't help a cynical laugh. "A case of possession would be good publicity for your movie."

Flurry made a sound of disgust.

Mercury laughed. "Might be. If we were making a different kind of movie." He rubbed the back of his neck. "But to tell you the absolute truth, I'd rather she'd haunt somewhere else. You don't happen to know any good exorcists, do you?"

Flurry snorted again. "Come on, Phillip. We've had this discussion before." She looked at Bree in appeal. "I am not, I repeat, *not* putting a woo-woo slant on this movie. I don't care what kind of ratings it'll bring in. This movie—and the book I'm writing—take a credible, serious look at a major injustice. We're going for the awards with this one, Phil. You promised me."

"Yeah. I did. But who knew?"

"I agree with Flurry," Justine said. "All this hocus-pocus. It's nonsense. That idiot girl is playing right into your bias, Phillip, and you can't see it."

"This isn't about Tyra necessarily," Mercury said.

"This is *all* about Tyra." Justine's cheeks were flushed.

"I'm not sure I have a clear picture of the problem," Bree said. "What is this about exactly?"

"I bring my movies in on budget and on time," Mercury said. "This movie is over budget and late. That's usually the director's fault. This time it isn't. Someone's engaging in sabotage. Might be Haydee. Might not." He glanced at Justine and away again, so quickly that Bree almost didn't catch it.

"Why?" Bree said.

"Why?"

Bree waited.

"Somebody hates my guts, is why. Tyra says it's Haydee. Haydee doesn't like the script." He ran his hands through his hair. Bree wondered what drugs his hair stylist was on. The orange color was truly bizarre. "And since I'm responsible for the movie, she's after me. The investors hate my guts too." His face sagged. "Everybody hates my guts. But the only person who hates my guts enough to want to destroy my film is Haydee Quinn. Everybody else has money riding on it."

Flurry sighed. "Phillip, your reputation is going to survive a two-million-dollar debacle, if this in fact turns into a debacle, which it won't. No." Her expression darkened. "No. The obvious answer is usually the right one. If anyone's trying to sabotage this movie, it's the Bullochs."

"The daughters of Alexander and the granddaughters of Consuelo," Justine said with a rather grand air.

"You wouldn't believe the ton of research I did for this script," Flurry said. "It's a terrific story. Just terrific. The Bullochs are petrified that my work could force the powers that be to reopen the case."

"That'd create a sensation of sorts, I suppose," Bree offered.

"You see, *they executed the wrong man*." Flurry jumped out of her chair and began to pace up and down. "I spent an entire year looking up old court records, the old police file, and all the old evidence. I even found an old guy that actually worked on the case. Robert E. Lee Kowalski. He was Eddie O'Malley's sergeant. O'Malley was the cop that forced a confession out of Bagger Bill Norris. Kowalski's parked out in a nursing home near Tybee Island." She smacked her hand into her fist. "He's, like, a hundred and three, or something, but he remembers the case like it was yesterday. I've been to see him a few times, and I'm going to see him a couple more."

"Ninety-two," Mercury said. "Kowalski's ninety-two."

Flurry had the light of a crusader in her eye. "There were payoffs. Bribes in the right places. They railroaded Bagger Bill Norris right into the electric chair. All so the real killer could go free."

Bree was momentarily at sea. "Bagger Bill was . . ."

"The murderer," Justine said tartly. "Owner of the Tropicana Tide nightclub. Unless you made that up, too, Flurry. I'm from Savannah myself, and I don't remember ever hearing a thing about it."

"That's because you weren't from the wrong side of the tracks," Flurry said flippantly. "Norris was Haydee's pimp," Flurry said to Bree. "Not a role model for your children or mine, but he didn't kill Haydee. I mean, why off the goose that laid the golden egg?"

"So who was the real killer?" Bree was interested in spite of herself.

"Consuelo Bulloch." Flurry sat down with an air of triumph. "Alexander's nasty mother."

"Nonsense," Justine said. "Utter nonsense."

Bree raised her eyebrows. "You can prove this, Flurry?"

"No. Not yet. I'm close. But I'm going to. It's all going to be in the book."

"Does your movie directly accuse Consuelo of the murder? If it does, I can see why the Bullochs are upset."

"It does not," Mercury said flatly. "The ending's ambiguous. My movie is a hell of a meditation on illusion and the nature of truth. Which is why this whole business about Haydee's spirit is such a grabber."

"I'm afraid you've lost me there," Bree admitted.

"Phillip's theory is Haydee's looking for justice. That she's trying to communicate with us through Tyra, to help us find the real killer." Flurry snorted. "Why doesn't she communicate with me, if she wants to get the record straight? I mean, Tyra's IQ isn't much higher than room temperature. You'd think a spirit would want a smarter medium."

Bree looked at Justine, who gave her a who-knows, who-cares sort of shrug. Then she looked at Flurry. "When does the spirit of Haydee appear? Does it ever happen when Tyra's alone?"

Flurry grinned. "Tyra doesn't do much of anything without an audience. Why don't you ask her?"

"I might," Bree admitted, "if you don't mind. I'm quite concerned about my client's well-being."

Justine touched the bruises darkening her throat. "I don't believe in spirits. What I do believe is that little jumped-up tart is out to get me. If you would just—"

"Tyra's not out to get you," Mercury said with elaborate patience. "We've been through this before, and I'm getting goddam good and sick of it. These fits . . . well . . . she doesn't have any more control over them than I do. Maybe it's Haydee's spirit, maybe not. I'm thinking that if it is, we've got one hell of an ending for the movie."

Justine trembled with indignation. "Tyra's no more possessed than I am."

Bree decided nothing would be gained by avoiding the question. "Why? Why is Tyra out to get you in particular? Or has Tyra exhibited this behavior with other people?"

"As far as I can tell, it only happens when she's in character as Haydee," Flurry said. "And no, the behavior isn't directed solely at Consuelo. She did her best to take a piece out of Craig Oliver's ear the other day . . ."

"Which means I've got to shoot him in profile until the bite marks disappear," Mercury said. "He's playing O'Malley. He carries a lot of the movie. It's a giant pain in the ass."

". . . He plays Lieutenant O'Malley, the cop who solved the case," Flurry said, as if Mercury hadn't spoken. "Then Tyra whacked Hatch Lewis with a cue stick in one of the bar scenes. He plays Alexander Bulloch, her lover."

"Which put Hatch out of commission for a week," Mercury said. "Kid needs to man up."

Hatch Lewis was equally famous for his action roles and his partying. Bree devoutly hoped Antonia didn't run into him.

"It's directed at me," Justine said stubbornly. "All this animus is to get me off this movie."

Mercury smirked. "Justine, sweetie, like every actor I've ever met, it's always all about you. Listen." He crouched down next to her chair. "You need to give serious thought to whether this is the right role for you. Talk to your lawyer about it. Tell her what we're offering you. I'm not going to hold out the big bucks for long." He gave Bree a considering look. "And I might have to get my legal eagles in from LA. You never know. That's gonna end up costing you a bomb." Mercury got to his feet, pulled out his cell phone, glanced at the time, and muttered, "Shit! You're wasting my time here, people. I'm at my trailer in ten, Flurry. I want those new pages stat. Justine, try to be ready to reshoot this scene in thirty. By the way, Justine, if you don't turn over that damn peacock pin, I'm going to rip it off you myself."

Bree worked this out. Ten: ten minutes. Thirty: thirty minutes.

Justine waited until Mercury had charged out of the room before she said, "Repellant little man."

Flurry shrugged into her hoodie and slung her tote over her shoulder. "He's making a pretty good movie, though, Justine. And he's right. You ought to consider his offer to buy out your contract. Catch you later, Bree? I'd like a little face time. See what you remember about your uncle."

Justine didn't wait for Flurry to disappear outside before she said, "The little slut's against me, too."

Bree bent forward and looked at the jewel on Justine's lapel. "Why does Mercury want you to remove the peacock pin?"

"I beg your pardon?"

"Why does Mercury want you to remove it?"

"Something to do with the lawsuit. The Bullochs want it back. Except for Dixie. Dixie's on my side. But Dixie had a perfect right to lend it to me. Consuelo wore it all the time. When I wear it, I get such a feeling that she's with me. It helps my performance tremendously." Her lips trembled. "I'm an excellent actress. Excellent. These people have no idea what great art is all about."

Bree personally thought that great art should be more about compassion than beating up on an octogenarian.

"Would you like me to handle this contract dispute for you, Justine?"

"There is no dispute. I am part of this movie."

"We want to keep it that way. I'd like you to find your performance contract for me so I can review it."

"My agent has it. She's in New York."

Bree nodded. She could find the address through the Screen Actors Guild website.

Justine fumbled with her handkerchief and pressed it to her lips. "I suppose it wouldn't hurt to have a lawyer on call. Do you think you can stop this persecution?"

"I'll do my best. There is one thing we can take care of right away. Might help to defuse the situation a bit."

"You want me to give up the brooch."

"Yes," Bree said gently.

Justine blinked away tears. Her fingers were surprisingly deft. She unpinned the jewel and laid it carefully on the damask cushion. "Will you see that it gets back to Dixie Bulloch?"

"Absolutely."

"Well. That's that." Justine closed her eyes for a long moment. Then her chin came up. "Do you remember what the *New York Times* had to say about my Medea? The 1965 production, on Broadway. I absolutely wiped Zoe Caldwell's eye. I stood in for her for two performances. I am capable of doing great work." She pressed her hands to her chest. "I *am* Consuelo Bulloch."

"You'll be splendid."

"Thank you, my dear. I'm going to freshen up in my trailer now. I need to ready myself for the work later on

72

today. Perhaps we can get the business of my will done tomorrow?"

"Certainly." Bree stood up politely and escorted Justine to the foyer.

She came back for the brooch.

For a few minutes, she stood looking down at it as it lay glittering on the couch. It was a beautiful piece of work. The peacock's body was set with diamonds. The tail feathers glowed with emeralds, tipped with sapphires. The bird's eye was a small round ruby.

Consuelo was wearing it when she died.

Bree's dead clients frequently came to her through such objects.

Bree bent and picked up the jewel.

She wasn't disappointed.

The apparition trickled from the jewel like water pooling from a narrow crevice. It was dark—more an absence of light than any particular gray or black—and formed itself into a shape that was vaguely human. A woman, Bree decided, or womanlike, at least.

"I'm Brianna Beaufort," she said. "Have you come to me for help?"

"Help . . ." The voice was less than a whisper, almost less than sound.

"You're Consuelo Bulloch?"

The shadow swayed. It might have been a nod. It might have been a wind from whichever circle of Hell poor Consuelo had been sentenced to. A faint echo sounded: "Yes."

Not for the first time, Bree was frustrated by the dysfunctional modes of communication between her and her clients. There didn't seem to be too much she could do about it, although she had filed a petition protesting the current process with Goldstein, the recording angel at the Celestial Hall of Records. Dead souls, she'd argued, should have the right to unobstructed dialogue with counsel. Goldstein had been amused, but at least he'd sent the petition on to wherever it was supposed to go.

"Have you come to me regarding the murder of Haydee Quinn?"

The shadow flared briefly into an angry flame.

"Haydee . . ." The malice in the shadow's voice came through loud and clear.

"You'd like me to file an appeal on your behalf, Mrs. Bulloch?"

"Yes. Yes. Help me! Treachery . . ." The shadow sighed. "Treachery . . ."

The shade of Mrs. Bulloch trickled away as slowly as it had arrived. Bree tucked the brooch into her briefcase and took out her cell phone. She'd call the Angelus office and get the staff moving on collecting the existing filings on the Quinn case. Flurry Smith would be a good source of background data, too. She'd schedule an interview with the scriptwriter as soon as possible.

"Ready to go?"

Bree jumped. She'd been so absorbed in planning the case that she hadn't noticed Dent come into the room. He held a small cardboard pastry box.

"Yes, I'm ready." She gestured toward the box. "I see you got the beignets."

"They gave me a couple extra. You look like you could use a good feed."

"Thank you," Bree said in surprise. "It's been a long day. I'd like a beignet."

"I like a woman with a little more meat on her bones than you have." He handed over the box. "There's one for your sister and your colored friend, too."

Bree took a deep breath. "Dent, please don't take this amiss. But in polite society there are acceptable ways to speak about other people and unacceptable ways. It borders on rude to refer to my weight. It is disrespectful to refer to Mrs. Billingsley as 'colored.' And to be perfectly candid, I have no interest, none, in what you personally like about women." *Good grief*, Bree thought, *I sound just like Francesca.*

"*That's* what I like to see," Dent said. "A nice big smile."

"I was thinking about my mother," Bree said stiffly. "Dent, you're past praying for. Let's round up Mrs. Billingsley and my sister and go back to Savannah."

"You didn't mean that. That I'm past praying for."

She'd hurt his feelings. Again. "No. Lavinia would remind me that no one is past praying for, and she'd be right. But do try to be less dense . . . I mean offensive, Dent."

"Who's Lavinia?"

"My landlady."

"Your landlady owns the Bay Street building?"

"I have a satellite office on Angelus Street. She owns the house."

She tucked the cardboard box under her arm and picked up her briefcase. "Let's go. I've got a lot to get through this afternoon, and it's late."

"You going to take on Mrs. Bulloch's appeal?"

Bree froze. The back of her neck prickled. "You mean Mrs. Coville. Justine."

"No," he said patiently, "Mrs. Bulloch. That was Mrs. Bulloch you were talking to, wasn't it? Just now?"

Bree set her briefcase down so that her hands were free, backed up a little, and faced him. "Okay, Mr. Dent. Spill it. Who are you? What do want? And what do you want from me?"

Four

This supernatural soliciting cannot be good.
—*Macbeth*, William Shakespeare

"Dent's a what?" Bree said to her paralegal, Petru Lucheta. Bree had arrived at the Angelus Street office well after four o'clock and called a quick staff meeting.

"An outcast angel." Petru had a thick black beard, black plastic-framed eyeglasses, and a thick Russian accent. He was the second angel Bree had hired on behalf of the celestial law firm Beaufort & Company. Lavinia Mather, her landlady, was the first. Ron Parchese, the third, fussed around the French press coffeepot at the other end of their small conference table. He was her secretary.

Three other members of the Company weren't there: Professor Cianquino almost never left his mansion flat on the outskirts of Savannah; Bree's dog, Sasha, was at home with Antonia; and Gabriel, who Bree privately thought of as the firm's muscle, never showed up unless he was needed to whack a few heads.

Bree propped her elbow on the table and sank her chin in her hand. Increasingly, the Angelus office was the only place where she felt completely at home. There weren't any secrets here, for one thing, and nobody commented on how thin or tough-looking she was getting. There was a price to pay for the work she did, and as long as she didn't completely lose her humanity, Bree didn't really mind. But she did mind when other people noticed how thin she was getting. How—hard.

Bree sat up, shook herself, and glanced around the table. "Dent says he's in rehab."

"Angels Anonymous," Petru said. "That would be correct. It's a traditional twelve-step program."

"But what's he in recovery for?"

Ron depressed the plunger on the coffee carafe. "Sounds like a bad case of incivility, if you ask me."

Bree made a face. "You can get kicked out for not being polite?"

"Ronald is kidding around. The poor soul's in treatment, and it'll be up to him to tell you why." Lavinia had a slight reproof in her soft voice. "Although it does sound to me like that ol' boy's handing out insults right and left."

"He doesn't seem to mean it," Bree said doubtfully.

"He'll find out if he means it or not," Ron said confidently. "Step Four is to make a searching and fearless moral inventory of yourself."

"What if he doesn't make it through all the steps?"

"What's he doing now?" Ron poured the coffee, dividing evenly into four cups, and handed them around.

"Right now he's a hire car driver for Savannah Drives. But he kicks around a lot. He's been a nurse's aide, washed dishes at a restaurant, that sort of thing." Bree looked at the coffee, picked up the cup and sipped at it, then set it down. "He's managing. It's a sort of life, I guess."

"There you are, then."

"He'll kick around here forever?"

"He can always opt out for a lower place in the Sphere, I guess." Ron shrugged his shoulders. "Up to him."

Petru took off his spectacles, polished them vigorously, and put them back on again. "I do not see that Mr. Dent has anything but a peripheral role in this case. Shall we address the needs of our new client? It's after four o'clock, and my sister Rose has promised borscht for dinner. Homemade. I will bring the remnants for you all tomorrow."

Bree had a sudden impulse to invite herself over for dinner. She wasn't wild about borscht, but she did wonder how her employees spent their nonworking hours. She'd never met Rose, for example, or Ron's partner, or seen Ron's apartment, although he'd insisted on her help choosing the paint for the walls. (He chose a color called Crystal Pink.) But they didn't ask, and she made it a practice not to pry. Instead, she moved on to their current case.

"As usual, the initial client meeting left a lot to be desired." She glanced at Ron. "I don't suppose we've heard anything about my petition to the courts to get better client access."

"That would be no," Ron said. "I play poker with Goldstein on Thursday nights, you know . . ."

"I didn't know."

"I nudged him about it last week. Fell about laughing at the thought of it, Goldstein did. Just before he laid down a full house, jacks high."

"We'll do the best with what we've got, then. First things first. I need to be sure we're representing the right client."

"You were embarrassed by the last case," Ron said. "No need. All of us were led down the garden path on that one."

"I wasn't embarrassed," Bree said testily. "I was taken aback."

"It would be as well not to be confused again," Petru agreed. Bree looked closely at him. He didn't look as if he were chuckling, but Petru's beard hid a lot. "What leads you to think Consuelo Bulloch may be the wrong client?"

"I half expected we'd be representing Haydee Quinn. Perhaps even William Norris. There's some evidence, anecdotal, to be sure, that Haydee's returned looking for some kind of justice. I made arrangements to interview Tyra Steele at her hotel tonight, just so we cover all the bases. As far as Norris is concerned, if Florida Smith is right, and he was executed for a murder he didn't commit, I would think he'd want reparations made."

"But it was Mrs. Consuelo Bulloch who asked for our help," Petru said. "You are sure it was she who approached you?"

"I asked her directly."

"The courts don't make that kind of mistake, anyway," Ron said. "She's who she says she is. You don't want to take the case?"

"Of course we'll take the case."

"Then we should proceed in our usual fashion," Petru said.

"That's fine. But I am going to check out Tyra Steele's claim to be possessed, if only to pursue this apparent vendetta against Mrs. Coville."

"It sounds like a temporal case to me," Ron offered. "Not a Company matter."

Bree looked at him thoughtfully. "You're probably right. It's time I paid some attention to the temporal cases, too. They're the ones that pay the bills. Anyhow, Consuelo wants to file an appeal—I'm assuming to get out of Hell altogether. Since I'm not sure what circle she occupies, or for that matter, how guilty she is, I don't know if we can accomplish that. Worst case, we'll fight to get her moved closer to the Outer Gates. Best case, she gets moved upstairs."

"It is not upstairs," Petru said fussily.

"I know. Sorry. It's a figure of speech."

"The Sphere is everywhere and nowhere."

"Got it."

"It is all things."

Bree rapped the table with her knuckles. She wished there was a twelve-step program for pedants. She'd shove Petru in it so fast his beard would fall off. "Let's move on."

"Did she kill somebody?" Lavinia asked. "Mrs. Consuelo Bulloch, that is?"

"It's possible," Bree said cautiously. "The director and the scriptwriter on *Bitter Tide* seem to think so. The state of Georgia executed Bagger Bill Norris for the crime."

"Mr. Norris is not our client, however," Petru said. "We are certain of this."

"As sure as I can be."

Lavinia set her coffee cup down with a clatter. "My goodness. I remember a bit about the Bulloch case. Consuelo was that boy's mamma, the one that got himself all tied up with that Haydee Quinn you mentioned?"

Bree had guessed that Lavinia's temporal body was at least eighty years old, but she hadn't considered that her landlady might be an original source of information about the Haydee murder. "My goodness, Lavinia. You bought this house in the late '50s, didn't you? So of course you were around Savannah then."

Lavinia nodded. "Happened before I started work for your Uncle Franklin, though. He was a good man, Mr. Franklin. Weren't that many folks in Savannah at the time that would have hired a colored secretary."

Dent's voice, unbidden, popped into Bree's head. *Lavinia says colored.*

"Did anyone make an issue of it?" Ron asked sympathetically. "Your race?"

Lavinia gave him a look. "Folks'll make an issue of just about anything, but back then they especially took on about the coloreds."

She said it again! What's the deal here, Beaufort?

Bree smacked the palm of her hand against her fore-head a couple of times.

"You got a headache, honey?" Lavinia asked. "You want some tea?"

"It's Dent," Bree said. "Or rather Dent's voice. He wants to know why . . ." She smacked her head again.

"Quit that," Lavinia ordered. "Wants to know what?"

Bree looked at them all in dismay. "I don't have a good feeling about this. What's Dent's voice doing in my head?"

"Depends on what he's saying, doesn't it?" Ron said with an infuriatingly reasonable air.

"But . . ." Bree gave it up. "He wants to know why referring to African-Americans as 'coloreds' is inappropriate when he does it but not when Lavinia does it."

Lavinia leaned over and shouted into Bree's ear: "Because I am colored! And you aren't." She thought a minute and shouted again, "Nobody cares when you insult yourself. It's a bit humorous, even."

Bree put her hands to her ears in protest.

Thank you.

Dent's voice went away, as completely as if it'd been switched off.

"It's gone," Bree said, mildly disoriented.

"He'll be back," Ron prophesied.

"What do you mean he'll be back? I don't want him back!"

"You sponsoring him?" Lavinia asked.

Bree reran the conversation with Dent in her head.

"He saw our new client. Temporals can't see the clients. Except for me. So I asked him who he was and where he was from. He said he was on rehab leave from the Sphere and wanted to go back. He asked me to help him, too. I said I'd see what I could do but I wasn't familiar with beings in his situation and I'd do some research and get back to him. Then," Bree added in dismay, "he asked if I'd be his sponsor. I said, 'Sure, why not, be glad to.' I mean, we don't turn anybody away from here, right? It's part of our job to help the dead, isn't it? Not just the condemned dead, but any dead."

"You're sponsoring him," Ron said. "No question about it."

"So he just gets to show up in my head like that?" Bree frowned. "I don't care for it. I don't care for it one little bit."

Lavinia patted her hand. "He didn't stay long, did he?"

"Well, no, but . . ."

"You can always tell him to leave," Petru said, "but under the circumstances, if the poor soul is attempting to achieve rehabilitation, it would be a kind thing to welcome him."

"Yes," Lavinia said, "you can tell him to hang up, like. Anytime."

"Perhaps in a softer way," Petru said. "I would advise Bree to have a candid conversation with Mr. Dent about the responsibilities of a sponsor, Lavinia. They are significant. Bree should be aware of this before she takes this on. Dent might be in a fragile state."

"Nobody seems to care about my fragile state," Bree snapped, a little unfairly. "I'll bring it up the next time I see him. I'll be sure to set some ground rules."

"If we are finished with Mr. Dent, I would like to say that my borscht is waiting." Petru laced his fingers across his substantial belly and peered at them over his spectacles. "May I ask that the new cases meeting proceed apace? We must first establish if there are grounds for an appeal."

"Of course, sorry. Hang on a sec. I made a list of action items while Dent drove us back in the car. I made him drop off Tonia and EB before he brought me to the office. Both of them wanted to see it . . . again." Bree sighed. Too many people in her life wanted to know why she never took them to the Angelus Street office. She dug into her briefcase and took out her Blackberry. "Ron, I'll need you to get the Bulloch case file from Goldstein. Early tomorrow morning is fine. Petru, if you can do the usual Internet search about the Haydee Quinn case, that'll be useful, but don't spend a ton of time on it. The scriptwriter's done a year's worth of original research, and I'm hoping she can help us. Thing is . . ." She paused. "She wants to interview me about Franklin."

"Hm," Ron said. "How smart is she?"

"Florida Smith? Very. Ambitious, too. She's writing a book about the murder. And she wants to interview me about Franklin's role in Alexander Bulloch's sanity hearing."

"I remember that, too," Lavinia said. "He grabbed her body right out of the funeral home and burned it up on the banks of the Savannah River. Right about where your town house is, Bree dear. There was a lot of hollering about that. Folks wanted to see him do some time."

"He ended up in a private hospital for a bit," Bree said.

Lavinia shook her head. "Not just because he burned the body up. There was talk he murdered that poor girl. That there was a cover-up."

"Yes," Bree said drily. "It's possible, isn't it? Can you see why I'm not wild about being grilled by Florida Smith about Franklin's part in all this?"

Lavinia looked stern. "You thinking that Mr. Franklin would have been involved in something like that? Setting up the boy Alexander as a lunatic so he'd escape justice?"

"I don't know what to think at this point." Bree's muscles were complaining. She felt like she'd been sitting all day. She got up, walked restlessly around the small room, then stopped and looked out the west window at the gloomy scene outside.

She'd rented the first floor of the house at 666 Angelus Street four months ago. It was beginning to feel like four years. She'd turned the dining room of the small house into this conference room, which was just big enough to hold a long oak table and six chairs. The window on the west wall, where she stood now, faced Angelus Street itself. Angelus was a tiny asphalt road set between Liberty and Mulberry. It was not to be found on any city map.

She rarely looked out the north window. That window overlooked Georgia's only all-murderers cemetery. When she'd first responded to Lavinia's ad for a tenant, she thought the rent was cheap because of the disordered graves surrounding the house. It didn't take her long to discover that the cemetery was there to accommodate the murderers she and the Company tracked down.

"You are concerned, perhaps, that a proper investigation of this case might reflect poorly on Great-uncle Franklin?" Petru asked.

"He's not my great-uncle. He's my father. Or was. And yes, I'm concerned." Bree turned back to them. "Lavinia, do you remember anything at all about the time Franklin represented Alexander at the sanity hearing?"

"I do remember that Mr. Franklin said that the Bullochs' a-hiring of him gave his business a boost."

"Great." Bree rubbed her forehead. "The Bullochs got his foot in the door of what turned out to be a very successful practice."

"It was hard for him, just starting out. You didn't have any of this lawyer advertising then, you know. With their faces on every bus in town. T'uh! ABA didn't allow it. Mr. Franklin didn't have money early on. Even if he was a Winston-Beaufort. That came later."

"The real money in the family came from Mamma," Bree said absently. "Francesca, I mean. The Carmichaels are loaded. Lavinia, is there any way we can get our hands on the client file from back then? I know we lost the dead souls' files in the fire that killed Franklin, but the temporals' files are in excellent shape. But they only go back for the last ten years."

"No need to keep the paper ones longer than that, unless it's an estate," Lavinia said. "I do recall putting a lot of stuff on microfiche, and the secretaries that came after me must have done it, too."

"I haven't looked at the microfiche tapes. I'll bet EB has. I'll ask her to do a search."

"A curious case," Petru Lucheta said. "We do not have to take on every client who comes our way. Perhaps this is one to refuse."

An expectant silence fell.

Bree drummed her fingers on the tabletop impatiently. "Of course we do."

Nobody moved, but she felt the relief like a breeze in the room.

"You didn't really think I'd back off because I might find out something I don't want to know about my father?" She didn't wait for an answer—her angels were painfully honest, but she held up her hand and ticked off the points one by one. "So far we've got three theories of this case: Consuelo did it; Bagger Bill Norris did it; Alexander Bulloch did it. We've got one client who may or may not be guilty of murder. If she is, we try our best to find mitigating circumstances and get her sentence reduced. If she isn't, we find out who did kill Haydee Quinn and present it in evidence. That sound about right?"

They nodded.

"Good." She shoved her chair against the table and picked up her briefcase. "I need some time to think about how we're going to approach this. I told Tyra Steele's representative I'd meet her at the Mulberry Inn right about now. It's just going on five o'clock. They agreed to give me half an hour. I'll be back in a bit."

The Mulberry Inn wasn't the grandest hotel in Old Savannah, but it was extremely comfortable, and situated so that the cast and crew of *Bitter Tide* were steps away from the river. It was also right around the corner from Angelus Street. The sun was down when Bree put on her coat and let herself outside, but the twilight that lingered meant she'd have little to fear from the Pendergasts. She glanced at the grave site as she passed by; Ron had closed it with a pile of rocks and good clay soil, and the mound looked undisturbed. Bree didn't know why Josiah was giving her a respite, but she was grateful for it.

The air was soft and chilly, heavy with threat of rain. Bree rounded the corner onto Mulberry. The entrance to the hotel was surrounded by clipped hedges and potted ferns. The foyer was small, carpeted in a pattern of dark navy squares with a floral design in the middle. Bree went through the double glass doors to a large atrium. A pleasant piano lounge with overstuffed sofas and chairs sat between the hotel restaurant and the long mahogany-faced reception desk. On her left, the lounge emptied into a proper bar. Bree had encountered Tyra Steele only once, but her voice wasn't easily forgotten. She heard it now, soaring over the rumble of conversation from the bar.

Bree checked her watch: five o'clock exactly. The meeting had been scheduled for the relative quiet of the lounge. She wasn't used to interviews with movie people, but she was willing to bet Tyra Steele would be late.

She was wrong.

The actress came out of the bar with her cell phone in one ear. She waved at Bree. Startled, Bree waved back. Tyra trotted across the expanse of celery-colored carpet and thrust the cell in Bree's face.

"Give a big hello to Team Tyra!"

"Team Tyra?" Bree said.

"You're that Justine's attorney aren't you? Winston something?"

"Yes, I am."

"Then say hello to my Facebook fans!" She settled into a comfortable chintz-covered chair and crossed her legs. She wore very brief denim shorts, a tight T-shirt that exposed her beautiful, astonishingly upright breasts, and flip-flop sandals.

Up close, she was exquisite, if overwhelming. Her skin was flawless, her teeth blinding white and perfectly shaped. She made Bree think of very high-quality polyester.

"Tyra, Ms. Beaufort didn't agree to the Facebook thing. So it'd be cool if you said 'bye-bye' and checked in with them a little later." Tyra's publicist, Mila Canterbury, had followed Tyra out of the bar. A nice-looking woman with short dark hair and a pleasant smile, she winked at Bree, took the cell from her client's hand, and said into it, "Check with the Big-T later, gang. This is Mila giving you all the big 'bye-byeee.'" She folded the phone, tucked it into a slim aluminum briefcase, and then shook hands with Bree. "Nice to see you again, counselor. We've got about a half an hour before we need to split. How can we help you?"

"This is about that old bat, isn't it?" Tyra said. "Mila said I had to talk to you, because otherwise we could get sued. The shoot's got a lot of problems already, Mila says, and Phil's not cool with any more lawsuits. So, like, ask me whatever." Her eyes were a true, limpid turquoise, as clear as seawater.

"Okay." Bree sat down across from Tyra and did her best to swing into prosecutorial mode. "Mrs. Coville is concerned about your attitude toward her. She fell this morning because you pushed her. She has bruises on her throat this afternoon because you put your hands around her neck and attempted to strangle her. I'd like to get to the cause of this behavior."

"Jeez . . . us," Tyra said. "Like, I don't know, okay? I mean, Justine is what, a hundred and three or something. She's older than my grandma. About as tough as my old grandma, too. But, like, you don't hurt old people. It's not something you do. It's Haydee you have to ask. Not me. I honest-to-God don't understand a thing about it."

"Okay," Bree said. "I'd like to talk to Haydee, if I may." She looked around the lounge. Some of the hotel guests had started to gather for the late-afternoon piano performance of Johnny Mercer songs. Some elderly couples, a few young families, and a sprinkling of men and women in business suits. They had all left a respectful space between where they sat and Tyra. "Is this the best place?"

Tyra's oak-colored hair hung to her waist. She flipped it back over her shoulders with a toss of her head. "I don't, like, choose the place. She just shows up."

"Any unusual circumstances surround her 'just showing up'? Are you holding something of hers, perhaps? Or near the place where she . . . um . . . passed away?"

"It's usually around Facebook time," Mila said. She dropped another wink in Bree's direction.

Tyra's turquoise eyes opened wide. "Like, you're right, Millie! Team Tyra is totally awed with Haydee. And that's what she likes, you know? She had fans when she was alive, and she needs fans now that she's dead." She leaned forward and said earnestly, "Team Tyra can't believe I'm so into the spiritual side of life. It's very awesome."

"You're the awesome one, Tee." The hearty voice was male, somehow middle-aged, and carried a hostile edge. Bree glanced up at a man in his midforties. He wore a tailored suit jacket and trousers in a slim European cut and a white shirt, open at the throat. He carried what looked to be a scotch on the rocks in his left hand. "This is the lawyer, Mila?"

"Mr. White." Mila got to her feet. "This is Miss Beaufort, yes. Bree, this is Vincent Victor White, one of our producers."

He didn't offer his free hand, so Bree didn't offer hers. He jerked his chin toward the chair Bree had been sitting in. "Sit down. I'll get you a drink."

"Now, why should I have a drink with you, Mr. White? As pleasant a prospect as that seems to be."

"Millie," Tyra said, "are we finished here? I gotta go." She uncurled herself from the chair. Her hair swung forward over her face. Bree noticed that she kept the chair between herself and Vincent White. She also noticed that White kept his eyes on Tyra. He had a greedy look, like a fat bully after a cake.

"We're finished here, Miss Steele. Thank you. I'd like to suggest that you have a little talk with Haydee, next time the two of you are in touch. Just remember that Mrs. Coville is a very old lady. She's fragile. Physically and emotionally."

"You mean she bruises real easy." Tyra nodded wisely. "My grandma does, too. I have to watch it when I hug her. I'll let Haydee know."

"Thank you," Bree said.

"You going to give me my cell back, Millie?"

"Only if you stop calling me Millie." But she said it with a smile. She dug the cell out of her briefcase and flipped it in the air. Tyra caught it with an easy, deerlike grace and turned to go back into the bar.

"Catch you around later, Tee?" White said.

She waved her hand without looking back. The guests whispered as she passed by, and the piano fell silent. Tyra disappeared into the depths of the bar. The piano started up again and gradually, the room filled with the subdued rumble of conversation.

"Amazing, isn't she?" White sat down in the chair Tyra had just vacated and wriggled obscenely. He grinned at her. "It's still warm from that cute little butt."

Bree felt a surge of intense dislike. White looked at

her face and scowled. Then, with an aggressive air, he challenged her: "You're representing Justine Coville, is that right?"

Bree nodded once.

"It's in her best interest to let us buy out her contract. You'd be wise to consider it."

Bree didn't say anything.

"She's past it, Br . . . Ms. Beaufort. Way past it. She wasn't much of an actress when she was younger . . ."

"Actually, that's not true, Mr. White." Mila, who seemed unaccountably nervous, glanced from Bree to White and back again. "She won a Tony for *A Little Night Music*. And she was nominated for a Golden Globe for her *Streetcar*."

"Christ! That was when, back in the '80s? Times are different now. There's no money in the stage, anyhow." He crossed one trousered leg over the other and balanced his drink on his knee. "I'll let you in on something you'll appreciate, Ms. Beaufort."

Bree didn't like this fake camaraderie any more than his hostility. Her dislike for this guy was growing.

"Money," he said. "Art is all about money. If we had a bankable actress in the role of Consuelo, we'd be looking at maybe digging ourselves out of quite a hole. Someone like Allison Buckley, say. Fact is, this production's in trouble. Not because of Tyra. The only reason we have a hope in hell of success is because she's such a draw. She could be big. Really big, bigger than Angelina. All she needs is the right vehicle." He dropped his voice to a confiding whisper. "I'm in on a production right now that could put her over the top."

Bree looked at her watch. Her face felt frozen.

White looked at her and glanced hastily away.

She relaxed her hands and said as calmly as she could manage, "You'll excuse us, Mr. White. Mila was good enough to give me a half hour of her time, and I haven't finished my business with her. I don't want to waste it."

He set his drink on an end table. "Yeah," he said uncertainly. "Sure. See you around." His gaze fell on Mila, and he said with abrupt viciousness, "I'm going to get Tee a drink. Call me if Phil shows up. I'm pretty pissed off about those cost overruns. You tell him from me that you're all in a world of hurt." He left without looking in Bree's direction again. Bree waited a long moment until her irritation was under control. She wanted to go back to the office, sit down, and try to put all of this stuff in order.

"You wouldn't be available to work on the shoot, by any chance?" Mila said.

"I'm sorry, what?"

"The way you routed White." Mila sighed. "We work with a lot of jerks in this business, as I'm sure you've heard. He's not the worst. Not by far."

"He's a predator," Bree said. "You're watching out for Tyra, I hope. She can't even stand to look at him."

"Tyra's no rocket scientist, Bree. But she hasn't gotten this far without being able to handle herself around men."

"She's going to handle herself better around Justine, I hope?"

"I think so. Tyra's a little idiot. She's halfway convinced herself that she is possessed by spirits. It started as a joke. But I have to admit she's taken it a little far."

"I don't want to see Justine hurt." Bree couldn't help but smile. "Or Tyra, either."

"Yeah, she grows on you." Mira sighed. "Now if you could just teach me that wrath-of-God look of yours, the one that reduced Vincent the Vile to a nice little jelly, I'd be a contented woman. For the next five minutes, anyway. Where did you pick it up?"

"Here and there," Bree said sadly. "Here and there."

Five

By the time Bree got back to the office, Lavinia had gone up to her apartment. Petru and Ron had drifted off to their own homes. She sat down in her small office to think and make notes.

It was close to eight o'clock by the time she was satisfied with her preliminary action plan. She closed down her computer, rinsed her coffee cup in the kitchen sink, and turned off the overhead light in the parlor she had converted into a waiting room.

Not that anyone ever actually waited there. She'd been incredibly naïve in those early days, imagining a raft of clients, all responsible about paying their bills, all with interesting tax problems, which had been her specialty in law school.

Instead . . . dead people. Who didn't seem concerned about her own need to pay the bills. And a career that seemed to be turning her into some sort of . . . what?

Ron's desk stood in the far corner. She'd purchased an old leather couch and chair from the thrift store down the block, and set them at right angles to the fine old brick fireplace. An old wooden chest acted as a coffee table.

Above the fireplace, over the Adams-style mantel, hung the painting of the *Rise of the Cormorant*.

Bree had to steel herself to look at it. A three-masted schooner rode flame-tipped waves. The sea was filled with the hands and arms of drowning men. The shadowed face of a dark-haired, silver-eyed woman hovered at the stern of the ship. Above it all was the slim, wicked figure of a seabird, beak open, and eyes glittering with hate, its hungry gaze on the dead and dying that thrashed desperately in the water. The cormorant, an avatar for Lucifer.

Who was the woman in the ship?

Who would try to help save the drowning souls?

Who was *she*, for that matter?

She knew the answer to the second question: it was the Company's job. Her job.

She suspected she knew the answer to the first. It was her birth mother, Leah, whom she longed to know. Leah had been an advocate for the damned, just as she was now.

As for the last question: Who was she?

She didn't want to think about it.

They had a small bathroom off the kitchen. It dated from the '50s, with a pedestal sink, toilet, and a tiny tiled shower. There was a mirror over the sink. The silver nitrate was wearing off the back, so it was speckled with black. Bree walked in, pulled the chain for the lightbulb, and stared at herself: A nice face. A face that had its share of admirers.

She thought of Vincent Victor White settling into Tyra's chair with that despicable smirk.

Her lips thinned. Her eyes grew hard and bright. And her face . . .

She reached upward, wildly, and wrenched the chain so hard it came away in her hand. The lightbulb flared and went out.

Not me. Not me. No way.

She was hit, suddenly, with a tidal wave of fatigue. She couldn't remember the last time she'd eaten. She wanted to go home, see her sister, and maybe give Sam Hunter a call. She hadn't seen him over the holidays, and they'd exchanged vague promises of getting together for a drink as soon as she was back in Savannah.

Time to go home. She walked into the small front foyer, with a glance at the frieze Lavinia had painted on the stair wall. Brightly colored Renaissance angels followed one after the other in a gorgeously hued procession. Their robes were scarlet, trimmed with gold, edged with celestial blue. The halos gleamed gold fire, and their wings were a silver prayer. The angel at the end of the procession had white-blonde hair piled in intricate braids underneath her halo. Lavinia was convinced the angel looked just like Bree.

She snapped off the foyer light, stepped outside, and locked the front door behind her.

The temperature had dropped into the thirties as soon as the sun was down, and the chill was welcome after the musty warmth of the old house. The night was clear. The moon was up, half-grown, the threat of rain gone. It threw a pale light that half illuminated the inscriptions on the gravestones nearest the little house. Beyond the waist-high wrought iron fence that encircled the property were the normal sounds of a Savannah night. Inside the fence . . . Bree gave herself a mental shake. It'd been a long day and she didn't want to deal with whatever lurked in the cemetery after dark on nights like this one. She looked hesitantly under the live oak that grew at the Pendergast grave; the ground was quiet. Then she heard the familiar tick-tick-tick of Sasha's paws on the brick path.

"There you are, Sasha. I was hoping somebody would show up to walk me home."

He bounced up the steps and nudged her knee with his head. She was grateful at how happy he was to see her. She scratched behind his ears and dropped down to kiss the top of his golden head. "I'm glad to see you, too."

Somebody coughed in the darkness. Bree's hand tightened on the fur at Sasha's neck. The dog's angelic powers only went so far. If she faced real trouble, she was pretty certain Gabriel would be around sooner or later, but there wasn't a hint of his presence. "Who is it?" she asked sharply.

"Didn't mean to scare you, young lady." There was a smell of cigarettes. A shoe scraped on the pavement, the cigarette butt flared out, and a big, dark figure shuffled on the other side of the gate.

"Dent," Bree said. She went down the three short steps to the pathway. "Good. I've been meaning to talk to you."

"Need to talk to you, too. Thought you might want to get a bite to eat or something."

"We need to get a couple of things straight first." She turned back to unlock the front door. "Why don't you come in for a minute?"

"Can't," he said shortly.

"You have another run to do for Sundowner?"

"No. My shift's over. Which is why I thought you'd want to grab a bowl of chili. Maybe a hamburger."

"It'd be nice if we talked in private," Bree said. "Everyone's gone home, except Lavinia. But once she's upstairs, she doesn't come down again until morning."

"I can't."

"You can't?"

"I'm Out, remember?"

"Out," Bree repeated. "Oh! You mean Outca . . . I mean, yes. Of course." Poor guy. Was it okay to refer to his status, or not? She didn't really have the right to ask, did she? "You're Out. And I'm In. Inside the fence I mean. Sorry to babble. You startled me. I'll be right there."

Sasha trotted ahead of her and waited while she un-latched the gate. He stepped into the road with her, gave Dent a brief once-over, and then ignored him.

"Nice dog," Dent said, looking down.

"He's part golden retriever, part Russian mastiff. The mastiff part is why he's so big."

"He works for you."

"Yes, he does."

Dent bent to pat him. Politely but firmly, Sasha moved away.

"Oh dear," Bree said. "He's usually very friendly."

"Yeah, well. It's part of the program."

"Part of being . . . Out." Bree bit her lip. "Well," she said brightly, "I'm so glad you dropped by. I was hop-ing we could have a frank discussion about my role as sponsor."

Dent had exchanged his black jacket for a tweed sports coat that was much the worse for wear. He wore the same baggy twill trousers. A grimy blue cotton fish-erman's hat was shoved back on his balding head. He stood with one hip cocked and his arms folded. He had on a pair of scuffed leather oxford shoes whose worn laces had been knotted and reknotted. He'd shaved re-cently, though, and he smelled faintly of strong yellow soap.

"So, how's about that hamburger?"

"I think we can get a hamburger at B. Matthew's," Bree said. "It's right across from the town house."

"That place? Too fancy. I want somewhere I can get a decent piece of meat. Not something ritzy."

"Pizza?" Bree said. "With meatballs? We can go to Huey's."

"Huey's is a little too snobby for me. Isn't there a White Castle around here somewhere?"

"Not for years," Bree said. "If it's junk food you're after, there isn't much."

"Huey's, then."

Bree and Antonia lived less than three blocks from Angelus Street at the end of a row of town houses overlooking the Savannah River. In the old days, when the city had been a busy port shipping cotton all over the world, massive brick warehouses lined the banks. The old Cotton Exchange still dominated Front Street, although most of the other warehouses had been converted to shops, offices, restaurants, and comfortable old apartments.

They walked the short distance down Angelus to Mulberry and turned right onto Bay. There was a button on the light standard for the Walk signal, and Bree punched it. When the little white figure flashed on, Dent took her arm with a Boy Scout determination that both amused and exasperated her. Sasha trotted along behind them. As they passed Bree's town house, Sasha veered off and disappeared around the back.

"He lets himself in," Bree said. "Antonia won't even know he's been out. Huey's is down this way." She shook free of Dent's proprietary arm and went down the wrought iron steps that led from Factor's Walk down to Front Street.

In the spring and summer, Front Street was usually

packed with tourists. Now, in January, the old cobblestone road was quiet, and the wooden market stalls that held the seasonal businesses were closed. The people that were there were locals, bundled up against the cold weather. As they passed the storefront for Savannah Sweets, Bree stopped.

Dent narrowed his eyes and scanned the quiet street. "What's up?"

"In 1952, Alexander Bulloch rolled a handcart down this street with Haydee's body in it." Bree wondered if she stood there long enough, if Haydee's shade would rise up from the cobbled stones.

"Nah, not here," Dent shook his head. "That'd have been the far end of the street. Just in front of that sign for the tourist bureau. Mercury got permission to shoot the scene there, but he hasn't done it yet. They were down here a couple of weeks ago, getting background footage. Your place is up there, right?" He turned and squinted up. "You should have seen the crew when they were set up. Those French doors of yours look right out on the river."

"Tonia and I went home to Plessey for the holidays."

"The old family plantation. That right?"

"As your sponsor, is it okay for me to point out that it's rude to sneer?"

He scratched his head. "Sneer, huh."

"Yes. You managed to shovel a world of contempt into your tone. About what you think you know about my family, and what you think about me. Not what you know. If you have a legitimate reason to sneer, let's talk about it. Otherwise, it's just attitude. There's Huey's. Let's get you something to eat. Maybe you'll cheer up."

Bree and Antonia were regulars at Huey's, and Antonia, at least, was always welcome. Bree had had another rather too physical encounter with Payton the Rat at Huey's several months ago, and the staff tended to deliver her meals and her bill in record time and encourage her not to linger.

Bree greeted Maureen the bartender with a wave, and headed for her usual booth. Dent took off his hat, settled himself on the side that faced the front doors, and looked the place over. When the waitress came up—even before Bree had sat down—he said abruptly, "Got a burger?"

"Sure do." The waitress, whose name tag identified her as Chelsea, handed Bree a menu but said, "Maureen wants to know if you want the regular?"

"Greek salad. And a cup of the black bean soup."

"Burger for you, sir?"

"With raw onions and fries. Make it a double."

Chelsea glanced from Bree to Maureen and back again. "That'll take a bit of time. Maybe ten minutes."

"So what if it does, sweetheart? You can bring us a couple of cups of coffee while we're waiting."

It was too late for coffee. Bree had enough trouble sleeping as it was. "Make mine a chardonnay, please. If you would bring my salad at the same time you bring him his sandwich, and not right away, I'd appreciate it.

Please tell Maureen I'm in no hurry. None. I'd prefer not to be rushed."

"Okay, I guess." Chelsea hesitated for a minute and then walked rapidly away.

Dent leaned back with a sigh. "You come here a lot?"

"At least once too often, I guess, as far as they're concerned," Bree said. "But I'm trying to make up for it."

He nodded seriously. "Making amends. Step Nine in most programs. It's number two in mine. The first is to make a list of all the persons I've harmed and become willing to make amends to them all." He gestured at his suit-coat pocket. "I've got the list right there. It starts with Bobby Lee Kowalski."

Bree frowned. "He was one of the cops on the Haydee Quinn case."

"That's right. I've got to get to Bobby Lee. It's important." Dent's big hands fiddled with the packets of Equal in the little ceramic jar. "How come they won't let you smoke anywhere anymore?"

"You know the answer to that. Same reason they give you the calorie and fat count on your food. It's better to be alive than . . ." Bree bit her lip. "Yes. Well. So. Mr. Dent. I agreed rather hastily to becoming your sponsor." At his look of dismay, she said, "No! No! I'm happy to help. I just didn't fully understand . . ." She stopped herself in midcourse. "You know, I'll ask you straight out what I want to know, shall I? What do you need from me?"

"I have to find out who killed Haydee Quinn. And I've got to get to Bobby Lee."

"So do we. The Company and I, that is. As the only surviving temporal involved in the Haydee Quinn case, Sergeant Kowalski's high on the list. Although I'm not sure what solving this old case has to do with your rehabilitation." She waited a moment while Chelsea set the wine and a coffee cup down. She filled Dent's cup from the Bunn carafe and slapped creamer on the table. Dent frowned at the creamer and barked, "Where's the sugar bowl, sweetheart?"

Chelsea blinked at him, then pointed at the packets of Equal. "Right there, sir. And please don't call me sweetheart."

"Maybe you could check in the back? Bring me some real sugar?" Dent reached up and patted her on the behind.

"Dent!" Bree said. "Stop that!"

"Stop what?" He looked genuinely puzzled.

Chelsea stepped away from the table, signaled to Maureen, and walked off.

Dent scowled after her. "What the hell was that all about?"

"For one thing, I think we're going to have a change in waitstaff. Probably EB's cousin Titus, if Maureen has anything to say about it. He's six-foot-six and played tackle for Georgia State when he was in school." Bree leaned across the table. "Dent, you cannot, cannot harass women in that way. No inappropriate touching. Got it? All that macho guy stuff went out in the '60s. Or it should have, anyway." She looked over her shoulder. Chelsea leaned over the bar, talking vehemently to Maureen. Maureen looked at Bree, her glance skidding away when she saw Bree looking at them. She disappeared into the back kitchen. Chelsea went around to the back of the bar, poured two glasses of red wine, and then served a couple at the far end of the bar. Moments later, a very tall guy in a chef's toque splattered with tomato sauce pushed through the swinging doors. He carried two plates, one in each hand.

He set the plate with the two hamburgers in front of Dent, the soup and salad in front of Bree, then leaned over and hissed in Dent's ear, "Cool it with the waitress, Jack."

Dent got to his feet. "Please tell the young lady I apologize."

"Yeah? Any more of this kind of hassle, you can apologize yourself right out of here." He turned and nodded to Bree. "Miss Beaufort."

"Titus," Bree said. "I'm sorry. My client here didn't stop to think."

"You aren't thinking of maybe switching your regular restaurant?"

"Of course not," Bree said earnestly. "I love Huey's, Titus."

"All I can say is goody, Miss Beaufort. As long as we keep things nice and quiet."

"Absolutely," Bree promised. "Sorry, again."

"Yeah. Right. Enjoy the food."

Dent sat back down as soon as Titus went back to the kitchen, and grinned at her. "You know, I don't think he was all that concerned about losing a loyal customer. I think you just got a heavy hint to move on."

Bree stared at him, dismayed. "Oh my. You're right. He was hoping I'd go somewhere else, wasn't he?" She craned her neck around. Maureen ignored her. Chelsea ignored her. Two middle-aged women splitting a pizza glowered at Dent. One of them said loudly, "Huh!"

"Lord," Bree said. "I can't believe I almost got banned from Huey's. My mother would just die. Antonia would kill me. EB would never let me hear the end of it." She sank a little lower in the booth. If she wasn't in sight, maybe everyone would forget about her.

"About the case," Dent prompted. "Where are we at?"

"The preliminary stages. I'll know more about the direction the case is going in a few days. But Dent." Bree hesitated and then said gently, "I'm not sure there's anything you can add to the investigation. I appreciate the offer, but we seem to have most of the bases covered pretty well. Why this case in particular?"

"If you haven't figured it out, you're not much of an investigator." He placed his hands flat on the table. "Do you know who William Dent was?"

"You mean, when you were . . ." Bree didn't know quite how to phrase this, so she said, "When you were a temporal, you mean?"

"William Dent was my favorite pulp writer. Bar none. Better even than Zane Grey. He wrote pretty damn good detective stories in magazines like the *Black Mask* and

Astounding Tales. Back in the '50s. I can't believe they aren't publishing those magazines anymore.

"I'm not William Dent, Miss Beaufort.

"I'm Eddie O'Malley. The cop who sent an innocent man to the chair back in 1952."

He put one hand over his eyes. It took Bree a moment to realize he was weeping.

Six

Justice delayed is justice denied.
—The Hon. Justice Learned Hand

"La, la, *la*," Petru said. He tsked again in dismay. "The poor fellow. The poor fellow."

"Dent said he was drunk most of the time he was on duty," Bree said. "He doesn't remember much about the case at all. He started drinking when he was fifteen, never really stopped, and died drunk, he said, in a car crash six years after Bagger Bill Norris was executed."

The conference room was bright with sun this morning, although there had been a light frost the night before. Savannah in January was a place of muted greens, soft browns, and silvery gray; rainy days and sunny days each had their own wintery kind of beauty. That beauty never came to the cemetery outside the windows. No matter how often Ron and Lavinia swept up the dead leaves around the gravestones, planted new sod over the graves, and weeded the flagstones, the place reverted to ugliness and decay within days.

Worst of all, it smelled. Of old grief, old sins, decayed bodies.

"Dent's sure Norris was innocent?" Ron asked. He poked at the slim file of information Petru had pulled off the Internet. "According to these old newspaper stories, they found Norris passed out in the back of the Tropicana Tide nightclub with a bloody knife in his hand and blood all over his clothes. They didn't have much in the way of forensics in those days, but they did match the blood type to Haydee's. And the two of them had been arguing for days. Norris had her signed to an iron-clad contract. She wanted out—possibly to marry Alexander Bulloch. She was a dancer, mostly, although the articles were coy about just what kind of dancing. Cootchie-cootchie, apparently."

Petru cleared his throat, which was usually the preface to a lecture. "The media was much less open then than it is nowadays. If a rape occurred, the reporters would write that the victim was 'interfered with.' This comes perhaps from a culture that was closed in upon it—"

"Really, Petru," Ron said crossly. "Enough's enough. It's perfectly clear what the newspapers meant."

Petru's thick eyebrows contracted. "What is this 'cootchie-cootchie,' then?"

"Hubba-hubba?" Ron said. "Don't ask me."

"Strippin'," Lavinia said. "Poor girl took her clothes off for men. Or most of 'em, anyway. Seems to me they had those little pasties things here and here." She gestured in the appropriate places.

"In Russia, I believe, they had these dances also."

Petru stroked his beard. "So, does Mr. Dent know who is guilty if it was not Bagger Norris?"

Bree, who had been waiting patiently for her employees to sort themselves out, shook her head. "He says he hasn't a clue."

"He is sure Norris is innocent because why?"

"He was a little vague on that. He's, um . . . Out, as he refers to his condition, until he makes amends on his performance in the Haydee Quinn case. That's all they told him at his intervention."

"Goldstein might be able to help us there," Ron said. "I'll ask him." He tapped at his Blackberry to make a note and then clicked his tongue in annoyance. "Look at the time. It's almost ten o'clock. I'd better get over to the Municipal Building."

"I'll go with you," Bree said. "I want to talk to Goldstein myself. Petru? Is there a way for you to get the microfiche files on Alexander Bulloch's sanity hearing from Mrs. Billingsley while I'm gone?"

"There is indeed."

"There are a couple of more things. Would you set up a time for me to see Mrs. Waterman? It'll have to be with Stubblefield, Marwick's permission, worse luck. They represent her. I've got to get that brooch back so they drop the theft case against Justine. I need to see Florida Smith, too. Schedule dinner with her if you can, as soon as possible. I'm assuming that Mercury gives her time to eat. I'll take her to B. Matthew's if you can get us a reservation. She'll like that. You can ask Dent to pick her up from the set and bring her here."

Petru's beard bristled with indignation. "This is a secretary's duty, I think. To schedule appointments and make dinner reservations is Ronald's task. I am a paralegal. I have been studying. I am almost ready to take the Georgia Bar examination."

"Um," Bree said unsympathetically. This was all about a long-running rivalry between the two. Petru and Ron had frequent spats. Petru was angelic enough to avoid falling into pride or arrogance, but he wasn't above a little petty nit-picking. Neither was Ron. "Ron's going to be busy recovering records with me this morning. I'd like those appointments set up as soon as possible."

"I will attempt to do so."

"What I've got to attempt is to clean," Lavinia said. "Y'all finished in here?" She wore two sweaters this morning instead of one. A brightly knitted cap perched on her halo of white hair. It was clear she felt the cold. "This conference room wants sweeping out."

Bree gathered up her winter coat. "Ron and I are off to the Municipal Building."

Lavinia tucked the collar of her sweater closer to her throat. "Y'all wrap up, now. It's bitter out there."

It was cold. Bree was feeling the lack of exercise over the past few days, and she'd walked to the office from the town house, but she wasn't sure she wanted to walk the eight blocks to the Municipal Building. "I left my car at the town house," she said as they went through the gate to the street. "Do you want to brave the cold? Or shall I walk back and get my car?"

"I think our transportation problem's solved." Ron

pointed down the road. The black Lincoln Continental was parked just past the intersection of Angelus and Mulberry. "That must be Mr. Dent. Or do we call him Lieutenant O'Malley now?"

"We call him Dent. He doesn't want anyone to start asking questions about him."

"Good grief. There can't be many temporals alive who would recognize him after all this time. It's been sixty years."

"There's Florida Smith. She's been looking at old newspaper stories about the case. Justine's still around and she remembers the coverage. And Dent says his old sergeant is still alive. His name is Robert E. Lee Kowalski. He's in a nursing home. Dent wants to see him, but he wants a witness present when he does, just in case Kowalski says something that breaks the case."

The Lincoln drew up to the curb. Dent got out and opened the back door. Bree let Ron precede her as she made the introductions. "Dent, this is Ron Parchese. Ron, this is William Dent."

Ron ducked his chin in acknowledgment and got in the car.

There couldn't have been a wider difference between the two men. Ron was dressed with his usual stylish elegance. He wore light gray trousers, a rep tie, and a pale yellow button-down cotton shirt. Dent looked like he'd slept in his uniform. It was more than that, Bree decided. Ron showed himself to temporals occasionally—he was good friends with Antonia and he seemed to like Cordelia Eastburn, the local district attorney.

To them, he appeared as he'd first appeared to Bree: a blond, well-dressed professional with a long-term partner and an easy charm.

But Ron had a subdued, shimmery aura. All Bree's angels did. She had gotten so accustomed to it that she barely registered it nowadays. It was the color of sunlight in a forest. It was very noticeable when he was next to Dent. "Well, for heaven's sake," Bree said aloud. Thoughtfully, she folded herself into the back seat.

Ron smiled at her, a little sadly, she thought. He put his lips to her ear. "If he makes it through the program, he'll get his light back."

"Do you think he will?" Bree whispered back.

"Depends on him."

"Where to?" Dent said loudly. The back of his neck was a self-conscious red.

Bree was embarrassed but didn't have a clue how to deal with it. So she said, "We're headed to the Municipal Building. Thank you for picking us up. You aren't needed out at the Rattigan plantation?"

"They're shooting on Front Street this morning. They brought the vans with the equipment about six, and they're setting up now. I'll be back and forth all day. But you need me, just call. I'll come and get you." He glanced at Ron through the rearview mirror. Ron gazed out the passenger window, ignoring Dent as thoroughly as Sasha had done. There didn't appear to be any malice in it. Dent simply wasn't there, in the same way that temporals didn't notice Ron or Petru were there, unless the angels wanted them to.

Out, Bree thought. *The poor guy is Out.*

"We're going to have to loop around Bull and go down Martin Luther King Jr. Boulevard," Dent said. "The cops have closed off the west end of Bay."

"Okay. You can drop us off on the corner. We'll walk from there."

He let them out a half block down from the Municipal Building.

Bree loved Old Savannah for a number of reasons, but high among them was the eclectic mix of architectural styles. James E. Oglethorpe had designed the original village as a series of twenty-four squares. Each square was to function as a mini-village, with a village office, a church, or a school among the houses, and a green park filled with trees and flowers in the middle of each square.

In the three-hundred-plus years since her founding, the city had been attacked and ravaged by pirates, damaged in several citywide fires, and occupied by General Sherman's troops in the Civil War. Each time a part of the city was destroyed, she grew back again. So Georgian homes sat next to Greek Revival churches. French Provincial vied with Carpenter Gothic. Queen Anne held pride of place next to Victorian. Bree's own favorite style, Southern Colonial, recalled her family's home in North Carolina.

The Municipal Building was an exception to this charm. A six-story concrete block that just barely escaped being taken for a prison, the building sat uncompromisingly between Montgomery and Martin Luther

King Jr. Boulevard. At least the color blended in with the soft Savannah tones of the old city. The block was a yellow gray, which mellowed in the sunlight to the color of milky scrambled eggs.

"You got an appointment? You want me to wait?" Dent asked.

"No thank you. I'm not sure how long we'll be. And it's warming up. The walk back will do us good."

Dent fidgeted with the steering wheel. "You want to set up a time to go out and see Kowalski? Maybe tonight? I'm off duty at four. I checked. Visiting hours are until eight."

Bree paused halfway out of the car. "Do you think we can risk it? Will he recognize you?"

Dent shrugged. "He's over ninety. I don't know if it matters whether he recognizes me or not." His face set. "I need to talk to him, though."

"Let me see how the rest of my day shakes out. We'll go soon, I promise you. I'll call you." Bree ducked her head back inside the car to look him in the eye. "Make sure your cell phone's on."

Dent muttered something she couldn't hear.

"What?"

"I said, right. Okay." He held his phone up. "It's on."

She caught up with Ron, and both of them entered the Municipal Building together.

The municipal courts had been in session for an hour or more, and the huge open foyer was jammed with people. A few young mothers pushed baby carriages.

Middle-aged couples in jeans, sweatshirts, and flip-flops wandered around in a bemused way. A couple of lawyers in suits acknowledged Bree with a wave. Guards in the dark blue uniforms of the combined Chatham County and Savannah police forces stood against the walls, wary, their hands near their gun belts. Bree tossed her briefcase onto the moving belt at the security gate. Ron drifted past the gate and stood waiting at the elevators. So he wasn't making his presence known this morning. She'd have to remember that if she ran into anyone she knew.

The elevator was full, and she edged herself to the back. A couple of secretaries got out on the sixth floor. One of them held the door for Bree, who shook her head, smiled, and said, "Forgot something downstairs. Thanks anyhow." She waited while the doors closed and the car proceeded up to the seventh floor.

The doors whooshed open. Bree was greeted by the familiar sign, with the winged scales of justice in the middle of the great gold seal.

Celestial Court of Appeals

She followed Ron down to the heavy oak doors labeled Records and into the cavernous space beyond.

Bree had developed a decided fondness for the Hall of Records. The huge room looked like a monastery (although for all Bree knew, it *was* a monastery). The walls were of cut stone, cemented together with thick mortar.

The vaulted ceiling soared high overhead, buttressed by thick, enormously wide oak beams. The Gothic-style stained glass windows let in little light. The angel scribes, each dressed in the coarse brown robes Bree thought of as typical monk garb, stood with quill pens at waist-high oak desks. Flaming torches were fastened to the stone pillars with fat bands of wrought iron. The whole huge room was illuminated by an evenly distributed mellow glow, like the light around Ron. Bree couldn't identify the source, but it generated a very restful feeling.

"If it isn't Parchese himself." Goldstein bustled out from between two desks. "And Bree. It's good to see you, my dear. It's been a while."

"Antonia and I went home for the holidays."

"Glad to hear it." Goldstein was short, round, and a little untidy looking. A fringe of black hair surrounded his otherwise perfectly bald head. "Got a new case on?"

"I think we do."

They followed him down the flagstone aisle to the very back of the room. The back wall was covered with thousands of wood cubbyholes, each containing rolls of parchment. A chest-high counter of a burled wood divided the wall from the rest of the room. Goldstein flipped up the hinged flap set into the counter and let himself inside. "I've been away myself, you know."

"Really?" Bree said with interest. Did he go home for the holidays, too?

"I'm at home here," Goldstein said in response to her

unvoiced thought. "No, I was away on a task that should bring joy to the heart of your colleague here."

"You're not computerizing!" Ron exclaimed. "Will wonders never cease?"

Goldstein's lower lip jutted out. He looked like a balked baby. "How did you guess?"

"Because this operation is so behind the times, Goldstein, it isn't funny. At some point you've got to give up and slog on in to the twenty-first century."

"Don't give me that, Parchese. You didn't guess about the computers. You knew."

"Okay. I give. It was an agenda item for Vatican IV. I got an e-mail."

"Hm. There *is* considerable pressure to modernize, as you call it." He cast his eyes upward in a pious way and remained respectfully silent for a long moment. "However."

"I knew there'd be a however," Ron muttered.

Goldstein folded his hands over his considerable belly and gazed benevolently at them. "I am resisting. I will resist until I am reassigned. I like it this way. How may I help you?"

Bree jerked to attention. The whole records room was very peaceful, almost lulling. It'd be easy to go off in a doze here. "Yes, of course. We have a client who'd like to file a Request for Appeal. Consuelo Bulloch."

"Bulloch," Goldstein mused. He turned and ambled down the row of cubbyholes. "Bulloch, Alexander . . . Bulloch, Alexander II . . . Ah. Here we are. Bulloch, Consuelo."

He brought the parchment back and laid it on the counter.

Bree picked it up and unrolled it. "Well, well," she said after a moment. "This is very interesting."

Ron looked over her shoulder. "How was she sentenced?"

"She's in the first circle, for a millennium. The charges are third-degree treachery, third-degree malice, bigotry in the fourth degree . . ." She looked up. "Nothing about murder."

"First circle," Goldstein said. "That's like temporal traffic court. Hardly worth your while."

"Now, now," Ron said. "We never turn away a client. Rather, we haven't yet."

Bree rolled up the parchment. "Good grief. Well, we have to proceed on the assumption that's she's innocent, right?"

"Florida Smith doesn't agree," Ron said. "She's doing everything she can to pin Haydee's murder on Consuelo."

"She sure is." This was a pickle. What if Consuelo had murdered Haydee? Bree could hardly investigate a case that might land her client a tougher sentence. Mitigating circumstances might help reduce the sentence. Get her into Purgatory, perhaps, which was a lot cooler. No manual labor, either. Perhaps her client would settle for that. "Goldstein, could we have the other Bulloch files as well?"

"Have they retained you as counsel?"

"Well, no. But the information might help us with our current client's case."

Goldstein tramped back to the cubicles, brought two more rolls of parchment, and handed them over. They were slimmer than Consuelo's.

"And the file for Haydee Quinn?"

Goldstein sighed.

"Please," Bree added.

Goldstein trudged back down the aisle with a put-upon air. His sandals slapped heavily on the stone floor. The roll he brought back was slim, too. "Anything else?" he asked. "Maybe the file on Idi Amin, which is all the way to the end of the row? And then on Xerxes II, which is all the way to the *other* end of the row and a back file, to boot?"

"If you got yourself a good IT system," Ron began.

"Hey!" Bree said. She had unrolled Alexander junior's parchment while the two angels squabbled. She flipped it around so that the other two could see it. "All this says is 'Pending.' "

Goldstein made a "so what?" gesture.

"There's nothing in this file but his personal data and this big fat red stamp that says . . . 'Pending.' " Bree's voice rose in frustration on the final word. She made an effort to lower it. "Alexander died in 1978. After working in a bank and having three kids. How come he hasn't had his Judgment Day?"

"Obviously, there are some unresolved temporal issues," Goldstein said. "When they've been taken care of, he'll be eligible for disposition."

"Where is he now, Goldstein?" Bree demanded.

"Limbo is as good a description as any."

Bree unrolled Alexander senior's file. "This one says 'Pending,' too. The poor guy's father! He's been dead a long time, too! He hasn't had his Judgment Day, either? Why aren't these folks guaranteed the right to a speedy trial?"

Goldstein opened his mouth to speak.

Bree held up her hand. "Stop right there. I know what you're about to say to me, Goldstein, and I don't want to hear it."

Goldstein said it anyway. "What is time to an angel?" Then, "Limbo's not so bad. I can think of a lot worse places to twiddle your thumbs. You don't start to serve time until the sentence comes down."

She eyed Haydee's file with misgiving. She unrolled it. She said, "Oh hell," which sent a rustle of disapproval around the room. She held out the parchment for Ron's inspection.

" 'Pending,' " Ron read aloud.

"That poor woman was stabbed to death in 1952 and her soul hasn't been disposed of yet!" Bree slapped the files together and then used them to smack Goldstein on the head. "I'm filing a complaint."

Goldstein took a prudent few steps backwards, out of Bree's reach. "What kind of complaint?"

"Not a complaint," Bree said. "Forget the complaint. The issue of time is a nonstarter. I can see that right away. I'm filing a petition."

Goldstein backed a few steps farther away. "Like your other petition? The one that demanded, what was it—'the right to direct and unambiguous communication between counsel and client'? Good luck with that one!"

"Tell me you're not snickering," Bree said in an ominous way.

"No, no, no," he said hastily. "You won't hear the slightest snicker from me. Actually, Bree, I admire your revolutionary spirit."

"You do, huh."

"Just as long as it doesn't go too far. After all . . ."

He *was* snickering, Bree thought furiously.

"Revolution has been known to be carried to excess. I refer you, of course, to case file 1.1 in the *Corpus Juris Ultima*."

"Case 1.1," Bree said. Her memory for famous temporal case precedents was a lot better than her recall of celestial ones. "Oh," she said flatly. "Right."

Lucifer v. the Celestial Courts.

She grabbed the only Bulloch file that was going to be of use to her. "Till the next time, Goldstein."

He twiddled his fingers. "Bye-bye."

"We should feel good about this, in a way," Ron said as they rode down the elevator to the first floor. "Look how important the caseload's getting. If we tie this one up, we're going to affect the disposition of at least three souls. Maybe even more than that."

Bree stamped her foot. "Damn. I should have asked for the file on Bagger Bill Norris, too. If he's in the eighth circle, we'll have a pretty good idea that he's involved somehow. It'll help the temporal investigation a lot to know who actually did it."

"Shall I go back up and get it?"

"Yeah. But look at it before you check it out. If it says 'Pending,' too, give it back to Goldstein and tell him to . . ." Bree stamped her other foot. "Oh, tell him I'm sorry I lost my temper. I suppose just knowing Norris is in Limbo along with everyone else helps a bit. But I *am* going to write out a petition, and I *am* going to see a little decent reform if it's the last thing I do. Jeez." Then she muttered, "Limbo."

Ron very rarely touched her, but he did so now. He put his hand on her cheek and smiled at her. "It's not just a flip saying, 'What is time to an angel?' It's a very profound truth. Time is meaningless. There is no past. No future. Just the now. If you're imagining Haydee in Limbo crying out for a justice that's been delayed, it just isn't so."

"I get the metaphysical part just fine," Bree said. There was something about Ron's smile that was better than any antidepressant devised by man, and that, Bree thought, included a nice slug of gin. She smiled back at him. "It's the people here in this time and this place that are waiting unfairly."

"Who, for example?"

"Dent, for one."

"Dent's problems are well within his control."

She was still arguing with Ron when the elevator doors opened on the first floor and she very nearly cannoned into Cordelia Eastburn.

"Hey, Bree! Back from your holidays, I see." The district attorney looked past Bree into the elevator. "It's Ron Parchese, isn't it?"

"Par-chay-see," Ron said. "Not like the game. How are you, Ms. Eastburn?"

"Finer than a frog hair, as my daddy used to say. Can I borrow your boss for a minute, Ron?"

"She's all yours. I've got to dash upstairs for a second anyway."

Cordy pulled Bree out of the current of people swirling around the room. She was in her midforties and had held the post of district attorney for just a few years. If Bree were a betting woman, she'd put a large sum on Cordy's stated goal: to become the first female black governor of Georgia.

"You're looking a little ruffled, girl. Everything okay?

"I'm pretty well, thanks, Cordy. How are you doing?" Bree cocked her head. "Love the new earrings."

Cordelia's one concession to fashion was an indulgence in handmade earrings; this pair was a handsome swirl of blown glass. Cordy touched them and gave her a cool smile. "Christmas present."

"Nice," Bree approved. "Is it a serious kind of present?"

Cordy wriggled her left hand. The third finger was ringless. "Might be. Might be at that. Speaking of might-be's, have you seen much of Sam Hunter lately?"

Bree gave a guilty start. "Lord. I was supposed to give him a call. Have *you* seen him?"

"More than I'd like. Not that I don't appreciate the

man. I surely do, and," she added, her tone a little more stern, "he's one of the best cops we've got on the force. But what with these movie people in town, we've been . . . what's a good way to put it . . . interfacing more than usual between the police and populace, which means Sam's been up to see me on a pretty frequent basis. Which brings me to the question I have for you, actually." Her tone was crisp, and slightly disapproving.

"Okay," Bree said. "What's up?"

Cordy's gaze was flinty. "You involved in dragging up a cold case?"

"The Haydee Quinn murder?"

"The very one. Are you involved with it?"

Bree hesitated. "Not officially."

"I don't think I heard you, Bree. Officially? Are you an employee of the State of Georgia? A member of my staff? Or, God forbid, of the police department?"

Bree's cheeks were warm. "No, of course not. But some concerns about that case have been raised, and I got interested. Are you upset with me, Cordy? If so, I'd like to know why."

"Who raised what concerns?"

Bree didn't say anything.

Cordy waited her out and then said, "We've been through this drill before. With the Skinner case and the Chandler case and the Lord knows what else you're getting into that I don't know about. So I'm saying again what you've heard before. You find anything out that should be brought to the attention of the State of Georgia you're going to let me know. Correct?"

"Correct."

"I don't have a problem with putting myself in the public eye, Bree. You've got to, if you're going to get anywhere with the kind of reform I want to have happen. But there's setting forward in the right way and then there's sheer opportunism. I'm not so fond of opportunism, and I don't think your daddy is, either. Am I correct in this?"

Bree was completely mystified, but she said, "Of course you're correct. Do you think I'm behaving unprofessionally in any way?"

"Not now. But I'd sure hate to see it in the future."

"I'm starting to feel a lot of sympathy for Alfred Dreyfus," Bree said a bit tartly. "Are you accusing me of something specific?"

"Just that you're the last person I'd accuse of being tacky. Ambulance chasing, so to speak."

"I should hope so," Bree said indignantly. "Who says I'm chasing ambulances? What ambulances?"

Cordy's fierce stance relaxed a bit. "Mind if I say something off-the-record?"

"I wish you would," Bree said fervently. Cordy off-the-record was much easier to deal with than Cordy the Crusader.

"Those Bullochs are not nice people. As for John Stubblefield . . ." She chewed on her lower lip for a moment. "One of these days that boy is going to regret his attitude. And it won't come soon enough for me. Anyway." She gave Bree's shoulder a friendly buffet. "Give Hunter a call one of these days if you feel like it. And it's been too long since the two of us got together for a girl's night out. Call me, soon, okay?"

"Soon," Bree promised.

Cordy walked away. On her way out the front door, she stopped and spoke to the security guards (leaving appreciative chuckles in her wake), greeted two attorneys with a nicely judged chilliness that didn't bode well for whatever pending cases they had, and patted three babies.

"You've cheered up," Ron said in her ear.

"Cordy always cheers me up, even when she's hollering at me." Bree thought about why, before she spoke again. "She's so decent, I guess. I'd sure like to know what set her off, though."

"An ally in the good fight," Ron agreed. "I always like to see her myself. Well, I took a look at the Norris file." He spread his hands to show they were empty. "Pending."

Bree sighed. "Great. Now we don't know if he murdered Haydee or not."

"Your day's about to get even better." He waved his Blackberry at her. "Petru sent me an e-mail. Last things first. Florida Smith will be glad to go to dinner. She'll meet you at today's shoot around seven, and you can walk on over to B. Matthew's from there. Right now, you've got a meeting at Stubblefield, Marwick in thirty minutes. They want you to bring the brooch."

"How is that going to make my day better? I've come back from every meeting I've ever had with John Stubblefield wanting to take a nice hot shower."

"You might feel better about meeting them if you read Petru's e-mail. Consuelo's will was probated ages ago."

"And?"

"Petru's read it, summarized it, scanned it, and sent it to you. You can bring the whole thing up on your iPod, if you want. But all you really need to do is read Petru's summary."

Bree took out her phone and pulled up Petru's message. She read it and then snapped the phone shut. "Well, well, well. This is going to make things interesting."

"Isn't it just," Ron said.

Seven

False face must hide,
What false heart does know.
—*Macbeth*, William Shakespeare

Bree thought of Stubblefield, Marwick the way she thought about designer shoes. A lot of glitz for little substance, and not worth paying full price. A cheat. The satellite office in the Bay Street building occupied the whole of the second floor. Bree pushed open the heavy glass door to the reception area and announced herself to the blonde receptionist at the front desk. Her name tag read TIFFANY.

"Mr. Stubblefield is in conference at the moment, Miss Winston-Beaufort," Tiffany said. "Would you care for a latte while you're waiting? Some Evian water?"

"Actually," Bree said, "what I would care for is not to wait."

Tiffany smiled glossily. Her hair was an improbable champagne pink. "I completely understand how busy you are, Miss Winston-Beaufort. Mr. Stubblefield will be just a few moments."

"I'm not particularly busy," Bree said. "What I am is averse to hanging around waiting for John Stubblefield." She looked at her watch. "Mr. Stubblefield has exactly five minutes. If we're not in a meeting by then, he can reschedule for a time better suited to his busy schedule." She held up her tote. "Just so you know, I have Mrs. Waterman's brooch with me."

Tiffany blinked. "I'll be happy to give him the message."

She picked up the phone. Bree sat down in a satin-striped fake Regency armchair and tried to avoid looking at her surroundings. The wall-to wall carpeting was thick, unnaturally clean, and the color of Tiffany's hair. The furniture consisted of ornate, stylized versions of antiques. Masses of silk flowers spilled from fake Tuscan urns. The drapes were Dupioni silk. The air thrummed faintly with the action of a white-noise machine, and somebody had gotten overexcited with a bottle of air freshener.

Within three minutes, the heavy mahogany door to the back rooms swung open. Payton came out first. Bree was mildly sorry to see that he favored his right knee when he walked, but not very. John Stubblefield stood behind him. Stubblefield wore a pale blue Oxford button-down shirt, the sleeves rolled to the elbow. Red suspenders held up beige cashmere trousers. His wingtips were polished to a spit shine. He looked as ersatz as the antiques in his foyer.

Stubblefield, with his crown of pure white hair and bright blue eyes, was the star of the firm's late-night infomercials. He came across as folksy, concerned, and not overly smart. In reality, he was self-interested to a pathological degree and greedy to a degree beyond that. He was also one of the smartest lawyers Bree had encountered in her short career. Bree hoped that one of these decades, the federal government would take a long, hard look at tort reform; until then, Stubblefield would continue to make a fortune bringing class-action suits against the manufacturers of floor wax and dentures.

"Miss Winston-Beaufort." Stubblefield's grin was wide, white, and about as trustworthy as a fox in a henhouse. "Please! Come in. Come in."

Bree avoided his hand on her arm and walked ahead of him down the thickly carpeted hallway to the conference room. Stubblefield, Marwick negotiated a lot of their class-action suits here, and it was set up with a grandiosity that always put Bree in mind of the United Nations, as interpreted by the descendants of Walt Disney. At least three former office suites had been knocked together to make one large room. Sixty feet long and thirty feet wide, it was dominated by a vast, highly polished round table surrounded by executive-style leather chairs. In front of each chair was a computer port, a water carafe, and old-fashioned yellow pads. Stubblefield, Marwick pens and pencils were placed neatly at the top of each pad. One end of the room was a stainless steel kitchen, complete with granite countertops, that could be closed off with plantation-style pocket doors. On top of the sleek kitchen island was a plate of cantaloupe, watermelon, grapes, and cheese.

Stubblefield indicated Bree should sit with a wave of his hand. "Can Tiffany make you a cappuccino? Or a 'Co-Cola?" He pronounced "cola" the Southern way, although Bree knew for a fact he was originally from Providence, Rhode Island. "We'll have to wait a few minutes for Mrs. Waterman, I'm afraid. Her driver called. Traffic's pretty heavy around the market. Apparently, Sundowner Productions is shooting some background footage. But you know all about that."

"Do I?" Bree pulled out a chair nearest the kitchen and sat down. Payton, who hadn't said a word and didn't seem about to, stationed himself behind the island and took out his Blackberry. She fought the impulse to holler, "Yo, steno boy," and turned to Stubblefield instead. "You're in a better position to know what's happening at Sundowner Productions, surely, John? Phillip Mercury thinks the place is full of your spies."

Stubblefield chuckled. "The ineffable Justine. Oh what a tangled web it is. Sister suing sister. Tsk, tsk." He settled on the tabletop and clasped his hands around his raised knee. Bree was familiar with the pose: Just-Us-Folks Stubblefield. "Nonsense. The Bullochs, as you know, are quite concerned about the slurs Phillip Mercury and his scriptwriter are casting on that fine family's name. But any information they have about the film has been gathered through ordinary legal channels. The truth will come out in court. In the meantime, I've advised the Bulloch family to stay at arm's length. You, on the other hand, seem to be closely involved in Sundowner's affairs."

"Well, I'm not. But I do represent Justine Coville. She's authorized me to discuss the return of the jeweled pin lent to her by Alexandra Bulloch, a member of the Bulloch family. And as all of Savannah knows, Justine has a role in *Bitter Tide*. I wouldn't characterize that as my being involved with the company."

Stubblefield frowned. "*Discuss* the return of my client's property? Your paralegal assured me that you were here to give Mrs. Waterman her property back. I wouldn't have dragged my poor client all the way down here for anything less. Of course, I'm always glad to see you. But I'm feeling very disappointed."

"Fib. Attack. Duck. That's a great tactic, John." Bree yawned for effect. "But it won't work with me. Torture might, though. This room is too hot. Do you think you can turn down the heat?"

"This is a climate-controlled facility," Payton said. "Everybody else is comfortable."

"How's the knee?" Bree asked sweetly.

Stubblefield's grin got mean. "How's about that knee, Payton? I'd surely like to know the story behind that little episode. I send my trusted associate down to see this little bit of a girl and he comes back all messed up."

A small chime sounded. Tiffany's voice floated into the room. The speaker system was a good one. It felt as if she were standing right there. "Mrs. Waterman is here, Mr. Stubblefield."

Stubblefield lifted his chin and spoke to the air. "Please escort Mrs. Waterman to the conference room."

Payton went to the door and opened it. Tiffany came in moments later. She stepped aside and held the door wide. Stubblefield leaped off the table, his arms open in welcome. "Samantha Rose! Aren't you looking like an English spring this morning?"

"It's after one' clock in the afternoon, John. And I haven't had my breakfast yet."

Samantha Rose Waterman was attractive in the way that women who could afford personal trainers, dieticians, and expert dermatologists were attractive. Her hair was brilliantly styled to minimize a large nose and a determined chin. Her makeup was discreet. She was in her midforties Bree guessed, maybe a little older. She wore a short mink jacket, a white silk shirt, tight-fitting Prada jeans, and red stiletto heels. A gold bracelet crowded with charms was wrapped around one wrist.

"There's a little fruit and cheese for you right over there," Stubblefield said. "Tiffany?" He patted the receptionist's rear end. "Be a good girl and fix a plate for Mrs. Waterman."

Tiffany dimpled prettily and went over to the kitchen island. Payton gave her a big smile and brushed up against her breasts as she took a small plate from the stack next to the fruit bowl.

So what's with this guy getting away with patting a woman on the butt?

"Dent," Bree said. "Dammit. Not now."

It's the fact the guy's got bucks, right?

"I said not now, Dent!"

Sammi-Rose looked at her with arrogant distaste. Stubblefield looked amused. Bree covered her mouth with her hand and scribbled aimlessly on her yellow pad.

One rule for the high rollers, and one for all the rest of it.

Bree dropped her pen and smacked her temple with the heel of her hand. "Will you just cut it out?"

"Sammi-Rose," Stubblefield said, "I'd like you to meet Brianna Winston-Beaufort. The next time you see Justine, you might comment on the professional quality of her counsel."

"Sorry," Bree said. She gestured vaguely at her ear. "Earache."

Samantha's smile was meaner than Stubblefield's. She accepted the plate of fruit Tiffany handed to her, picked over the grapes and the cantaloupe, and handed back the plate. "I don't eat watermelon. I'd appreciate it if you'd slice up the other fruit a bit more." She narrowed her eyes at Stubblefield. "Did she bring the brooch?"

Stubblefield looked at Bree. "She brought the brooch."

She snapped her fingers. "I want to see it."

Bree opened her briefcase and held up the jeweled pin. The overhead lights struck small rainbows from the diamonds. "Is this the brooch? You can identify it?"

"Of course I can. It's a Louis Comfort Tiffany. An original."

"Thank you." Bree put it back in the briefcase and snapped it shut.

Sammi-Rose looked directly at her for the first time. "That's mine," she snarled.

"It's not yours," Bree said cordially. "It's your grandmother's."

"My grandmother—bless her heart—passed a long time ago. And she left that brooch to the family. That old bitch got her hands on it, stole it, and we want it back."

Bree cut her eyes at Stubblefield. "Consuelo Bulloch's last will and testament directed that she be buried with the brooch."

Stubblefield smiled a little.

"Your grandmother's buried at Belle Glade. I've got the brooch. Which means it's not in the casket."

"So?" Apparently Tiffany had cut the fruit into sufficiently small pieces. Sammi-Rose picked up a square of melon and chewed it. "It would have been ridiculous to bury that fine a piece."

Bree stretched back in the chair. "Whoever decided to keep the jewel committed grand felony theft."

Sammi-Rose stopped chewing. "What the hell are you talking about?"

"Can you tell me who made the decision not to inter the brooch with Consuelo's body?"

Stubblefield spoke up. "She's not going to answer that, are you, Samantha?"

"I guess not." Sammi-Rose put another piece of melon in her mouth and chewed mechanically. Bree thought she was worried, but it was hard to tell. Botox took her Aunt Cissy the same way.

"It's the duty of the executor of the estate to pursue

this," Bree said. "I'm afraid until it's resolved, the executor will have custody of the peacock."

"The executor?" Sammi-Rose pushed the plate aside and stood up. "That's all right, then. My father was the executor of Grandmother's estate. And he was the one who decided what a waste it'd be to bury it with the old cat anyhow."

"Your father was co-executor," Bree corrected her. Out of the corner of her eye, she saw Stubblefield frown suddenly. "And your father was derelict in his duty, I'm afraid. Which is another kettle of fish altogether." Bree jumped to her feet. "I'll leave you and Mr. Stubblefield to hash this over, Mrs. Waterman. In the meantime, the brooch remains with me."

"God damn it," Stubblefield hissed. "You're going to regret this."

Sammi-Rose's face flushed red. "You can't just let her walk right out of here. That pin is worth twenty thousand dollars."

"And a beautiful piece to boot." Bree reached the door, opened it, and paused on her way out. "You haven't asked, John, but it *is* pretty obvious. You should have read Consuelo's will more carefully. Whatever else you are, you're a capable man, so I'll cut you some slack and assume that you had someone else do it for you." She very pointedly avoided looking at Payton. "There's a reason why he's not looking too pleased, Mrs. Waterman. The law firm of Franklin Winston-Beaufort was your grandmother's co-executor, too. She chose him because he helped your father through a rough patch after the

Haydee Quinn murder. My great-uncle, bless his heart, turned his legal obligations over to me when I took over his practice. Which is why I have the brooch, will keep the brooch, and will dispose of the brooch according to the rule of law. I'll let you know what the courts decide about the disposition of your grandmother's property. I'm going to petition that it be reburied with her." She touched her brow in a half salute. "See ya!"

Bree jogged up the four flights of stairs to her own office, reflecting there were few things as satisfying as a complete (admittedly temporary) victory over chiselers and cheats. EB would enjoy the story. EB would also remind her that the Bullochs in general and Stubblefield in particular were bad enemies to have.

Except EB wasn't there. It was after two o'clock. EB went home at noon. The Bay Street practice was still too new to carry a full-time assistant—other than Justine Coville, the only other clients Bree had were clients who'd already made out their wills. Bree stood in the middle of the room and tried to look at the room through the eyes of a prospective client.

A bamboo screen split the room into two parts; the two-thirds in front held EB's desk and her computer, three gray metal filing cabinets containing Franklin's old files and Bree's very few new ones, and a visitor's chair. Bree's desk was behind the screen, set under the double-hung window that looked out over Bay Street.

The carpeting was the standard industrial type that Bree mentally thought of as "no color," just like the walls. All the furniture was secondhand—maybe even third. EB had picked it up from Second Hand Rows down on Whitaker Street. Paint, pictures, plants, Bree thought. When she had time.

She sat down at her desk to pick up her messages. There was a note in EB's distinctive handwriting:

> *Went through the storage cabinet. Found transcript of December 13th 1952 file on Alexander Bulloch. Ron came to pick up. Left case file for you to read before you meet Florida Smith at 7:00 p.m. What a nice smile that boy has. Calls from Lt. Hunter— please call back. Dent wants to see you. Heard from Ron you'd be here today so I told him stop by. See you tomorrow I hope.—EB*

The transcript of the sanity hearing was on top of the pile. Bree picked it up, surprised to discover she was nervous. Her memories of Franklin were good ones. She had known him as a tall, rather reserved man with a mane of white hair and a deep, resonant voice. She was about to see him again, through his words on the pages she held.

She reviewed the list of witnesses first. The consulting MD was a Dr. Pythias Warren. Bree frowned. He was a GP. His credentials didn't include psychiatry. The presiding judge was a man she'd heard about but who'd died long before she was born: Bulwar Kinney. She was vague about his reputation, but undoubtedly he would have been part of the city's Old Guard. The Kinney family certainly was.

Eddie O'Malley was listed as a witness. He'd been part of the team that had arrested Alex's pitiful journey with the burning cart.

The witness testimony about Alex's behavior after Haydee's death was consistent. He was tragically distraught. Consuelo, Alexander senior, Dr. Warren—their testimony didn't have the sameness of agreed-upon lies. Alex wept, scarified his face and chest with a table knife, couldn't sleep, and then, finally, relapsed into a sort of stupor, neither eating nor responding to the people around him. It made Bree's eyes sting with tears just reading about it. It must have been horrible in the courtroom.

She came to Alex's own testimony:

JUDGE KINNEY: You say that Miss Quinn asked you to purify her, Mr. Bulloch? How did she come to do that?

DEFENDANT BULLOCH: She called to me.

JUDGE KINNEY: She called you? Where did she call you from, son?

DEFENDANT BULLOCH: In my room. She was in my room. At night. With her hair down. Calling me.

JUDGE KINNEY: This was the night of July 3?

DEFENDANT BULLOCH: No response. Weeping.

JUDGE KINNEY: She came to you the night of July 3?

DEFENDANT BULLOCH: In my bed! In my bed!

Bree set the transcript aside. No real answers there. Tyra Steele's behavior had put paid to the notion that Haydee's spirit had returned to seek justice. The young actress may have fooled herself into thinking she was possessed, but Bree was willing to bet most of her sorry bank account that that notion would disappear once the Facebook fans lost interest. As for a ghostly appearance in Alex Bulloch's room all those years ago?

Maybe.

She picked up the thick manila packet that contained the downloads from the Internet. There were three separate bundles inside, labeled MURDER, BEFORE, and AFTER. She picked up the MURDER file first. The lead story was from the *Savannah Daily News* dated July 1, 1952:

GRUESOME DISCOVERY IN RIVER!
Haydee Quinn Found Stabbed
Beautiful Danseuse Dies of Wounds!

The photographs attached to the story were typical of the time. There was a smeary black-and-white shot of the riverbank, showing the old pier and the blurred outline of the opposite shore. A white arrow pointed to an area in the water just beyond where the Savannah Tourist Bureau was now.

The photograph that really drew Bree's interest was of Haydee herself. It was a black-and-white head shot, obviously a studio pose for publicity purposes. Haydee looked into the camera over her left shoulder. Her hair was dark, coiled on top of her head. She wore a jeweled cap, with feathers sweeping down her cheek to the tip of her chin. Her eyes were light—someone, it might have been Justine, had said they were blue. Bree was willing to bet her eyelashes were fake; they were too thick and lush to be natural. Her lips were distinctive; she had a triangular smile with a seductive curl that reminded Bree of the actress Vivien Leigh in the old movie *Gone with the Wind*.

Below the head shot was a photograph of Haydee in full theatrical costume. She wore a net bodysuit covered with spangles. She looked a little chubby to Bree's eyes and definitely underexercised. But she supposed beauty standards in the Cold War era had differed from those now. And in any era, her face was dazzling.

The article stated the facts right up front. An early morning fisherman cast his line over the banks. The hook caught in Haydee's hair. As soon as he realized what was on the other end of the line, the dismayed fisherman ran for the beat policeman, Patrolman Herbert Wilson. Bleeding and unconscious, Haydee was pulled from the river. An ambulance rushed her to Savannah General Hospital. Every effort was made to save her, but she died of a dozen wounds to the chest six hours later.

The articles subsequent to the discovery of the victim herself concerned the police investigation. Haydee was the star attraction at a nightclub called the Tropicana Tide in the docks area east of Old Savannah. Shipping was a dying industry at the time, but the area was home to what the newspaper referred to as "the rougher elements of our fair city." (Bree was struck with the reticent tone of the reporting when it came to sex and drugs.) Her manager, a "notorious gangster, three times convicted of illegal gambling," was Dysart William Norris, known as Bagger Bill. A helpful sidebar indicated that he'd come by this nickname after running numbers for "gentlemen from up North." Bagger Bill was suspected of the crime almost immediately by "our fair city's crack homicide team," Lt. Edward O'Malley and Sgt. Robert E. Lee Kowalski.

There was a black-and-white photograph of O'Malley—Dent, to her—and another of a square-jawed man with slicked-back hair. Bree examined the picture of Dent closely. This was an official police photo taken in a studio, like Haydee's. It showed a younger Dent, with a lot more hair, staring directly at the camera. Florida Smith must have come across this photograph, too. But most of the lenses at the time flattened faces out and added weight to their frames. It would have taken a highly skilled professional a lot of fiddling to get a genuinely representational portrait. And by the time Dent died in the car crash years later, alcohol had taken its toll on his face.

Two days after Haydee's death at the hospital, O'Malley and Kowalski charged Bagger Bill with the first-degree murder of Haydee Quinn. In the statement given to the press, the police claimed Norris was found dead drunk with "blood on his hands" and a knife at his side. According to the bartender at the Tropicana Tide, the accused and the victim had a "knock-down, drag-out set-to" the night before Haydee was found in the river.

After undergoing extensive interrogation, Norris confessed. A few weeks later, he recanted his confession, and ultimately went to the chair loudly claiming his innocence.

Confessed.

Bree sat back and thought about this. There was no mention of the accuser's lawyer until some weeks after the murder. The police weren't required to Mirandize suspects until 1964. As far as police interrogation techniques at the time, there was a lot less oversight than there was now.

She wondered if Dent had been capable of beating a false confession out of William Norris.

Bree paged through the rest of the articles, pausing at the news stories about Alexander Bulloch's tragic odyssey on the riverbank. The stories were remarkably restrained. Maybe not so remarkably, Bree thought, since the Bulloch family was reverently referred to when they were referred to at all. There were no photographs of Alexander himself, although Petru had researched a picture of Consuelo. Bree found it a little eerie to see a temporal representation of her client. The woman was quite thin, with a tight mouth and an even tighter perm. The peacock pin rode high on her right shoulder, fastened to the collar of her prim dress. The small headline below her picture read, *Mrs. Alexander Bulloch at the Red Cross Relief Fund-Raiser.* Bree studied Consuelo's face. She certainly didn't look like a woman who would welcome the lush curves of Haydee Quinn at her dinner table. She recalled the charges that had sent her client to Hell: spite, malice, bigotry, treachery. Yes, that face looked capable of all those behaviors. But murder?

On an impulse, Bree took the peacock jewel from her briefcase and held it between her palms.

"Mrs. Bulloch?"

A faint sigh went around the room. The blinds at the window stirred, although there was no breeze.

"Mrs. Bulloch?"

Somebody rapped on the office door. Bree, absorbed in the frustrating task of summoning her client, thought for a wild moment it was Mrs. Bulloch herself, released from the Sphere.

It wasn't.

Eight

There's husbandry in heaven,
Their candles are all out.
—*Macbeth*, William Shakespeare

"Oh," Bree said. "It's you, Dent."

"Got a minute?" He stepped into the office. He held his driver's hat in one hand.

"Sure. Come in." She gestured at the visitor's chair. "Have a seat."

"This your office?" He looked around at the bare walls and the sparse furniture. "Business doesn't look too good."

"It'll be even worse if you keep bouncing into my head at inopportune moments. I behaved like an idiot this morning."

"What d'ya mean?"

"I mean that episode this morning. In John Stubblefield's office? In front of Sammi-Rose Waterman?" She thought a moment and then added indignantly. "Not to mention Payton the Rat."

His brow cleared. "Oh. You mean the ass-grabbing incident. Yeah, well, it's something I want you to keep in mind."

"That you want *me* to keep in mind?" Then, she added automatically, "Please don't call women's asses, asses. It's demean—oh forget it. Just what am I supposed to keep in mind?"

"That there's a standard for the muckety-mucks and a standard for the rest of us down here." He pursed his lips. "Thing is, you're one of the muckety-mucks, so . . ."

"Dent!" Bree took a breath, stared down at her knees, and counted backwards from ten. "Okay. So you've got a self-esteem problem. I'm your sponsor, right? It's one of the things we can work on. 'We hold these truths to be self-evident,' remember? 'That all men are created equal?'"

"Except some are more equal than others." Dent wasn't smiling. "Look, I want to go out and see Bobby Lee and I want you to come with me."

"Sergeant Kowalski?" Bree glanced at her watch. "Not enough time today. I've arranged to meet Flurry Smith at seven tonight, and I'm hoping that she'll have a lot of useful information. But let's talk about the case a little bit, shall we? We can make up a list of questions for him. I'll make sure we see him tomorrow or the day after, at the very latest." She pulled a legal pad from her desk drawer and headed it SUSPECTS. "Now, I know you think you don't remember a lot about the case, but I'd like to try."

"I was drinking then. A lot."

"So you told me. But it's not a total blur, is it?" The

newspaper photograph of Lt. Edward O'Malley was on top of the pile of papers on her desk. "You remember this?"

Dent picked it up. His hands trembled slightly. "The department took that when I made lieutenant."

"When were you promoted?"

"About a year before the Haydee Quinn case. Maybe less."

"You must have been a good cop, to get promoted," Bree said encouragingly.

Dent's smile was cynical. "I was a Marine. The police commissioner was my CO at Iwo."

Bree felt chilly. She'd read about the war. "Iwo Jima?"

Dent scratched the back of his neck. "What the hell does this have to do with the Quinn case?"

"Just trying to get a handle on you and the times." Bree's long hair was a nuisance during the day, so she braided it and coiled it around her head. Sometimes after a long day, the weight of her braids gave her a headache. She was getting a headache now. She pulled out the tortoiseshell pins, let her braid fall over her shoulder, and tugged absently at the end. "I think we have two tasks here. The first is to find out the facts."

"And if Consuelo did it, after all? That's not too good for your client. Lawyers are supposed to get people off."

Bree wound the tip of her braid around her finger. "I've thought hard about this. The state—or in this case, the Celestial Sphere—has an obligation to turn over any and all evidence of a crime to the defense. There is an extraordinary obligation to turn over exculpatory evidence. We have a different standard of duty as the defense. Our obligation is to our client. If we find out that Consuelo is guilty of murder, and that the miscarriage of justice here is that she's not being punished enough, we are not obliged to turn her in. It's the plaintiff who has to prove it."

"And the second job?"

Bree smiled at him. "To present an alternative theory of the crime. Sometimes a successful defense is built on getting the judge to entertain the notion that someone else did it. To establish reasonable doubt. But you can bet that the defense is going to be ready to tear those doubts apart. That's why I need to know everything you can possibly remember. Especially about the William Norris confession. I'd like to start there. Even if it doesn't . . ." She paused, searching for the least brutal way of phrasing her suspicions about Bagger Bill's confession. ". . . reflect very well on you or Sergeant Kowalski."

Dent sat up a little taller in his chair. "Right. 'Continue to take personal inventory and when we are wrong, promptly admit it.' "

"I beg your pardon? Oh! Of course! The steps." Bree did her best to look both encouraging and sympathetic.

"You want to know what kind of encouragement we gave Norris to get that confession."

"That'll do for starters."

"We didn't touch him." Dent's grin was a little crooked. "I can see what you're thinking. You're remembering what Eleanor Roosevelt wanted to do with us Marines."

Bree tried to look as if yes, she certainly was.

"Keep us all on an island for a year after the war."

"Eleanor Roosevelt said that?" Bree was astonished.

"We weren't saints, most of us. Not during the war. Not afterwards. But you do what you have to do. So you're thinking Bobby Lee and I found this lowlife drunk out of his mind at the back of that scummy bar, planted a bloody knife on him, and beat a confession out of him because he was the most likely perp."

"Yes," Bree said. "The thought crossed my mind."

He shook his head. "Nope."

"Nope?"

"He confessed, fair and square.

"You have to know what it was like back then. This was what the commissioner called a high-profile case. Lot of muckety—sorry, a lot of influential people were involved with Haydee Quinn and Bagger Bill one way or another. Norris bootlegged liquor in the '30s, in the black market during the war years, and supplied a lot of the upper crust with whatever dope they needed after that." Dent set his jaw. "Marijuana and worse. Anyhow, this nightclub of his, Tropicana Tide, had been a thorn in the city's side for years. Gambling mostly, along with the drugs. Norris signed Haydee on as a dancer a year and a half before all this happened, and I'll tell you, I knew even then she was trouble. She slept around a lot. Mostly men who could give her a hand. Rich men. Power brokers.

"As far as Haydee herself." His face softened. "She reminded me a lot of Ava Gardner."

"Ava Gardner the actress?" Bree asked. The name was familiar from the occasional crossword puzzle.

"The movie star," Dent said, as if it made a difference. Maybe it did back then. "Haydee had that same hardscrabble background. Her daddy was a dirt-poor cotton farmer from the Low Country. Haydee got herself out of that dirt-floored shack and never looked back. How she did it, when she could barely read and write . . . well, you would have had to have seen her in the flesh." He reached over and tapped the news photo of Haydee in costume. "That doesn't begin to show you how drop-dead gorgeous she was. When she walked into a room, everything stopped. With those eyes and that hair and that white, white skin. She had a perfect face, you know. Perfectly proportioned. They did an article on it in one of the big newspapers after she died. Anyhow, she hit Savannah like a Mack truck on a mud slide. Everybody was nuts about her. The men, that is. The women not so much.

"So she got herself hooked up with this kid Alex Bulloch. He was a couple of years younger than she was. I never saw them together, but those that did seem to think they really loved each other. That's what the argument was about. The one Haydee had with Norris just before it all happened."

"Norris told you this?"

"Oh yeah. The man was crazy jealous. She was a bit of a hellcat, from all accounts. Told Norris he could shove his contract where the sun don't shine, or words to that effect, and that she was going to marry the kid come hell or high water. Norris said he grabbed the first thing that came to hand when she started to walk out the door. A knife they used to slice up the ham at the club." Dent sucked his lower lip reflectively. "Always had a big old ham on the bar at Tropi. Norris said it made people thirstier for the booze. Worked like a champ on me, that's for sure."

Bree nudged the conversation back to the night of the murder. "Norris attacked her with the knife?"

"Stabbed her in the heart, or tried to."

"Then what happened? Did he take the body to the river?"

"Norris? Hell, no. Said he felt so bad he dropped to his knees and begged her forgiveness. She ran off, he said, and the next thing he knew, they were pulling her out of the drink."

"The river," Bree said, just to be clear. "What did the autopsy show? She didn't drown, according to the newspaper. Although, to be absolutely accurate, she was alive when they pulled her from the water. She may have died from the effects of inhaling river water, I suppose."

"Stab wounds," Dent said. "Near as they could tell."

"Why couldn't they be certain?"

"You're the one that's nitpicking here," Dent said. "I'm just damn glad you never cross-examined me in court." He pitched his voice higher. " 'Although, to be absolutely accurate, she was alive when they pulled her from the water.' You sound like Norris's lawyer."

"God is in the details," Bree said with a smile. "And I want to get to Norris's lawyer in a minute. So the coroner's office wasn't certain of the cause of death? What did it say on the death certificate?"

"Alex Bulloch broke into the funeral home and grabbed her body before the autopsy was done. By the time the coroner got it, the chest tissue was pretty burned up. So the cause of death was listed as probable stab wound to the blah, blah, blah. I don't remember that part. What I do remember is once the death certificate was entered into evidence, Norris was lawyered up, and the lawyer made a big to-do about how she might have drowned instead of bled to death and Norris only wounded her. Got Norris all excited. Didn't mourn her very long, old Bagger Bill. Recanted his confession. Said he was drunk and didn't know what he was saying. Blah, blah, blah." Dent eyed her distrustfully. "So his lawyer did what you just said. Presented an alternative theory of the crime. But the judge didn't buy it. Condemned Norris to the chair. And to the chair he went."

"When did you decide he was innocent?"

"Me?" Dent said. "I never thought so. He had the knife, he was covered in her blood, and he said he stabbed her. If I thought he was innocent I would have done something about it. I may have been a drunk, but I would have pulled myself together long enough to keep an innocent man from the chair."

"But . . ."

"That's what they said at the intervention," he said. "That I let an innocent man go to the chair. If I'd run a better investigation, he wouldn't have died the way he did. So that's why I'm here. I have to fix this. I've got to make direct amends to those I've offended whenever possible, except when to do so would injure them. Can't get much more injured than being sent to the chair.

"I need to talk to Bobby Lee. He's going to remember a lot more than I do. Sober, churchgoing man, Bobby Lee was."

He was also ninety-two years old. Bree hoped the poor old guy's brains were in good shape. She scrawled a few more questions to herself on the yellow pad: *Norris atty—Who? Trial trsnpst—Smith?*

Dent looked at his watch and shook it next to his ear. It was a large inexpensive one, with a wide chrome band. The dial was labeled TIMEX. "Give it a licking and it keeps on ticking. That's what the ads say. But it's stopped."

"It's quarter to seven." Bree got up out of the chair. She was stiff from sitting. "May I ask you to run me down to the shoot? Flurry expects me there around now. We've got a dinner date."

"Mind if I come along?"

"No," Bree said. "I don't mind at all. As a matter of fact, it might be a very good thing. I'm not sure how easy it's going to be to pry those files out of Florida Smith. I'm going to have to wing it. If anything occurs to you, just jump right in. And Dent, try and keep your hands off the waitresses."

Nine

Who can control his fate?
—*Othello*, William Shakespeare

"Fish tacos, for sure. And a half bottle of a Pinot Grigio." Florida Smith dropped the menu on the table and looked around appreciatively. "I like this place."

B. Matthew's wasn't overly large—maybe sixty feet long and thirty feet wide, but the tables had been placed so you didn't feel you were going to back into the diners next to you. The old wooden floor was made of narrow-planked pine, stained a comfortable brown. A long bar ran the width of the back of the restaurant. Large windows looked out over Bay Street. The walls were hung with a variety of found objects from the nineteenth century: cast iron griddles, etchings, sepia-toned photographs of women in wide hoop skirts.

"I like it, too." Bree looked up at the waitress. "I'll have the fish tacos, too. And a cup of the black bean soup. And a nice dark beer. Whatever kind you think would be good."

"You have burgers?" Dent demanded.

The waitress was young, cute, and patient. "Be happy to make you some."

"Make it two, rare, with raw onion and fries."

"Sweet potato or regular?"

Dent reared back in his chair. "Sweet potato? You're kidding, right? You have hash browns? No. Then just the regular kind. And a lot of coffee. Black." He drummed his fingers on the table. "I take sugar in my coffee. You have sugar, hon—I mean, ma'am?"

"Just the Equal. That's the blue packet on the table. But I'll see if I can find some real sugar in the back for you."

She stood at Dent's shoulder, one hip cocked to help support her as she wrote on her order pad. Dent's right hand came up, hovered around her hip, and retreated. Flurry and Bree looked at each other.

"Thank you, darl—ma'am."

She smiled sunnily at him. "A pleasure, sir."

Bree raised her glass of water in a mock toast to Dent as soon as the waitress was out of earshot. "See? You get happier waitstaff that way."

Dent grunted.

"Bree's right. Happy waiters don't pee in your soup back in the kitchen. Bree! If you're the one who's cured him of inappropriate fanny patting, more power to you." Flurry rummaged in her backpack as she spoke. After setting most of its contents on the table—an HP mini-notebook, an iPod, a Blackberry, two sets of earphones, a half-full bottle of Saratoga Springs mineral water, and a wallet, she withdrew a fat red-brown accordion file. "Here we go." She handed the file to Bree and returned all the other stuff to the backpack item by item.

Bree picked up the file and set it down again. This was too easy.

"It's like the magician's hat," Dent said. "How did you get all that stuff in there in the first place?"

"We have our ways."

Bree looked at the accordion file but didn't open it. "Is this all your research on the Quinn murder?"

"The part of it I haven't gotten on disk yet. Actually, it's copies, not originals. I'm scanning those whenever I have free time. I've got most of the stuff on hard drive, or stored on flash drives."

"How extensive is your research?"

"Oh, I went way back. If poor Haydee had lived past the age of twenty-three and achieved something more than becoming a B-girl, I could have written a whole book about her. She was bound for glory, that girl was. As for William Norris—I have a raft of stuff on him, but he's your average small-time gangster. Hoods, they called them then. A lot of other writers have been there, done that. No, what's really interesting about this case is the role the Bullochs played in it."

The waitress set down a half bottle of the Pinot, poured Flurry a sip, waited for her approval, and then poured the wineglass half full. She did the same with Bree's beer. Dent's coffee was accompanied by four sugar cubes. The only time Bree ever saw sugar cubes was at Plessey, because her mother loved to soak them in lemon and put them in her tea.

"So what do I have, you ask? I've got the transcripts of both trials—the Norris trial for murder and the sanity hearing for Alexander. I've got every magazine and newspaper article ever written about the case, or the principals in the case. I've got the autopsy report, photos of the crime scene, and photos of the burning cart with Alexander pushing it."

Flurry paused to drink her wine.

Bree still didn't open the folder. "What about the murder book?"

Flurry raised both eyebrows in a query.

"The police file," Dent said by way of explanation.

"The O'Malley-Kowalski investigation? I've got photocopies of that. For all the use it is. I mean, sure, I picked up on a couple of witnesses that weren't mentioned anywhere else. But O'Malley was a drunk. I found a source that said the only reason the commissioner kept him was that they were old Army buddies during the war." Flurry raised her hands and fluttered her forefingers in tandem. "The Big One. That's World War II for us girls, Bree. O'Malley wasn't much use. It looks like the partner, Bobby Lee Kowalski, did most of the work."

"Marines," Dent said shortly. "O'Malley was a Marine."

"Marine, Army, whatever."

Bree didn't want to see the look in Dent's eyes, so she

stared straight at Flurry. "Did you get any useful information from Sergeant Kowalski?"

"I only saw him once, but I'm going to go back as soon as I get the time. The old guy's just this side of the grave, but boy, is he smart. Remembers the case like it was yesterday. I got a lot of good stuff on O'Malley. The guy was a total loser. He'd be out of any decent police force in twenty seconds flat nowadays. It's amazing to me how much less oversight there was on the cops back then. Some of them literally got away with murder."

"You don't think the police had anything to do with Haydee's death?" That sort of stuff happened, back in the day. And it wasn't confined to the South.

Flurry emptied her wineglass and poured herself another. "I've got this theory. More than a theory. A conviction." She thumped her slender chest.

"Based on more than hearsay, I hope." Bree's voice was dry. She was stinging over the insults to Dent.

"Oh yeah. The cops turned up a witness that never appeared in court. I've got the interview notes."

"From Kowalski?" Bree guessed. They didn't tape interviews back in the '50s, did they? The junior partner took notes by hand.

Flurry smiled and shook her head. "Not another word out of me, Bree. We've got some negotiating to do."

"The cops turned over every piece of evidence that they had to the DA," Dent said abruptly.

"How would you know?" Flurry wasn't being rude, just inquisitive. She looked at Dent, really looked at him, and for a moment, Bree wondered if she'd make the man at last. "Were you a cop in a past life, Dent?"

"It's their job," Dent said shortly.

"Ha," Flurry snorted. "Like crucial evidence that makes the cops look bad doesn't go missing every day of the week."

"You've been watching too much bad TV," Bree said. "Or reading the wrong newspapers. Every system, in every year going back to Day One and going forward to the Last Trump has or will have corrupt human beings in it. It's who we are. The human race. But it's not pervasive, and it's not worse now than it's ever been."

Flurry put her hand over her heart. Then she saluted. "Hear you loud and clear."

Their food arrived. Dent picked up his hamburger and put it down again. He slumped in his chair and stared at the bottle of Pinot Grigio. Bree was glad it wasn't rye whiskey. Rye whiskey had helped bring poor Dent to his current state. She nudged the conversation back to the case. "Crucial evidence, you said. From this unknown witness."

"Yep. It's going to make one hell of a book, one hell of a book. Did I tell you I got interviews with two of the three Bulloch granddaughters, too? I got them before Sammi-Rose Spiderwoman slammed the door shut in my face. Marian Lee's pretty lame. She married a guy who runs a very successful car garage. He's a perfect sweetie. But she's miserable, just miserable, not living the life of a Bulloch. Now, Dixie Bulloch's pretty cool. She never married, and she remembers her grandmother pretty well. She's the oldest, and she also remembers that her folks fought over Haydee when she was a little kid. Haydee had been dead for years. She claims that Alexander never got over her." Flurry picked up her fork and stared at her fish taco. "Isn't that the saddest thing? I mean, this guy fell in love with a woman when he was nineteen and that was it. He never fell in love again. The rest of his life was just going through the motions."

Bree, who was not particularly sentimental, tended to doubt stories of everlasting love. Now, everlasting guilt was another story. Hatred lasted, too. She'd believe in a heartbeat that Alexander never got rid of his sense of guilt.

"Anyhow, I've made up a time line, tracking the chief suspects twenty-four hours before and twenty-four hours after Haydee kicked the bucket." Flurry bit into her fish taco, chewed, swallowed, and said, "This food is *fabulous*!"

Dent had reconsidered his hamburger and eaten his first one, and was now moving on to his second. Bree added a little mango salsa to her own taco and began to eat with the others.

"So," Flurry said, after a long moment spent on the food. "What do you think? I prepared all this because I want you to be so impressed with my researching skills, my writing skills, and my all-out competence that you'll agree to an interview about Franklin Winston-Beaufort. What do you say?"

"I'm not sure I'd be any help at all."

"Of course you will. He's a bit of a mystery, you

know, even to folks I've found in the court system who knew him well. Haven't been able to dig up a whole lot about him. He had a pretty decent run as a state court justice. Seemed to have been respected by his peers, as they say. But I've got nothing on his private life. Why did he agree to take on the sanity hearing? You knew the man. You could take a guess. How close was he to the Bullochs? Did he ever socialize with them after Alexander went off to the booby hatch? How much did he know about who really killed Haydee Quinn? He was a young, struggling attorney when the Bullochs handed him this high-profile case. After that, his reputation and his revenues soared." She regarded Bree over the rim of her wineglass. Her smile was steady, but there was a determination in her eyes that made Bree wary.

Dent broke his long silence. "I've got a question."

"Lay it on me, brother." Flurry beamed, on top of the world.

Bree recognized these particular high spirits. Flurry was young, in the middle of a project she hoped was going to make her reputation, and best of all, doing work she believed in. Antonia got like that when she'd landed a wonderful part. Bree silently amended that: whenever she landed any part.

"Why do you think we . . . that is, Miss Beaufort here, needs any of the information you're offering?"

"Why?" Flurry seemed taken aback. "You were the one who invited me to dinner, remember?"

Bree fought the urge to leap over the table and give Dent a kiss. She'd been so caught up in the pursuit of this background information she'd forgotten that none of the temporals involved had any idea she'd taken on Consuelo's case. She was moving too fast. She wasn't getting enough sleep.

She was slipping.

"Yes. But I'm representing Justine Coville's interests, Flurry. I'm handling her will, I'm going to be representing her if Mercury tries to fire her unfairly, and I volunteered to handle the return of the peacock brooch." She smiled at Dent. "That's the extent of my interest, I'm afraid. This is wonderful research. It sounds like it's going to be a wonderful book. But you've leaped to an unwarranted assumption here."

"That's not what I heard."

"What did you hear? And from whom?"

"That you're poking your—sorry, that you've taken an interest."

"In the murder? Why in the world should I?"

"You've done it before, I guess. Turned perfectly usual client cases into moneymakers for yourself. The Chandler family hired you to handle the defense of the teenager accused of shoplifting—"

"Petty theft," Bree corrected her.

"And it turned into this big huge deal about a murder with a very high fee. Tully O'Rourke hired you to handle some real estate contracts for her theater, and all of a sudden, you were involved in a murder case, again with a very high fee. And there was that billionaire, Skinner. His heir hired you to handle a dispute over the will and—"

"I also ended up charging a very high fee? Is that what the gossip is?" Bree had a tight rein on her temper. "The accounts of the size of the fees are inflated. I charged the usual hourly fee. It's average for an ABA member in my situation."

Flurry blushed a little. "Sorry. Personally, I think you're terrific, and having met you, I'm wondering just what kind of line my source is feeding me."

"Your source wouldn't be that slick piece of . . ." Bree bit her lip so hard she tasted blood. "You ever meet Payton McAllister?"

Flurry's eyes slid sideways and down. "The name's familiar."

"His firm represents the Bulloch interests, I believe."

"Yes. I believe they do."

"So you think I'm chasing a large fee for myself by involving myself in this case."

"Jumping on the bandwagon, yeah." Flurry shrugged. "You have to grab the opportunity when it comes by. I understand that better than anyone."

"Who's paying this huge fee I'm supposed to be after?" Bree was so furious the room around her was beginning to tilt. "The Bullochs maybe? Justine Coville?"

"Don't be silly," Flurry said uncomfortably. "The Bullochs hate the book and the project. Poor Justine doesn't have a pot to piss in. Payton thinks maybe you're after a TV deal." She looked hopeful. "If you are, you can't do it without me."

Suddenly, Cordy's disapproving attitude made sense. Somebody was accusing her of jumping onto the Haydee

Quinn murder to make a name for herself in Savannah. An accusation like that would have consequences. The better law firms wouldn't send her referrals. Clients who required discretion would be scared off. She could be ruined even before her temporal practice got off the ground. Someone wanted to see that happen.

She was absolutely certain she knew who that someone was.

"Payton McAllister's no friend of mine, Flurry. There's some history there."

"He hates her guts," Dent said. He grinned. "She keeps beating him up, and he keeps losing."

Bree frowned Dent into silence and turned to Flurry. "So you can take anything he says about me with a large grain of salt."

Flurry twiddled with the stem of her wineglass. Her dark skin had a deep red cast. "I've had the wrong take on this, totally. I apologize. You sure don't act like somebody that wants to hang on celebrity coattails. Which means I guess there isn't any real reason why you'd want to talk to me about your uncle."

"I wouldn't say that. I do understand," Bree said. "This is an exciting project. More than that, it's a worthy one."

"It is, isn't it?" Flurry's high spirits returned in a flash. "Proving a man innocent is a pretty cool thing to do."

"Yes," Bree said soberly. "It's a life's work, isn't it?" She was silent for a long moment, thinking of her face in the mirror at Angelus Street.

Flurry tapped the table impatiently. "Earth to Bree."

"Sorry. I was just thinking of the consequences of all this." She took a deep breath. Whatever her ultimate decision about her own life's work was going to be, she was already in the pool with this case. "I'm fascinated by what you've told me so far. And I'm very curious about my uncle's part in it. I would like to help you, if I can. *Quietly*, though. I'd rather my name was not associated with this in any way."

"You want to help?"

"Yeah. I would. I'm afraid I don't really understand the big picture, though. Tell you what. If you like, I can take some of these materials here—and maybe you can e-mail some of your other research, as you suggested, and I'll run it by my dad. He's seventy-two, and I'll bet he remembers the circumstances of the case, especially if my uncle had some minor involvement in it. He might be able to come up with some things we've never considered."

"You're not interested in writing your own book about this, are you?" Flurry said suspiciously.

Bree shook her head and borrowed a phrase from Antonia. "I'd rather eat a rat. I have enough trouble settling down to write a brief, much less a manuscript. How long do you think it'll be?"

"Hundred thousand words, easy."

Bree's dismay was entirely sincere. "No thank you, ma'am. I do like puzzles, though, and so does Dad. And since this has some of our own family history in it, it's going to be really interesting to get a handle on things."

"So we have a deal?"

"We do." Bree reached across the table to shake her hand. Dent, to her surprise, grasped her wrist and drew her hand away. Both women looked at him.

"Restaurant's filled up," Dent said. "Take a look-see."

Flurry twisted around in her chair. "Oh my God. It's Phillip."

"Tyra and Hatch, too," Dent said. "Bunch of people from the shoot." He scowled. "And there's that jerkola Vincent White."

Bree waved at Justine, who sat with Craig Oliver at her side, apart from the others. She looked lost.

Dent grunted. "They must have wrapped for the night. Now, what I want to know is who are those people over there against the back wall? From the looks they've been shooting at us, they're the Indians. And we're Custer."

Flurry spluttered in a combination of laughter and nerves. "Where do you get these expressions, Willy?"

Bree said wryly, "I'm surprised you don't recognize him, Dent. That's our very own Payton McAllister. And he's sitting with my favorite client of the year, Sammi-Rose Waterman."

"The one in the polyester pantsuit is the second sister," Flurry said. "Marian Cicerone. Have you ever seen a crabbier face?"

Bree leaned forward to get a better look. "You're right. If mental messages could kill, we'd be sprawled on the floor, dead as doornails. They are not happy to see us together, Flurry. Hm. The two sisters are getting up. Rather, Sammi-Rose is getting up, and Marian's pulling at her."

"They're not going to come over here, are they?" Flurry asked nervously. "I hate scenes. Well, not all scenes. Just scenes where I get yelled at. Some scenes are quite interesting."

"Shut up," Dent said, not unkindly. "You're babbling. And no, they're not coming over here. They're leaving."

"I want to get out of here, too." Flurry drained her second glass of wine. "But I don't want to go out the same time they do. I'm going to have another glass. I want to wait until they've . . ." She sank lower in her chair. "You said they weren't coming over here. And they're coming!"

Sammi-Rose Waterman seemed to have dined on more wine than food. Her eyes were a little glassy, and her red lipstick was smeared on her front teeth. Marian Cicerone looked sober, worried, and discontented. She had on a cheap pink pantsuit with a flowered tee that didn't do a lot for her waistline. Payton trailed behind.

Dent rose to his feet as the group approached the table. Payton hung back, looking like he'd just received an audit notice from the IRS.

"You think you're so smart," Sammi-Rose said. She swayed a little on her stilettos. "So smart." She swayed in a semicircle and shook her fist at Flurry. "And you, you little bitch! I'm going to get you, too! Accusing my poor old grandmother of murder. Deaf—deaf-defaming the family. He's going to sue you for slander."

"That's right," Marian said. "We're going to sue you for every penny you've got."

"It's libel," Flurry said pertly. "And it's not libel if it's true. I've got proof, Mrs. Waterman."

"The hell you do!"

"The hell I don't."

"So what is this proof?"

"You'll find out when you read the book."

"Screw that goddam book!"

"Mrs. Waterman," Payton said, "we really ought to go."

"Go away. I'm talking to Miss Fancy Pants Beaufort, here. Jewel thief." She leaned forward. Her winey breath was in Bree's face. "We're going to get you. When you least expect it. You got that?"

"Time to move on," Dent said. For a man as tired and weary as he was, he moved quickly. He had Sammi-Rose's right arm around her back and his hand on her shoulder before she could say a word. In moments, he'd moved her across the floor and out the front entrance. Payton had to trot to keep up. Marian stamped along behind them.

"Slick," Flurry said. "Hey, you suppose I was right? That Dent was a cop in his checkered past? That was a cop move if I ever saw one."

"I hope he was one of the good ones," Bree said. The missing witness worried her.

Dent reappeared after a few moments outside and stopped briefly at Mercury's table to talk to Justine. Justine drew on his arm, and he bent his head, nodding occasionally at her urgent whisper.

"Now what does the old dear want?" Flurry demanded. "You should have seen her on the set today. She didn't have that damn pin that supposedly belonged to Consuelo, and we had to take and retake this one shot that should have been a snap. I'll bet we spent an hour on it. It was a reaction shot, for God's sake, not even any dialogue."

"Reaction to what?"

"She's standing on the river's edge, watching Hatch, as Alexander Bulloch, of course, wheel Haydee down the road."

"She's not a bad actress, surely," Bree said. "She made some notable movies in her day."

Flurry moved irritably. "I suppose so. You ever watch those old movies from the '60s? Not the new-wave stuff, like *Easy Rider* or *Five Easy Pieces*. Those hold up pretty well. But the junk from the old-style studio system? Just try and sit through *Three Coins in the Fountain* or *Twelve O'Clock High* or any of that middlebrow stuff. The acting's stagy, the color balance way off, the direction's stale, and the women all look like they're wearing girdles."

"They were wearing girdles," Bree said. "My grand-mother wore girdles."

"That's Justine's reference point, and she's not about to change." Flurry sighed. "I don't know, maybe if she were about forty years younger, she could relearn her craft. But it's too late now. And really, Bree. You ought to think about suing her plastic surgeon. I mean, I know she wants to look younger, but really! One face-lift's enough."

"You're being unkind."

"Am I? Yeah. I am. It's a tough business, movies."

Justine released Dent's sleeve, and he made his way back to their table. "She's upset," he said as he pulled out his chair. "Says she can't do her job without the brooch. I told her that you still had it, but you couldn't lend it to her. She couldn't see why."

"I wish I could," Bree said. "I'll have to file an affidavit tomorrow. I'll request a speedy disposition, but it'll probably go back into the coffin with Mrs. Bulloch."

"You mean that thing is real?" Flurry said.

"Twenty thousand dollars' worth of real."

They didn't stay long after Dent got back to the table. Bree settled the bill. She accepted, with a show of reluctance, the accordion folder Flurry had brought with her, and promised to download the e-mail files when she got into the office the next morning.

Flurry declined the offer of a ride back to her hotel. "It's just the Mulberry Inn. It's right around the corner," she said and, with that, drifted over to the tables filled with the cast and crew of *Bitter Tide*.

"Let's call it a night," Bree said. "It's been a long day. All I want to do is go home, curl up on the couch, and watch something mindless on TV."

Dent sat slumped in his chair.

"Are you going to be all right?"

"Sure."

"Flurry mentioned a witness who never appeared in court. Does that ring a bell?"

He dragged both hands over his face. "Sort of. I told

you. I was drinking a lot at the time. I also told you we have to get out to see Bobby Lee." He was quiet a minute and then said, "She said my investigation sucked."

"Yes, she did." It wouldn't do to duck the painful parts of Dent's past.

"You think all that stuff about my being a drunk came from Bobby Lee?"

"Possibly. But it doesn't matter all that much, does it? What matters is that we're going to find out what really happened and fix what we can fix. We're in this case for good reasons, Dent. To represent Consuelo's interests and to help you get through the program." She touched his arm. "Why don't you go home and get some sleep? We'll set up some time to talk together tomorrow."

"All right." He stood up. "You need a ride back to your town house?"

Bree looked out the window. "I can see it from here. I'll just jump right across Bay and be right home."

"See you tomorrow, then."

She watched him as he wound his way out through the tables. Lonely. She'd never met a man who was as alone as William Dent seemed to be. A big, tired guy who'd lost the battle. Well, if she had anything to do with it, he was going to win the war. She glanced at the corner where the *Bitter Tide* cast and crew had gathered. Justine and Craig Oliver were gone. So was Phillip Mercury.

Suddenly, she really missed Sam Hunter. She pulled out her cell and hit the speed dial. He answered on the first ring, which could be a good thing (he was missing her) or a bad thing (he was irked she hadn't called him before this).

"Bree!" he said. Which meant it was that good thing. He was missing her.

"Hey."

"How long have you been back?"

"Tonia and I got home just after New Year's Day. But you were out on that school shooting. I heard you wrapped it up, though. Did the case go well?"

"As well as anything can that involves a jealous step-father, an overconcerned high school history teacher, and a teenager barraged by too many hormones."

"But nobody died."

"Nobody even got seriously hurt. You weren't by any chance calling to say that you're free tonight?"

"Not only am I free, Antonia's over at the theater until late. Would you be able to come over?"

Bree hoped she read the silence on the other end of the line correctly. But she and Hunter had been dancing around long enough. She wanted a real person in her life, in her bed, in her heart. She wanted a life of her own.

"I can be there in five."

"Movie speak," Bree said. "Ugh."

He laughed. "You don't know the worst of it."

"We'll swap horror stories." Her heart was beating a little faster. She was swept with a wave of happiness. "Have you had dinner yet? I'm at B. Matthew's right now. I can order something for you."

"Fish tacos," he said promptly. "I'll meet you at your front door."

———— ∞∞∞ ————

The night outside was warmer than it had been. Bree left her winter coat unbuttoned. She tucked the take-out bag under her arm, stood at the crosswalk, and punched the Walk button. Somebody waved at her from across the street. Bree narrowed her eyes to see better. It was Hunter. He wore a black leather jacket. Like hers, his coat was open to the warmer air. He looked good to her: solid, tall, reassuring, and very dear. She waved. He threw her a kiss, which was so uncharacteristic for Hunter she had to laugh.

The little white running figure beeped at her, and she set one foot in the street. There was a whisper of sound behind her.

Then she didn't remember anything else for a long time.

Ten

More needs she the divine,
Than the physician.
—*Macbeth*, William Shakespeare

Bree woke up flat on her back, staring at an unfamiliar sky. Her arms were at her sides. A pale mist blanketed her breasts and legs. The light was soft, golden, like sunlight through trees in a forest. The air was scrubbed with the scent of roses.

I'm in the Sphere.

Happiness welled up in her.

She was surrounded by five columns of intense color. The columns varied in height and width, but they were spinning, eddies in a whirlpool of soft air.

"Well, child." The voice from the violet column was soft and known to her.

"Lavinia?" Bree said. Or tried to. Her lips were stiff. And she hurt, terribly, all over. She narrowed her eyes against the violet glow. For some reason, it was much brighter than the others.

The silver-ash column that was Petru said, "My dear Bree."

Bree reached out to him, but her arm wouldn't move.

"We are all here," Professor Cianquino said. His form was a steady blue flame. "There is nothing we can do for you, my dear. Except hope."

"I don't believe it." The green-blue column that was Ron sounded testy.

"You know the rules."

That fiery column. Was that Gabriel? She hadn't seen him for such a long time. Gabriel and his coin-colored eyes.

"This is a temporal matter," Gabriel's voice was calm. "We cannot interfere."

"We can hope," Ron said.

She felt his smile. All their smiles. Better than hope . . .

She drifted away.

Bree woke up flat on her back, staring at an unfamiliar ceiling. Her arms were at her sides. A white sheet was drawn up across her breasts and legs. The light was strong, bluish white. Stainless steel railings barred her on either side. The air was scrubbed with an unpleasant odor. Disinfectant of some kind.

She shoved her hands flat and sat up. Something tugged at her arm like an angry wasp, and she slapped at it reflexively before she had a chance to look. A piece of opaque tape covered a tube and the tube held a needle.

The needle disappeared into skin that wasn't her own: bright pink, slightly charred at the edges, covered with an oily goop.

She hurt. All over.

"Well, there you are. How are you feeling?" A mournful face hovered in the air above her. The face—which resembled a basset hound more than a person—was attached to a body dressed in hospital whites. Bree registered his name tag: Ollie.

"I don't know," she said cautiously. Then, "Where am I, Ollie?"

"The hospital," he said reassuringly. "Savannah General. Which is in Georgia," he added unnecessarily, "although I shouldn't tell you too much before you tell me who you are."

"You don't know?" Bree said.

"Of course I do, dear. But we need to know if *you* do, you see. Name, age, and current date. It's called being oriented times three." He smiled, which lifted his jowls. He was in his late forties, perhaps—Bree wasn't very good with ages—and his face was a roadmap of hard living.

"Brianna Winston-Beaufort. I'm twenty-eight, and I'm a lawyer, with a practice in Savannah. And it's the fifteenth of January."

"You are so right," Dent said. "Except it's the seventeenth. Are you in any pain?"

"The seventeenth!" She felt dizzy. Where had two days gone?

"You *are* in pain," he said sympathetically.

"Not much." This wasn't strictly true. Pain was there all right, waiting to jump on her, but she was pretty sure the IV glugging whatever into her arm had some pain-killers in it. "Thank you for asking." Bree sank back. There was a pillow, but it was hard and flat. She hated being horizontal when everyone else was vertical. Hospital beds could be elevated, couldn't they? She fumbled around the mattress. No buttons.

"You want to sit up," Ollie said in a kindly way. "I think that'll be okay." He pressed a button and Bree raised partway up without any effort at all.

The room was small. Grayish tile covered the floor. A half-open door led to a bathroom equipped with a tall toilet, stainless steel handholds, and an efficient-looking shower. A narrow floor-to-ceiling window with vertical blinds looked down on a parking lot. From the slant of the sun Bree judged it was late afternoon. An orange chair of molded plastic held a bulging tote. Bree knew that tote. It belonged to her little sister, Antonia. She did know who she was and where she was. Bree sank back against the pillows. It was a slight effort, this examination of the room, but it exhausted her.

"Oh my God! You're awake."

Antonia swept into the room, stopped short, and flung up her hands. "I take two seconds to go down to the Coke machine, and what happens?"

"I wake up?"

"You wake up!"

Antonia looked like she hadn't slept for a week. Her gray University of North Carolina sweatshirt had coffee stains on the front, and it looked as if she'd bitten off a couple of her carefully manicured fingernails. Bree took all this in with a glance and said, "I'm fine, you know."

"Of course you are," Antonia said heartily.

She burst into tears.

"Oh dear," Ollie said. He lifted Antonia's tote off the orange chair and put a gentle hand on her shoulder. "Sit down, sit down. No, don't go mauling your sister around. Leave go of her foot, dear. You don't want to fool around with burn patients. Scarring. Infection. You just leave her be."

Antonia released Bree's foot and sank into the chair. She swiped her forearm under her eyes. "Right, right."

Bree put her hands up to her cheeks. The skin on her face was tender but intact. Her left forearm was wrapped in gauze, but her hands seemed to be okay. Her right forearm, the one with the IV in it, was one step beyond a bad sunburn. She shifted her legs under the light sheet that covered them. Both legs were in immobilizer casts.

"She's awake now," Antonia said. "She should see a doctor, Ollie. Go get one. Right now."

"Tonia. For heaven's sake. You can't just order people around like that."

"Don't you for-heaven's-sake me! Push that little thing-gummy, Ollie, the emergency button."

Ollie winked at Bree. "Don't go anywhere, Ms. Beaufort. I'll be right back." He closed the swinging door gently behind him. It opened again, almost immediately. Hunter stepped into the room. The skin around his eyes was drawn tight. Like Antonia, he looked exhausted.

"Not you again," Antonia said. "Not now. She just woke up. Come back later, Lieutenant. Unless you came to tell us you shot the guy that did this to her."

"Not yet." Hunter stepped to the foot of the bed. He took in the bandages, the IV, and Bree herself. His face was expressionless, but there was a glitter in his gray eyes Bree hadn't seen before. Rage? "I'd ask how you're feeling, but you look pretty doped up."

"I'm fine," Bree said. "A little drifty maybe." She smiled. "Sorry I didn't get to deliver the fish tacos."

"Yeah." He ducked his head. Was he crying? Bree struggled once more to sit up.

"Lie down, sister!" Antonia sprang out of the chair and joined Hunter at the foot of the bed. "I don't know why you've been hanging around here, Hunter. You should just leave and go shoot the guy like I said before. She needs to sleep. She needs to see a doctor. She needs my mother, who'll be here any second. She doesn't need you."

"Oh dear," Bree said. Francesca and Royal lived at Plessey, some two hundred miles away in North Carolina. "Did you really have to call them, Tonia?" Then, "What guy?" She closed her eyes in an effort to remember. "What happened?"

"Oh my God." Antonia bit off another fingernail. "Brain damage. I knew it. Where's that damn doctor?"

"Right here." The door to the room swung open and a portly man Bree didn't know walked in. He was dressed in hospital whites. A stethoscope hung around his neck.

He was followed by a slight, dark-haired familiar figure. "Dr. Lowry!"

The pathologist grinned and wiggled her fingers in a half wave.

The other doctor picked up the chart at the foot of the bed and flipped through it. "You know this patient, Dr. Lowry?"

"Bree Beaufort? Sure. I've given her a hand with a case or two." She went up to the head of the bed and peered into Bree's eyes. "How're you doing?"

"Pretty well," Bree said cautiously. "How are you, Megan? Have you been appointed to the coroner's office?"

"You mean, am I here to see how fast I can get my hands on your corpse? Nope. Still working there part-time and helping out with my brother's live practice."

"Excuse me." The other doctor, whose name tag read ERIC CAUSTON, moved Megan aside. He flicked his oph-thalmologic scope on and shined it into Bree's eyes.

"You're doing remarkably well," Megan said reassur-ingly. "Just what I'd expect in a patient with the kinds of vital signs you walk around with. I've never seen burns heal so fast in my life! I thought maybe you'd let me take a few tissue samples and haul them on down to the lab."

"Hoping for another Latts cell culture, Doctor?" Causton's tone was sarcastic. He snapped the light off, felt the sides of Bree's throat with cool dry fingers, and then put his fingertips on the pulse at her wrist.

"You never know," Megan said eagerly. "Cells are amazing things."

Megan Lowry was exceptionally thin, very tiny, and wore thick tortoiseshell spectacles. Bree bet she wasn't much older than Antonia. She'd suspected that Megan was some kind of medical wunderkind when she'd first met her on the O'Rourke case, and the irritated attitude she was getting from Causton bore that out. Established physicians didn't like competition from brash young newbies anymore than anyone else. "Causton's taking your pulse himself because he doesn't trust the machines. You're going to be amazed, Causton. This woman's the fittest patient I've ever had."

"Ever treat real athletes, Lowry? The kids on the basketball team at Duke, for example? You wouldn't believe how fast they heal. Youth, good health, motivation. It all goes into the picture."

She pushed her spectacles up her nose with her forefinger. "Can't say that I have."

"Then I'd keep my bright ideas to myself." He looked down at Bree. "But you're healing remarkably quickly."

Sam moved to the other side of the bed and took Bree's undamaged hand in his. "The intake report documented extensive burns on the legs, forearms, back. She has a tibia plateau fracture of the right leg and a cracked collarbone. I want a prognosis."

"And a concussion," Megan said with relish. "You got a whack on the occipital area that should have felled a horse. But it just put you in la-la land for a few days!"

"I want to know the origin of each of the injuries, too," Hunter said.

Causton glanced at Megan with dislike. "She can tell you that."

"I don't think so," Hunter said. There was something in the tone of his voice that made Causton straighten up. "Cooperation makes better medicine, same as police work. I'd like to hear what both of you have to say."

"You didn't see her at intake, Causton," Megan said. "There was some question about whether or not she was going to make it."

Sam's hand tightened painfully on Bree's.

"So I got over here as fast as I could. I mean, she's a patient of mine, for goodness' sake. Plus, I thought I could maybe get a tissue sample right off. She checked in with concussion, fractures, et cetera, et cetera. What he said. You gave a very accurate summary, Lieutenant. Hunter. Anyhow, I talked to one of the EMTs, and in the twelve minutes that it took to get you here, you already had visible signs of burn healing."

"Nonsense," Causton said.

"You didn't go over her with a magnifier, like I did. I mean, it was barely visible, even under a strong scope."

"Healing begins immediately," Causton said disapprovingly. "There's nothing unusual about that."

"Not visible to the naked eye!"

Causton made a disgusted movement.

"Tell me about the head wound," Sam said. "Now."

Causton's fingers were surprisingly gentle at the back of Bree's head. "A depressed fracture, right here."

"Could that have happened when she was hit by the car?"

"I was hit by a car?" Bree said.

Causton frowned. "Possibly."

Megan said, "Absolutely not."

Causton reached the end of his patience. "What the hell, Lowry. You seem to know it all. Go ahead."

"I took a few bits and pieces when she was in the ER, just to get a head start. The blood and tissue sample from the occipital area showed evidence of . . . guess what?"

The silence in the room was heavy, and not encouraging.

"Cast iron!"

"Cast iron?" Hunter said.

"Yes. The kind of cast iron you'd find in a frying pan. As a matter of fact, I'm pretty sure that's what it was."

"Somebody hit me with a cast iron frying pan?" Bree closed her eyes. "You know what? There was a cast iron frying pan on the wall of the restaurant. Along with a lot of other stuff."

"Do you remember anything else?" Antonia asked.

"Don't bite your fingernails," Bree said. "No. I don't remember a thing about the accident. What happened?"

Hunter's hand still gripped her own. His voice was a little hoarse. "You punched the Walk button to cross Bay to come home. A beer truck went through the intersection just as the light turned green. When the truck passed, I saw you lying in the street. A car came zipping around the corner, swerved to avoid hitting you, flipped up onto the sidewalk, and burst into flames. I went across the street and got you out from under the car."

"What about the driver?" Bree asked.

"Jumped free. And there was no one else in the car, thank God, or I would have been patching up two victims instead of one." Causton tucked the end of his stethoscope into his jacket pocket. He crossed his arms. "You think someone hit her from behind before she was hit by the car?"

"I'm sure of it. Knocked her into the path of the car. We cited the driver for failure to yield, dangerous driving, and a couple of other infractions."

"I'd like to get my hands on him," Antonia said.

"He's in the Chatham County Jail at the moment, pending the results of the traffic investigation."

"Anyone I know?" Bree asked.

Hunter nodded slowly. "Phillip Mercury."

"Really." Bree absorbed this for a long moment.

"Claims he did what he could to avoid you."

"The newspapers said he was drunk," Antonia said. "Or high. You cited him for DUI, didn't you, Sam?"

"We did."

"So he's going to jail for a long time. Of course, not as long as if . . ." Antonia's voice choked with sobs.

"Well, I didn't die," Bree said tartly. "Get a grip, sister."

The door to the room burst open. A small, red-gold whirlwind spun into the room, followed by a tall, handsome man with gray hair.

"Mamma!" Antonia threw herself into Francesca's arms. "You're here, Mamma. She's going to be all right. She's not going to die! I was so sure she was going to die!"

Bree smiled at her heart's true father, Royal Winston-Beaufort. "Hey, Daddy. That's my diva sister for sure. I'm fine. It's like they say. The whole thing was a long way from my heart."

"Darlin' girl," her mother said. "We've come to take you home."

Eleven

"I'm not staying in this bed a minute longer!" Bree shouted. She wasn't in the best of tempers. Sasha was curled on the floor nearest her right hand. Once in a while he lifted his head and bumped her hand.

It'd been a three-day hassle to get out of the hospital, and it was even more of a hassle to resist the efforts of her parents to take her back to Plessey. At least she was set up at the town house. Her mother and father had taken over Antonia's bedroom. Antonia was set up in the living room on the pull-out couch. Bree herself was in her own room, propped up in her bed, feeling like a turkey trussed for stuffing.

It wasn't the disruption of her days that bothered her so much.

The peacock pin was missing. And she couldn't get up to search for it.

Bree had discovered it as soon as she'd managed to go through her purse and her briefcase at the hospital. Flurry's accordion folder was there. Her cell phone, credit cards, and driver's license were there. She had a hundred-some dollars in cash, and that was there, too.

The missing jewel led to a lot of questions, and Bree wanted some answers.

"You hear me, Sasha? I'm getting up." Her bedroom door was half-open. She could hear her mother rustling around in the kitchen. "And my folks are going back to North Carolina if I have to stuff them in their car myself. I'm going nuts cooped up here."

Bree liked this room, but she didn't like it well enough to stay stuck in bed for however many days her mother was planning to keep her there. The town house had been in the family since before the War Between the States; two hundred and fifty years ago, it had been an office for the warehouse below it. The room still had the original narrow plank floors, now covered by a rose-figured carpet. There was an old chest of drawers directly across from the bed, the kind with a mirror attached. Bree could see herself. Her hands were pink, but not as red as they had been. Her hair was hidden beneath a gauze cap. She felt carefully under the edges at the back. They'd shaved off part of her hair. Her cheeks were a shiny pink; Causton had told her this was from the heat of the flames that had burned her arms and legs.

Her legs. Her mother had thrown a light blanket over her. Bree twitched it aside. They'd removed the immobilizer cast from her right leg, since the burns were healing well. Her left was now in some sort of a resin cast. Her knee was bent at a slight angle. They'd put a pin across the top of her tibia. She'd be up and weight-bearing in a few days, with any luck.

"I'm getting up," Bree said to Sasha, "and I'm not kidding."

"What's that, dear?" Her mother bustled in with an armload of fresh towels. Francesca was small, comfortably round, and the sunniest woman Bree knew. The red-gold hair that caught Royal Winston-Beaufort's eye thirty-odd years ago across the main dining room at Duke University was helped a little nowadays with a rinse. But the light, pretty voice that was so much of Bree's childhood was untouched by time.

"How are you feeling, darling?"

"Fine. Just fine."

"You're looking so much better. Who knew that you had such speedy cells!"

Bree laughed. Her face didn't hurt as much as it had before. "You've been talking to Megan Lowry."

"She's quite delighted over the whole business. She said your bones are healing faster than a little kid's. I'm somewhat vague on the details, but apparently very young bones heal faster than ours."

Bree tried to bend her knee. It hurt like hell. "Not fast enough."

"Patience, dear. Would you like some soup?"

"I would like to get up."

"I don't think so."

"Among the many things Megan Lowry told you, I'm

sure, is that it's fatal to sit around. For your muscles, I mean."

Francesca did what she always did when she needed to call in the troops. "Royal! You get yourself in here! Your daughter's acting up again. Royal! Where is that man? You stay right there, Bree. Don't you move!" Francesca trotted out of the room. Bree leaned over the edge of the bed and looked into Sasha's golden eyes. "Help," she said. "I mean it, Sash. They have to go home. I've got to find that pin. You know what I think, don't you? I think Justine clocked me over the head with that handy frying pan and grabbed the pin out of my briefcase. This"—she swept her hand over her face and legs— "was an unintended consequence."

Sasha cocked his head, yawned, and got to his feet. He considered her for a long moment, then turned and trotted off.

Her father, long, lean, with his curious eyes and gentle smile, edged into the room, followed by her mother. "Feeling antsy, pet?"

"I'm feeling less and less like an adult and more and more like an infant. If I don't get up right now, I'm going to revert to my childhood permanently. By the way," she added crossly, "where's my stuff?"

"Those old files," Francesca said. "Your father's been looking through them, just like you asked."

"And he got the downloads?"

"Mrs. Billingsley brought them right over."

"She didn't say anything about them when she came to visit."

"We asked her not to. You need to rest, dear. Your work is far too stimulating."

Royal put his hands on Francesca's shoulders. "I think we can give her a hand out of bed, Chessie."

"But the doctors said—"

"The doctors simply come in to marvel at our good old girl. They say she's doing splendidly. Okay, Bree. Swing yourself over."

"Here!" Francesca shrieked. "The crutches!"

Bree stood up, gave herself a minute to adjust to the crutches, and then swung into the living room, Sasha patiently behind her. Antonia was out. A tag end of a bedsheet peeked from underneath the cushions on the sofa. Her poor sister. Bree had slept on that sofa bed herself. It had a pesky iron bar right across the middle of the mattress.

Bree headed for the rocking chair by the fireplace, swung herself around, and lowered herself into it. Sasha sat down next to her and then suddenly leaped to his feet, his tail wagging furiously.

The doorbell chimed.

"Oh, for heaven's sake," Francesca muttered. "Not more flowers I hope. And if it's Sam Hunter again, he can just turn right around and go back where he came from. He's positively been haunting this place, Bree."

"I thought you liked Hunter."

"I love Hunter. But all he does is hold your hand and glower. Then Antonia asks him if he's shot Phillip Mercury yct. None of it conducive to proper healing." Francesca disappeared into the foyer, trailing words, and reappeared moments later, looking happy. Sasha bounded past her, ears up. "I never thought I'd actually meet him," she said. "He's such a good-looking boy in person. You have callers, Bree."

Ron and Lavinia came into the room. Bree made an effort to get to her feet. Her father placed both hands on her shoulders and kept her in her chair.

Ron was his usual vital self. He smiled at her mother, who smiled happily back. Lavinia looked— "transparent" was the best word Bree could come up with. Bree knew that her angels had to make an effort to appear in the temporal world. She hoped it wasn't taking a toll on her old friend.

"You poor child," Lavinia hobbled forward, her worn wool cardigan pulled tightly across her chest. "Ron didn't want me to come, but I just had to see for myself." She smiled proudly. "So I come out. I haven't been out for years."

"Mamma, Daddy, this is Lavinia Mather, my land-lady at the Angelus office and a dear friend. Mamma, you've spoken with Ron on the phone. Ron, this is my father."

Ron shook hands with Royal, gave Francesca a hug, and leaned over Bree. "Lavinia insisted on coming," he said into her ear. "I won't let her stay too long."

"She looks—worn," Bree said worriedly.

"It's an effort, at her age." He stepped back and raised his voice a little. "You're looking pretty spry, boss."

"I'm feeling fine. You guys want to see something impressive?" She hopped out of the chair on one leg, grabbed the crutches, and swung herself up and down the room.

Lavinia beamed. "Well, they told me you were coming along fine and I guess it's true."

"I'll be back in the office in no time."

"We'll see about that," Francesca murmured. "And here I am, forgetting my manners. Please sit down, all of you. Let me get you some tea, Mrs. Mather."

"That would be tasty," Lavinia said. "But I'm not staying long, so please don't fuss yourself."

"Sit down right here beside Royal on the couch. Do you take lemon or sweet?"

"I do love my sugar, thank you kindly." Lavinia perched on the edge of the couch and looked around the room. "My goodness, my goodness. This place hasn't changed much at all."

"When were you last here, Mrs. Mather?" Royal asked.

Oh, about 1754, Bree thought. *Coming in with the rest of the auctioned slaves to the paymaster's office.*

"A while ago," she said with a sweet smile. She accepted the cup of tea from Francesca. "Just had to come and see with my own eyes that she was doing as well as Ron said. I do like to see for myself, when it's important." She settled the fragile cup on the end table and turned to Royal. "Bree told us you were taking a look at all that history Florida Smith dug up about the Haydee Quinn case."

Bree hadn't really intended to turn the case notes over to her father—despite what she'd told Florida Smith—

but he wouldn't leave her mother to go back to Raleigh, and her mother wouldn't leave her. He was a restless man by nature, especially when he didn't have any real work to do. The case files had kept him out of the rest of the family's way for days.

"Yes, indeed. Very interesting. Very."

"Is the case making any more sense to you than it is to Bree, here?"

Royal patted his pockets, realized yet again that he'd given up his pipe years ago, and settled for stroking his chin reflectively. "I was eight years old in 1952, and as a matter of fact, I was a witness to the burning of Haydee's body."

"You were?" Bree said. "Good grief."

Francesca shuddered. "What a sight for a young boy."

"Yes, well, as you know, we usually spent the fourth of July here on the river." He smiled a little. "And the—ah—spectacle—was one of the reasons we don't any-more. In any event, I saw him. I'll never forget it. The poor boy was wild with grief. Of course, I was more than usually interested in the handling of the case, so I read everything about it I could put my hands on. And I eavesdropped whenever I could on the adults' conversation. Your grandmother and grandfather, Bree, knew the Bullochs socially, and of course, the whole thing was a huge scandal and the topic of every gathering for weeks. And of course, you knew that Franklin represented the boy at the sanity hearing. It was a big break for him."

"Yes," Bree said. "I knew that."

"So my own theory of the case may be tainted by

what I recall. Although I did my best to set aside whatever bias I may have picked up as a youngster when I looked at these notes. She did a good job, this young woman. Very thorough."

"So who killed Haydee Quinn?" Francesca asked.

Royal steepled his fingers and tapped his chin. "There are two questions that need to be answered before I have a legitimate theory of the case. Bree? What would those questions be?"

Bree answered promptly. "Where did she go after she staggered away from the Tropicana Tide with the knife wounds to her chest? And who went with her?"

"Mercy," Lavinia said. "You brought this girl up right, Mr. Royal."

"Thank you, Mrs. Mather. I did, didn't I?" They smiled delightedly at each other. Bree's heart contracted a little. They were both so dear to her. "Daddy," she began. She stopped and chewed at her lower lip.

"What is it, my dear?"

"Do you think . . ."

"That young Alex had anything to do with it?" He tilted his head to one side. "This case has been getting at you . . ."

Bree made a dismissive gesture.

"Well, something's been getting at you. But if it's a concern that Franklin was involved with a coverup, it shouldn't be." He frowned with distaste. "Not Franklin. No. Not knowingly, at any rate. That kind of dealing just wasn't in your . . . uncle. You're not thinking logically about this, Bree. Again, what do you need to do before you can come to a rational conclusion about whether an injustice has been done?"

"Follow the body," Bree said.

"If an injustice has been done—and I suspect it might have been—the answer lies there. Follow the body, Bree."

"The missing witness," Bree said. "Of course. Ron, do you think Petru could come up with a list of the employees at the Tropicana Tide?"

"From 1952?" Royal said. "That'd be quite a feat of research."

"It would," Bree agreed. "But you don't know Petru. If it exists in a record somewhere, he'll dig it up."

"You're thinking that the barkeep or one of the dancers might have seen Haydee after she staggered off into the night?" Royal patted his pockets for his long-gone pipe.

Bree had the flutter in her chest that meant there just might be a crack in the case. "The odds are pretty good, aren't they? The Tropi was what Dent calls a hangout for lowlifes."

"Who's Dent?" Francesca asked. "That poor sorry soul who keeps leaving you daisies?"

"Is that where they came from?" Bree said. "Anyhow, Daddy, I doubt that any employee of William Norris's would be all that interested in helping the police."

"I like it," Royal said.

Lavinia murmured in admiration. Bree looked at her. Was she imagining it? Or was Lavinia fading, just a little? She glanced at Ron, a worried question in her eyes.

"Oh my," Ron said promptly. "Do I hear the phone?"

"I didn't hear it, but then, I turned the ringer down so it wouldn't bother Bree," Francesca said. "It's probably Florida Smith again. She's been trying to reach you, but I told her business would have to wait until the weekend was over."

"Mother," Bree said, "you can't just summarily dispose of my phone calls."

"Oh! There it is. Such sharp ears you have, Ron." She rose, crossed the small living room, and picked it up.

Lavinia put her hand on Royal's knee. "Is this child getting around okay, Mr. Royal? Able to take a shower and such?"

"She's made a remarkable recovery."

"She looks good," Lavinia said judiciously. "Needs fattening up, but that's nothing new. I made her another batch of my Brunswick stew, by the way. Soon as she gets back to the office, I'll make sure she eats a pint or two."

"Not much going on at the office at the moment," Ron said with a casual air. "She'll be able to ease back into the caseload. Of course, if she's out too long, things will begin to back up."

"Now that'd be stressful," Lavinia agreed. "Waiting too long to get back."

They both smiled at him. Bree knew those smiles. She looked down at Sasha, who thumped his tail in a rather mischievous way.

Francesca hung up the phone. "That was home, dear. There's a tax question come up about the assessment on

Plessey. And that big old live oak fell over and dammed up the creek. Art Johnson's raising a hullabaloo. Says it's going to flood his cow pasture. Gurney thinks we should come home, but I told him not while my darling girl is laid up like this."

"Your darling girl is doing just fine," Ron said. "She has me to run her errands . . ."

". . . and me to stuff her full of my good food," Lavinia added, "and to wash her hair if she needs a hand."

"And Antonia to take care of everything else," Bree said. "Please, Mamma. I love you. You're driving me crazy. I have to get back to work."

"It's time to go, Chessie." Her father got up and enveloped her in his arms. "She's going to be just fine."

Francesca sighed, looked from Ron to Lavinia and back again, and threw up her hands. "Okay, okay. I give. But the *instant* something else goes wrong, I'm all over you like a Persian rug."

Like much of what Francesca said, it made sense. Sort of.

Twelve

There is a divinity that shapes our ends,
Rough hew them how we will.
—*Hamlet,* William Shakespeare

"I do not see how Beaufort & Company can be concerned with the missing jewel," Petru said. "This is a temporal issue. The Beaufort & Company charter is for celestial matters only. The missing witness? Absolutely."

Bree's right leg was propped on a chair. She, Ron, and Petru sat around the conference table at the Angelus Street office. Lavinia was upstairs, and Sasha was outside in the cemetery, poking around the gravestones. Her parents had finally gone home.

Ron and Petru both agreed that the Company couldn't support the search for the missing peacock pin. Bree thought they should.

The cast was itchy. Her knee hurt like the devil. She was glad to be back at work, but her temper was short. "The jewel is the contact point for our client, Petru. How else can I get hold of her?"

Petru shook his head no. "Whoever took it committed a theft. This thievery will weigh in the balance at the end of the thief's days, of course, but there has been no miscarriage of celestial justice."

"True." Bree stuck her pen down the top of her cast and scratched at her leg. It didn't help. "Okay. So I'll handle the investigation of the theft from the Bay Street office."

"Did you tell Lieutenant Hunter the pin was gone?" Ron asked. "This is a case for the police, don't you think?"

"I didn't, no." Bree doodled circles on her yellow pad. "I'd like to avoid talking to the police for the moment. I think Justine clocked me over the head."

Petru's eyebrows shot up. "The old actress?"

"She was desperate to get the pin back. She's worried about losing her job. She didn't stop to think. She certainly didn't intend to push me into the path of Mercury's car."

"Hm." Petru tugged at his beard.

"I support our justice system, both temporal and celestial. You know that. But I don't want to feed Justine to the wolves, so to speak. The poor woman's suffered enough."

Ron said, "Maybe it wasn't Justine. Maybe it was Sammi-Rose Waterman. She was drunk enough to do something stupid, from what you've told me. Or that mean-looking sister of hers. Marian Lee."

"Payton was with Sammi-Rose when she left the restaurant," Bree pointed out. "I suppose Payton could have done it or even the three of them together, but it doesn't make much sense. Payton's a creep, but he's not violent. And he'd be in a heap of trouble with Smilin' John Stubblefield if he let one of their clients launch into an assault with grievous bodily harm. I'm not saying it isn't possible, but it's unlikely. Besides . . ." She paused. Parts of her memory were coming back. Justine wore a distinctive perfume. Gardenias. She was sure there had been an odor of gardenias in the air. "Either way, I'll look into it." She put a final flourish on the doodle and sat back. "Anyhow. Let's move on to the Haydee Quinn case. I had a long chat with my fa—with Royal before I finally got him to go on back to Plessey. I finally reviewed Florida's material. She did a sensational job on the background, and she made a time line of the events leading up to Haydee's death. I've made notes in places where I think we might pursue things further."

She moved to the whiteboard that hung between the windows facing the cemetery, balanced herself on her crutch, and picked up a red marker.

JUNE 30, 1952

7:30 p.m. The Tropicana Tide: Haydee and Bagger
Bill Norris quarrel about her affair with Alexander
Bulloch.

"There were several witnesses," Bree said. "A young chorus girl, Charis Jefferson; a waitress, whose only name was Darcy, no last name; and the bartender Moses

Busch. Busch states: 'Billy said he'd kill her and himself before he let her go.'"

She picked up the marker again and wrote:

8:00 p.m. Haydee performs Dance of the Seven Veils
   for a full house. Alex Bulloch is in the audience
   with three friends. He stays through all three
   performances.

"There were over forty witnesses to this," Bree said. "Plenty of verification. His three friends all went on to other bars. Their whereabouts after the assault on Haydee are all verified."

JULY 1

12:45 a.m.: Haydee comes out from backstage with Alex
   Bulloch. Tells Norris she's quitting to marry Alex.
   Loud argument ensues. Haydee sends Alex home.
   Alex leaves in his 1952 Buick Roadster.

"This is what Moses Busch says." Bree read aloud, "All three of 'em had been drinking up a storm. Haydee kicked the kid out to keep Billy from pounding him to a pulp." She looked up at them. "Alexander's 1952 Buick automobile was seen at the Bulloch home within thirty minutes. This was verified by a routine patrol car."

1:00 a.m.: Norris closes bar. Sends all employees home.

1:15 a.m.: Presence of 1952 Buick Roadster (red) verified at Bulloch mansion, 742 Washington Square, by police car on routine patrol.

1:20 a.m.: Norris and Haydee argue violently. He grabs a butcher knife from the bar, stabs her repeatedly in the chest. Haydee runs out the front door.

2:00 a.m.: 742 Washington Square: Alex Bulloch and his mother, Consuelo Bulloch, argue violently over his affair with Haydee Quinn.

"There was a witness to this," Bree said. "The housekeeper, Marie Toussaint. Here's her statement from the murder book: 'They was at it something fierce. Woke me up. They was a-throwing ashtrays at each other, I guess. There sure was a mess in the morning.'"

4:30 a.m.: Haydee's body discovered in the river.

"Alvin Carpenter was fishing off the banks at 230 Front Street when his line became entangled in Haydee's hair. He called the foot patrolman to the scene. Haydee's body was pulled from the river. She was barely alive." Bree turned to the whiteboard and wrote down the rest of the time line.

5:15 a.m.: Haydee arrives at Savannah General.

6:20 a.m.: Alex Bulloch, Consuelo Bulloch, and the family doctor, Pythias Warren, arrive at Savannah General.

8:20 a.m.: Lt. Eddie O'Malley and Sgt. Robert E. Lee
    Kowalski arrive at Tropicana Tide. Discover William
    Norris passed out on barroom floor. Discover knife,
    later assumed to be murder weapon. Norris covered in
    blood later determined to be same blood type (A pos)
    as victim's.

11:20 a.m.: Haydee pronounced dead.

JULY 3

12:15 p.m.: Body removed to private mortuary, Ernest
    Cavanaugh Funeral Home.

3:00 p.m.: Norris confesses to murder.

JULY 4

5:00 a.m.: Funeral home attendant Cecil Brewster discov-
    ers Haydee's body is missing.

7:05 p.m.: Alexander Bulloch arrested for desecration
    of a body. Remains of corpse brought to Chatham
    County Morgue.

JULY 5

Official autopsy of Haydee Quinn.

Bree tossed the marker on the conference table. "So
the question is: where was Haydee between the hours of
one thirty and four thirty the morning of July 3?"

"The police did a canvass of the city?" Petru asked. "Finding out where she was seen?"

"They made a stab at it. The Tropicana was about three-quarters of a mile downriver from where the body was found. The tide was coming in. She could have stumbled around in the dark, fallen down the banks of the river, and been unable to get out. But I find it hard to believe she could have kept herself afloat for very long. Flurry did a great job mapping out the way the city was laid out at the time." Bree smiled. "In many ways, Savannah's an eternal city; everything changes, and yet nothing changes. But the area to the west of us was dedicated to a pretty vital shipping industry then. A lot of warehouses, a lot of heavy equipment to move containers, cranes, and such. O'Malley and Kowalski interviewed three or four night watchmen, a security guard or two, and several of the patrons Norris kicked out of the bar at one thirty. But!" Bree held up a finger. "This is really cool, gentlemen. And I hope that when her book is published, Flurry has a huge best seller. Because she worked her rear end off tracking down the witnesses. Listen to this." Bree had made notes on the case on her Blackberry. She tapped on the keyboard and read aloud: "Lucille Baxter, bar cleaner. Says she didn't see nobody, nowhere. Lucille's wages at the time were thirty-five cents an hour. She was returning from her nighttime job cleaning at around two thirty in the morning. Six months after the murder, Lucille bought and paid for a house on Flatiron Road. She paid four thousand six hundred and fifty dollars, cash. And here's this one. Lionel Woods, garbage collector. He was out on his usual run at three in the morning, didn't see a thing, according to O'Malley and Kowalski. He earned forty-five cents an hour."

"And what luxury was he able to purchase, in cash?" Petru asked.

"A brand-new Cadillac Eldorado."

Ron ran his hand through his blond curls. "Wow."

"Wow, indeed. Now . . . oof. I've got to sit down." She landed rather heavily onto her chair and positioned her crutch awkwardly across her lap. "Florida Smith has dug up a witness statement."

Ron's eyes lit up. "Someone who saw Haydee before she went into the river?"

"I think so."

"And this statement will indict Consuelo Bulloch?" Petru asked.

"She claims it will."

Petru pointed out the obvious. "You do not have this statement."

"She's saving it for the book."

"Oh dear," Ron said. "Whatever for? I mean, if she could bring a murderer to justice, she's morally bound to bring the statement to the authorities."

Bree was exasperated, and let it show. "But to what authorities, Ron? Consuelo's long dead. Let's assume it wasn't Consuelo, and that our client is innocent. Well, whoever killed Haydee is long dead, too. Flurry's not tracking down a murderer to bring him to justice. She's solving a historical mystery. From her standpoint, she has every right to keep this to herself until the book comes out."

"Sergeant Kowalski's still alive," Petru said. "Perhaps he is the one who dispatched the dancer?"

"Flurry thought of that. Police cover-up? Savannah shields one of its own? It'd make a heck of a true-crime book. But Sergeant Kowalski was headed back into Savannah that Saturday night. With a school bus full of Boy Scouts, no less. He got into town just in time to join O'Malley for his shift. Besides, you haven't seen the murder book. Poor Dent may have been out of it as a cop, but Kowalski was dedicated. You can see it from the notes he took. Very complete. Very neat. And he saved everything that could possibly be connected to the case. If Dent ever wonders why he wasn't kicked off the force, the answer lies in his partner's competence." Bree scratched at her cast. "This is going to drive me crazy."

"Get a knitting needle," Ron said. "Lavinia must have one."

This was perhaps the only thing that could divert Bree's attention from the job at hand. "Is she all right? I was so thankful to see you two, Ron, when you came to the town house on Saturday. But she looked . . ." Bree searched for the right word. "Frail. And she isn't at the meeting this morning."

Ron and Petru looked at each other. Petru made a slight gesture with his hands, as if to say "Go ahead."

"Our time in the temporal universe isn't infinite," Ron said.

"What do you mean?" Bree asked sharply. "Lavinia's fading. Fading into what?"

Petru pursed his lips. "For lack of a term more comprehensible to you, we could say she is travelling up. All existence is a journey. The journey ends in peace and stillness for those on the celestial path. In fire and stillness on the other."

Sudden tears sprang to Bree's eyes. "What are you saying?"

"A joyful thing." Petru leaned forward and patted her hands. "Lavinia will not pass by for some time yet. But the energy she used to meet your parents pushed her a little further along. It pushes all of us a little further along. Now, I think, we will not talk about this anymore, but you are having an unsuitable reaction of sadness."

"Unsuitable!" Bree dug a tissue from her skirt pocket and blew her nose.

"We have a client to represent," Petru reminded her. "I would suggest we turn to the case. If you have more questions about these other issues, I would suggest that you bring them up at the next meeting of the Company. You should address them to Professor Cianquino."

"For all the good that will do me," Bree muttered. Cianquino was prone to the self-discovery school of knowledge. He liked you to figure things out for yourself. She blew her nose one more time, tossed the tissue into the wastepaper basket, and said, "Okay. Back to work. There's a good possibility that Kowalski might remember something. From what Dent says—and from the background Flurry got on him—I can't imagine a less likely candidate for corrupt cop. So we're going to see him, Dent and I, late this afternoon."

"Suppose he does recall the witness who has disappeared," Ron said. "And this witness fingers Consuelo?"

"Yeah, well, that's a risk we're going to have to take. I'm off to the Bay Street office. I have," she said with a pleased air, "a new client coming in to see me at eleven. Then Dent and I are on to see Sergeant Kowalski this afternoon. In the meantime, I'd like you and Petru to go over Consuelo's past life with a fine-tooth comb. We need to find every decent thing she ever did in life and hope like heck we can come up with enough to mitigate her sentence."

"Will do, chief." Ron put his hand beneath her elbow and helped her get to her feet. "Dent's outside. He's going to take you over to the Bay Street office."

"That's great." Bree had hopped the three blocks to the Angelus office on her crutches. She wasn't looking forward to hopping the six blocks more. "Did Mercury give him some time off?"

"Vincent White fired him."

"What a jerk." Bree swung through the reception room. The *Rise of the Cormorant* remained in place over the mantel. The sea seemed to have a redder glow than usual this morning. Good. She was in a fairly fiery mood herself.

"So Dent's driving your car. Hang on while I get the door for you."

215

"Hm."

Bree paused in the small foyer while Ron propped open the front door. She looked at the procession of angels on the staircase. The last one in line, the one with silver hair, had a bandaged foot and a plain wooden cane in her right hand. Bree gave her a tiny salute and swung out onto the small front porch. She waved at Dent, who was standing next to her car on the other side of the wrought iron fence, and turned to Ron. "I can take it from here."

"You're sure?"

"I'm sure."

"We'll see you when you get back, then."

Bree had discovered that of all the annoyances that came with being on crutches, going up and down steps was the worst. She didn't have the patience to keep one foot elevated while she hopped down each step with the unsteady support of two skinny aluminum poles. The fastest way was to sit down with her cast extended and descend—rather inelegantly—on her rear end. She was in a hurry, so that's what she did.

"Would you care for a hand up?"

The hand in front of her face was male, hairy, and had sharp yellow nails encrusted with a dark red substance Bree never allowed herself to think about.

"Mr. Beazley," she said. She accepted the hand, rose to one foot, and steadied herself on her crutches. "And Mr. Caldecott."

The two attorneys for the Prosecution hovered just above the brick path. Beazley was tall and thin, with those disgusting hands. Caldecott was short and bald. It took some determination to look Caldecott in the eye; his pupils were black vertical slits; the iris was yellow, like a cat's or a goat's.

"Delighted to see that you're doing so well," Beazley said. He offered to put his hand under her elbow. Bree stopped him with a look. She swung herself down the walk to the gate, where Dent was waiting for her, with a look of alarm on his face.

"There was some mention of burns, Caldecott," Beazley murmured. "Not so bad, really, now that I see her in the flesh. And her hair will grow back." He stopped and craned his head around to view the back of her head. "Good idea, that. The bun. Covers up the shaved bits. Write that down, Caldecott."

"Appearance . . . not . . . generally . . . affected . . ." Caldecott read aloud to himself as he scribbled in a small notebook. "Mobility. . . . excellent . . ."

Bree brought herself to a halt. She didn't have time for this. "What's up, gentlemen?"

Caldecott tucked the notebook into the breast pocket of his suit coat and then withdrew a small camera. "Photographs, do you think, Beazley?"

"Not as much use as they used to be," Beazley said. "Not since Photoshop. Juries are skeptical. Too easy to crop, trim, and otherwise fake it."

Bree stared at a spot behind Caldecott's head and said in fake surprise, "Why if it isn't Gabriel himself! Gabriel! Good to see you, and your nice sharp sword. It's been way too long."

Caldecott jerked in alarm and looked around nervously. "Gabriel? Where!"

"Just kidding," Bree said. "But it got your attention." She scowled at them. "What do you two want? If it's about the Bulloch case, I'm nowhere near ready to file an appeal, and I'm certainly not ready to talk a deal."

"The Bulloch case," Beazley murmured. "No, no. We aren't ready to talk about that yet."

"Like you," Caldecott said smoothly, "we have a temporal practice . . ."

"One does need to pay the bills," said Caldecott.

"Our card," Beazley said, handing it over.

Bree took it, read it, and glared at them. "You're representing Armguard Insurance Company?"

"We're on retainer." Caldecott took the card back. "We're here on behalf of poor Mr. Mercury."

"Who is devastated by the accident . . ."

"But not in any way liable for your injuries."

Bree limped to the gate. "Forget it. I'm not suing Mercury, and I'm not dealing with you two. Go away."

"Do think she means it, Caldecott?"

"She may, Beazley. She may."

"I do," Bree said firmly. "I have no interest in suing Mr. Mercury." She reached the gate. Dent stood there, his hands clenched. He looked rough. "Mr. Dent," Bree said pleasantly, "I remember how efficiently you removed Sammi-Rose Waterman from B. Matthew's the other day. Do you think you could perform the service again?"

Dent took his sports coat off and hung it over the wrought iron fence. "Be glad to try."

"No need to get irritable," Caldecott said.

"We'll send you a release to sign," Beazley said.

"Don't forget to have it witnessed," Caldecott added. "Notarized, too. Say good-bye, Beazley. Keep in step, Dent!"

They were there, and then they weren't. The only thing left in the air was Caldecott's snigger.

"They're gone," Dent said.

"None too soon. Thanks for your assistance. Those two can be a real pain." Bree hopped through the gate and onto the sidewalk. "Let's get on to Bay Street."

Dent took his sports coat from the fence and slowly put it back on. Bree didn't think she'd ever seen anyone look so tired. "You know those two guys?"

"I wish I didn't. They're opposing counsel. I've been up against them in court three times, now."

Dent seemed to focus with an effort. "Yeah? How's your track record?"

"Against those two bozos?" Bree smiled. "Pretty good so far. But I'm not sure about winning *this* case." She stopped and leaned against the side of her little Ford Fiesta. He opened the passenger-side door for her. She swung herself around, sat down backwards on the seat, and swiveled her legs inside the car. Dent got into the driver's seat and pulled out onto the road with less than his usual expertise. Bree glanced at him. She didn't know whether to bring up his jobless state or not. He looked awful. He hadn't shaved. There were dark shadows under his eyes, and the lines in his face were deeper than before. She'd talk to EB about putting him on the payroll as a driver. She had no intention of suing Phillip Mercury, but his insurance company owed her a driver at least. "This witness that seems to have disappeared. Do you have any recollection of that at all?"

He jerked a little and brought his attention back to her. "What?"

"The missing witness?"

He ran one hand over his chain with a rasping sound. "Oh, that. I've been over it in my own mind, over it and over it. Maybe she went straight to the defense lawyers? I think it was a woman. Her statement never went through the department at all, or if it did, I don't recall it. She never did show up for the trial, and I seem to remember that her statement was ruled inadmissible. There was some talk about the judge in the case owing the DA's office a favor."

"So it wouldn't be in the trial records."

"Might be with the defense counsel's office."

"Good idea. I'll get Petru on it. If it's a matter of public record somewhere, anywhere, we're allowed access to it. There's another thing. There's three hours gone missing, between the time Norris stabbed Haydee and the time her body was discovered in the river. Did you and Kowalski try to account for that at all?"

"I don't remember." There was a world of self-disgust in his voice.

"Kowalski might," Bree said calmly. "We can see

him this afternoon, if you're . . . if you can spare the time."

He pulled up in front of the Bay Street office and double-parked. There was a lot of traffic this morning; the wail of sirens cut through the air, and the normal traffic routine seemed disrupted. There must have been an accident down by Montgomery. The Lexus behind them hooted angrily at Bree's car. Dent stuck his hand out the window and motioned the Lexus driver forward. "I'm going down to the Municipal Building and see about getting a handicap sticker." He looked into the rearview mirror as the Lexus made an elaborate show of backing up and then swung wide to get around them.

"No need," Bree said. "I'll be weight-bearing next week. I'm sure of it."

He shrugged. "Okay by me. You want a hand into the building?"

"No," Bree said crossly. She shoved the car door open and then paused. "I'm sorry I snapped at you. I'm feeling irritable this morning."

"There's a lot of that going around."

"So I hear."

There was an awkward silence. "I'm sorry you lost your job, Dent."

"What?"

"Your job? Ron told me this morning that Mercury fired you."

He blinked. "Yes. Yes, he did." He didn't look at her but stared ahead through the windshield. There was something more here than a job loss.

"Tell me what's wrong," she said quietly. "Please. Maybe I can help."

He rested his head against the steering wheel. "Florida Smith is dead. They found her body in the river about less than an hour ago."

Thirteen

What's past is prologue.
—*The Tempest*, William Shakespeare

No accident down by Montgomery, then. The traffic was being diverted to let the emergency vehicles get down by the river. Bree slammed the car door shut, grabbed Dent by the shoulder, and made him face her. "How?" she demanded. "What happened?"

"Somebody said she was shot. Somebody else said she was stabbed. You know what the crowds around a scene like that are like. Can't be sure of anything. But Lieutenant Hunter drove up just after they pulled her out of the river. And he's homicide, isn't he?"

Bree remembered what Cordy Eastburn had said: *Nobody better.*

So it was murder.

"Tell me exactly what happened, Dent. From the beginning."

"The crew's back at the riverbank this morning, reshooting a couple scenes. I went down to report at seven.

223

I was on seven to three today. Before I got fired. Which happened as soon as I got there. Vincent White was on set; I went over to see if he had any assignments, and he said, 'Yeah, get lost. How's that for an assignment?' "

"This was about seven this morning?" Automatically, Bree checked her watch. It was just after eleven. "Did you see Florida?"

"No, no I didn't. It doesn't mean she wasn't there. You know what a shoot's like. Everybody and his second cousin's running around like chickens with their heads chopped off. She could have been there, I guess. She is . . . was . . . always on time."

"Who else was there?"

"Ah." He ran his hand over his face again. "I don't know. Everybody, I guess." His eyes narrowed to slits. "Mrs. Waterman, for sure. She and her smartass lawyer. And Vince White, like I told you."

"Which lawyer? Payton McAllister?"

"The slimy one. Stubblefield."

"Dent. You were a cop. You've been trained to pay attention." She tapped him on the shoulder. "Would you look at me, please? What are you staring at anyway?" She followed the direction of his gaze out the windshield. It was fixed on a building about halfway down the street: Bartlett's Bar and Grill? Drinks Any Time. "Forget it, Dent. You don't drink anymore. You're going to help me find out how Flurry Smith died. Right?"

"Right."

"Do you blame yourself for this in some way? How could you?"

His face was bleak. "If I'd been a better cop sixty years ago. If I'd been a better *man*, none of this would have happened."

"You think Flurry's dead because she knows something about Haydee's murder that we don't?"

"What the hell do you think?"

Evasion never helped anybody. "I think you're right. Not about your value as a cop or a man, but about the link. It has to be connected to the missing witness."

Bree was getting very nervous about the answers this case was presenting to her. "Listen to me. I need a driver. You want the job?"

"Sure. Fine. Whatever."

"Dent, I don't have time for you to slide into this . . . this valley, or wherever you are. You don't happen to know *how* Flurry died? Did you see the body for yourself?"

"I saw. Couldn't tell."

"Okay. We've got to get down by the river. I'm going to call EB and cancel my eleven o'clock appointment. I want you to figure out a way to get me as close as you can to the scene." Bree looked over her shoulder. The traffic was still heavy. And the Lexus was back. Bree waited impatiently for it to pass. It didn't. The vehicle pulled up and came to a stop. A chorus of angry horns greeted this maneuver. A plump middle-aged woman in a bright purple caftan got out of the backseat and rapped on Bree's window, charm bracelet jangling.

Bree opened the window, ready with an apology.

"You're Ms. Winston-Beaufort, aren't you?"

"I am. And I apologize for blocking traffic, but don't you think it'd be a good idea to have your driver move—"

"I'm Dixie Bulloch," she said. "The third sister. I have an eleven o'clock appointment to see you, but Morris couldn't find a place to park and couldn't find a place to park so we circled the block about a million times. Then I said, 'Morris! That's Ms. Beaufort herself. We'll just have the meeting right in her car, and then she can run me back home.' I hope that's acceptable to you, Bree—it's Bree, isn't it? Then Morris can take the car on home. So we don't have to worry about parking at all." She opened the back door and thudded into the backseat. She was wearing a lot of heavy perfume that flooded the car with a sharp, very unpleasant scent of flowers.

"You're my new client?" Bree said.

"Figured nothing would make my sisters madder. You've got quite a reputation." She thrust a plump, freckled hand over the headrest. "Call me Dixie."

The Lexus found a break in the traffic and moved off, with Morris at the wheel.

Bree looked helplessly at Dent.

"So," Dixie said brightly. "Shall we drive around a bit, or do you just want to sit in the car and chat?" She stuck her head between the two front seats. Her hair was dyed a bright, brave red. "My goodness, you did get banged up in that accident with Phillip, didn't you? Although I have to say you're looking much less awful than I thought you would. Sammi-Rose said your face was about burned right off. But that's Sammi-Rose all over. Never lets facts get in the way of a good story. Your leg's broke though, is it?"

Bree looked down at the infuriating cast. "That it is. Miss Bulloch, Dixie. Before we go any further, why don't you tell me why you wanted to see me?"

Dixie wriggled comfortably into the backseat. "Now that is quite a story. I would have been along to see you before this, but I've been kind of tied up lately, what with one meeting and another."

Dent cleared his throat. "You wouldn't be a friend of Bill W's, by any chance?"

"I surely would," Dixie said. "You a friend of his, too? Now, isn't that a coincidence. You know, I thought I'd seen your face before."

Bree was happy to see Dent pulled out of his slump, if only momentarily, but the morning was wearing on, and she didn't care at the moment what friends the two had in common. "Dixie? Could you just summarize the reason you wanted to see me? I'm a bit short of time at the moment." Bree figured there was little if any chance that Dixie was fond of brevity, but it wouldn't hurt to give it a shot. "Dent is going to drop me as close as he can to the *Bitter Tide* shoot, and then he's going to take you on home. Aren't you, Dent?"

"Sure." He put the car into drive and pulled into the street.

"Aren't they making that movie down by the river? That's where all the commotion was a little bit ago, wasn't it? What do you suppose that's all about? Some tourist fell off of one of the tour boats, I should think.

They get into those bourbon sours and fall into the river like that." She snapped her fingers. "My sister went on down there this morning fixing to take Flurry Smith's head off with an ax. Maybe she's the one fell into the water. That'd be no loss to the country, that's for sure."

Dent pulled up in front of an unmanned police barricade and said bluntly, "Florida Smith is dead."

Dixie gasped. "That sweet child? Down there?" She craned her neck out the window and looked down at the activity beyond the barricade. "What in Sam Hill happened?"

Florida was a lot of things; sweet wasn't one of them. Smart, curious, ambitious—all that lively intelligence taken out of this world—for what? "We don't know yet," Bree said.

"So you're going to the river to find out?" She worried at her lower lip. "Holy crow. You don't suppose Sammi-Rose really did up and shoot her, do you? My goodness. And here I thought my morning was going to be taken up with boring old legal matters."

"I'm afraid that it wouldn't have happened in any event, Dixie. I've inherited the obligation to dispose of your grandmother's effects according to the directions she left in her will. The likelihood that you and your family are going to be on the wrong side of any legal action I might have to bring is pretty strong."

Dixie blinked. She wore a lot of mascara, just like her sister, but she wasn't as adept at application. She had dark smudges beneath her eyes. "I'm tryin' to work out what you just said. You mean you can't take me on as a client?"

"It's called a conflict of interest," Dent said. Dixie amused him. Which was a lot better than Dent, depressed.

"Well, that's all right, then, because like I told your Mrs. Billingsley, I didn't come to see you about me; I came to see you about Justine. Justine is your client, right?"

"Justine?" Bree had switched her briefcase out for a large tote bag with a strap. She hung it around her neck, opened up the passenger door, and collected her crutches. "We can't talk about her, either, Dixie."

"Why ever not?"

"Conflict of interest," Dent said. He put the car in park, then got out and came around to Bree's side of the car. "Let me give you a hand there, boss. This is as close as I'm going to get. It's a hike to the scene, but at least you won't have to go down any steps."

Bree took stock of her surroundings. Front Street ended in a cul-de-sac near the open-air market on Montgomery. Old, deserted warehouses loomed on either side of a narrow road leading down to it. The road had a fairly steep slope, but it was asphalt rather than cobblestone, which would make her descent easier.

Dent handed over her crutches. "I'll run Dixie home and then be back for you."

"Keep your cell phone on. I'm not sure where I'll be."

"Hello!" Dixie yodeled. "Remember me? So you're just takin' off without talking to me?"

"I'm sorry, but I'm sure you can see it wouldn't be appropriate." Francesca's Southern-girl training kicked in and Bree smiled at her. "It was very nice to meet you. Thank you for taking the time to come and see me."

"Is it a conflict of interest to tell you the real reason why my sisters have it in for Justine?"

"No," Bree said promptly, and with sudden, intense curiosity. "It isn't. If it turns out to have a bearing on the case you and your sisters are bringing against Justine for theft, it would be sneaky. Sneaky is not a conflict of interest."

"Boss," Dent said in a warning way.

"The case is going to be set aside until the actual disposition of the brooch is settled, anyway," Bree grumbled. "But you're right." She sighed. "You can't tell me that, either, Dixie." Her smile broadened.

"But you can tell Mr. Dent."

<hr />

Bree found that resting her weight lightly on the iron bar across the bottom of her foot steadied her enough to get down the asphalt path, using her crutches, of course, at a fair rate of speed. A patrolman stepped out from the warehouse overhang and stopped her at the bottom.

"Sorry, ma'am. You're approaching a crime scene."

The patrolman looked familiar. He had blond hair and very fair skin that turned pink under her puzzled scrutiny. A collection of police cruisers, emergency vans, and rescue equipment were gathered an eighth of a mile or so beyond him, down the cobbled street. Suddenly, recognition kicked in. "It's Officer Banks, isn't it?"

"So my ID tag says, ma'am."

"No. I mean we've met before. You helped me rescue my dog. Remember? About five months ago. He was caught in a steel trap just off Mulberry, and I called for help and you came. I'm Bree Beaufort."

His face lightened. "Sure. I remember. What happened to the dog?"

"He's fine. Healed up in record time. You'd just started on the job, as I recall."

"That's correct. Been on the force ever since." He looked a little wary. "You're a lawyer, right?"

"Yes. Is it true that you discovered Florida Smith's body this morning?"

"Can't confirm that, ma'am."

Bree decided it wouldn't hurt to stretch the truth a bit. "Ms. Smith was my client. Lieutenant Hunter should have been asking for me already."

"I'd have to confirm that, ma'am."

"Thank you," Bree said. "I'd appreciate that."

Banks spoke into the transmitter on his collar. "Arnie? The lieutenant handy? There's a Miss Winston-Beaufort wants access to the scene."

After a short delay, the transmitter erupted into a series of squawks. Banks looked at Bree's cast. "Yes, sir." Then he peered up the sloping road to Bay Street. "Yes, sir." Then, "I'll do that, sir. Ms. Beaufort?" It took her a second to realize Banks was addressing her. "You're supposed to wait right here."

One of the cruisers in the distance started up and bumped slowly toward them. It came to the end of the road and reversed before it stopped. Banks held the rear door open for her. "You're to go on up with Officer Arnold, Ms. Beaufort."

Bree backed into the seat and sat sideways while the cruiser bumped its way back. Officer Arnold was a stone-faced woman in her midthirties with bottle-blonde hair. She looked back at Bree once or twice but never said a word.

The walkway in front of the hotel was roofed and open on three sides. All of it had been cordoned off with yellow police tape. A crowd of onlookers on the far side were held back by the presence of two patrol officers. A few tourists, a clutch of media people with cameras, and the shopkeepers and regulars who were usually present on Front Street throughout the year milled around behind the tape. The crowd on the side closest to Bree was backed into a small section in front of a seafood shop specializing in buckets of oysters and cold beer. It was composed of the cast and crew of *Bitter Tide*. Hatch huddled with a couple of his handlers. Tyra Steele stood with her hairdresser, her makeup man, and a woman carrying a small white dog under one arm and holding up a cell phone with the other. Tyra, occasionally tossing her hair, was talking into the phone. A video feed, Bree guessed, with a direct link to Facebook. Justine sat on a camp stool, head erect, back straight. Craig Oliver stood behind her, his hand on her shoulder. Mercury—out on bail—and Vince White stood shoulder to shoulder, arms folded, with identical scowls.

A red-faced John Stubblefield harangued Sam Hunter. Stubblefield had one arm around Sammi-Rose Waterman. Her cold self-possession was gone. She was furious. And scared, Bree thought. Hunter's red-headed sergeant Nancy Markham stood at his back.

Stubblefield shook his finger in Hunter's face—a mistake, for anyone who knew anything at all about him. Hunter turned, nodded at Markham, and walked away. Markham pulled Sammi-Rose's hands behind her, cuffed her, and propelled her toward a patrol car.

"Good grief," Bree said.

"That got right up Stubblefield's rear end," Officer Arnold said gleefully.

"They've arrested Mrs. Waterman for the murder of Florida Smith?" Bree said.

Officer Arnold clammed up. "I wouldn't know anything about that, ma'am. Lieutenant Hunter wants to have a word before I take you home. You can ask him."

"Hang on a second." Bree swung her legs to the floor and tried the door handle. It was locked. "Hey," Bree said. "Would you let me out, please?"

"Sorry. The lieutenant doesn't want any civilians at the scene."

"You've got civilians all over the scene," Bree said furiously. "Either arrest me, Officer Arnold, or let me out. You can't do this." She whacked her hands on the glass. "Right now!"

"She giving you a little trouble, Arnie?" Hunter

opened the back door. "I didn't give in to the temptation to leave you standing on one leg at the end of the street, but right now, right here, I'm asking myself why the hell not."

Bree glared at him.

Hunter didn't twitch. "Arn?"

"Yes, sir."

"Get yourself a cup of coffee."

"Yes, sir." Officer Arnold touched her finger to her Stetson. "Ma'am. Pleasure driving you." Then she ambled off in the direction of the clam bucket restaurant.

"Pleasure driving me? Was she being Southern-polite or sarcastic?"

"Since she's from Detroit, I hazard a guess at the latter. Come on, Bree. Move over." He eased in beside her and took her hand in his. "This is a bad business. You're in no shape to take it on."

"I'm fine."

He cocked his head. His eyes were gray, with fine wrinkles at the corners. He looked older than he was; most cops did. Sometimes, Bree thought she might love him. Sometimes she thought she could never love anyone, given the job she had to do. Mostly, she wasn't sure. "You don't look as bad as you might." He touched a finger to her cheek. "You're peeling."

"Really?" She strained to catch a glimpse of herself in the rearview mirror. "Yikes. So I am."

"You've made a remarkable recovery. No doubt about it. But it's a little soon to be back in the game, don't you think?"

"What I think is, I'm capable of making that decision myself."

"Fair enough. So what's with the intemperate invasion of my crime scene?"

"Intemperate?" she flashed.

"Yep. As in ill-considered. What's your real interest in this case?"

I'm trying to solve a sixty-year-old murder on behalf of my client, who's been dead for more than thirty years wasn't going to cut it. "Florida Smith was a friend of mine. And a client." Bree thought a bit and improvised. "She had me on retainer to defend her against the Bulloch lawsuit."

"I thought the *Bitter Tide* attorneys would take care of that."

"As far as the script is concerned, of course. Flurry was worried about the book deal."

"Wouldn't her publisher pay for her defense?"

"She had an advance, Hunter. She didn't want anything to jeopardize publication. It was her first big break."

"Fair enough."

"Was she murdered, Hunter?"

"I don't know. I won't know until the results of the autopsy are in."

"But you arrested Mrs. Waterman."

"Mrs. Waterman arrived on the set this morning about nine thirty, with her lawyer, John Stubblefield, and an injunction to stop filming *Bitter Tide*. She got into a shouting match with Florida Smith and assaulted her."

"With what?"

"She picked up a folding chair and hit Ms. Smith on the back of the head."

Bree's hand went to the back of her own head. The area was still tender. And she was really angry about the shaved patch at the base of her skull. Criminals were known to stick with the same MO. Maybe Sammi-Rose had clocked her after all. "Is the back of the victim's head a usual target for Mrs. Waterman?"

Hunter's smile was faint, but his eyes were cold. "That possibility occurred to me. Florida left to get a cold compress. She wasn't seen again until they pulled her out of the river at ten fifteen."

"Did anyone go with Florida, to give her a hand?"

"Two of the grips. Mercury's got a trailer here. The grips—Grant Thomas and Hudson James—got her settled with an ice pack and offered to call the paramedics. Florida said she was fine. They left her there."

"Then what?"

"We're interviewing the cast and crew, one by one. So far, no one admits to seeing her between the time the grips left her at the trailer and the time she was found in the river."

"Could she have been disoriented? Wandered off and fallen in, then been unable to get out again?"

"It's possible. You're thinking like a defense lawyer. Anything's possible at this point. I don't have the autopsy results back, we aren't finished with the interviews, and we don't have enough information."

Bree scratched irritably at the top of the cast.

"You need a knitting needle," Hunter said.

"So Ron tells me. Sam, you must have a theory of the case. What do you think?"

"My gut tells me it's murder."

"I think so, too." She glanced at him. His eyes were on his team. They were moving methodically through the crowd of restless cast and crew members, taking names, statements. "Why? Her death isn't going to stop the movie going forward. It might not even stop the book. She had a first draft. She told me so. If it's in decent shape, her publisher could hire another writer to finish it off."

"If they find it," Hunter said. "We searched her trailer. Her laptop, her zip files, her CD files. They're all missing."

Fourteen

Rest, rest, perturbed spirit.
—*Hamlet*, William Shakespeare

Bree sat and stared at the whiteboard in the meeting room at the Angelus Street office. She'd added a question mark above her previously scrawled *4:30 a.m.: Haydee's body discovered in the river*, and it seemed to leer at her. What had happened between Haydee's running out of the bar at one thirty and her being pulled from the river at four thirty? "I'm missing something here," Bree said aloud.

"I'm sure you'll think of it," Lavinia said placidly. Her gnarled fingers whipped rapidly along. She was knitting a cardigan out of soft violet wool. Bree's request to borrow a knitting needle had reminded her of the unfinished project. Her skin had taken on a faint, bronze glow, as if she were lit from within. She looked happy, and it eased Bree's heart.

"I looked through all of the police documents available at the time," Ron said. "Florida Smith didn't miss a thing."

239

"It would be more accurate to say that there is nothing in the police files that is not in the deceased's files. Those that we have in our possession," Petru corrected him.

Bree scratched at her cast with the knitting needle. Her team politely avoided looking at her. "Nothing about a possible witness to Haydee's whereabouts after she left the Tropicana?"

"Notes of the persons interviewed only." Petru drummed his fingers on the tabletop. "That scratching is most annoying, my dear."

"Sorry." Bree tucked the needle into the tote at her side.

"As far as this current case is concerned, Lieutenant Hunter is of the opinion that Florida's death was motivated by a desire to stop the publication of the book?" Petru asked.

"If she fell into the river because Sammi-Rose gave her a concussion when she smacked her over the head with that chair, it sure was. He didn't come right out and say it, but he's thinking a manslaughter charge, for sure. And maybe that's what it is." Bree rubbed her forehead. "Maybe I'm totally off base about this. Maybe it's not murder."

"Could be. You're still recovering from your own concussion," Ron said cheerily. "All of Flurry's original files have been stolen. If she *was* murdered, whoever did it doesn't know that we have copies."

"That lets out just about everybody," Bree said crossly. "All of our possible suspects—Waterman, Cicerone, White, Mercury, Stubblefield, and even Justine were in B. Matthew's the night Flurry handed over the stuff to Dent and me. For all they knew, a copy of the manuscript was with it."

"And all of those suspects were present this morning," Ron said. "Why look for intelligent conduct from a killer?"

Bree stared at him. "Now, that's given me an idea."

"I don't see why it should," Petru said with a look of slight disapproval. "The evidence we do have points to a person who thinks logically, albeit with immoral ruthlessness."

"Something must have happened yesterday," Bree said. "Flurry turned something up. I wish I'd answered her call last night."

"She called you?" Ron said.

"Left a message on my cell phone. I figured I'd call her back sometime today." Bree rubbed her eyes. She wanted to cry with frustration.

Lavinia tilted her head, as if listening to something only she could hear. "I do believe Mr. Dent is outside."

"Is it time to go see Kowalski already? All right." Bree heaved herself to her feet. She needed something solid to do. Something that would give her some facts. It was way past time to see Kowalski. The missing witness was a solid lead, and with just a little bit of luck, Kowalski could get her further ahead.

"He's going out to see his old friend at last?" Lavinia asked.

"It's more than that, I think. He feels awfully guilty

241

about the way he treated Kowalski when they were on the force together. I spent a little time last night thinking about how to help Dent with that, and I believe I've found an answer. So we'll see."

"But you are going to inquire from him about this missing witness," Petru asked.

"You bet I am. I hope we get some kind of lead. It's about time we had a break in the case. Speaking of the case . . . Ron, I want to find out where Florida was yesterday, all day, and all the time."

"Sunday?" Lavinia murmured. "I hope the child was in church."

"If she was, I hope it wasn't an all-day service." Bree slung her tote strap around her neck and started out the door. "That last night at B. Matthew's, Flurry kept saying she needed a last little bit of proof, right? Maybe she found it. And if she found it, so can we."

━━∞━━

"I take it you got Dixie back home without any trouble." Bree adjusted her cast so that it was elevated on her tote. The whole leg throbbed, the knee worst of all.

"Depends on what you call trouble." Dent had written out directions to the Sweet Briar Adult Care Facility on his lap. His refusal to use the GPS system in Bree's car was absolute. "The only woman I ever met who talked as much as she does was my ex-wife."

"You were married?"

"Before the war," Dent said curtly. "She wasn't long

on patience. Wasn't there when I was shipped home." He shrugged. "Happened to a lot of guys."

Bree wanted to ask what had happened to her, if Dent had any children, if he still missed her. She didn't.

"She did tell me why her family hates Justine so much."

"I figured it was part of the Bullochs' total harassment plan. Stop the movie, stop the book, and get the actress playing their mother fired. There's more?"

"Justine worked for the Bullochs. Did you know that?"

Bree was taken aback. "Justine Coville? When was this?"

"The mid '70s. Dixie's recall isn't much to write home about. She says Justine left Savannah to make it big on the New York stage, ended up broke, and came back to Savannah with her tail between her legs. Mrs. Bulloch took her on as sort of a secretary. Dixie says her mamma remembers that the family treated her like a queen. They lived out near Rattigan's old mansion at the time. Dixie said it was gorgeous. There was some kind of horse house out back that Justine lived in."

"Horse house?" Bree said. "Do you mean a carriage house?"

"That's it. Mrs. Bulloch had been sick sometime before Justine showed up. Bad heart. The daughters 'bout run themselves ragged lookin' after her, and then Justine took over taking care of the old lady." He snorted. "That nursing didn't last too long. A week or so after

Justine came in, Mrs. Bulloch ended up falling in the bathtub and eventually dying from the effects of the fall. Justine took off right away for Hollywood. Left the family high and dry at the worst possible time, Dixie said. Sammi-Rose never forgave her, either. They were just kids at the time. Dixie thinks maybe six or seven years old. Dixie's mamma, the woman Alexander married after Haydee died in '52, ended up nursing Mrs. Bulloch right through to the end, which wasn't long in coming after that fall. Liked to have killed Dixie's mamma, all that nursing. Dixie thinks maybe it did. Her mamma keeled over from a heart attack at a Stuckey's just after Dixie went into middle school, and they figured Consuelo had just wore her heart right out. The old lady was pretty demanding. Anyhow, there's no love lost over Consuelo, that's clear as crystal. They slung her body into the cheapest cemetery they could find, out to Belle Glade, and that was that."

"Oh dear." Belle Glade was where Haydee was buried. What was it Justine had said? With an angel watching over her tomb. Bree had a brief vision of the two bitter enemies lying side by side in their graves. Ugh.

"Families," Dent said. "They'll kill you, if you let them. I told Dixie that you just have to rise above. It's all there in Step Four." He braked at a red light and looked at the directions in his lap. "We're on Skidaway. We take a left here, go down a quarter of a mile, and that should be it."

"GPS is much easier, Dent. There's a little voice that tells you exactly where to go."

"I got enough little voices telling me exactly where to go."

They rolled along in silence for a bit. The area was what real estate people called "mixed use." They passed a strip mall containing an auto parts store, a Denny's restaurant, and a Michaels craft shop. A development of small, one-story frame houses was next. Then on the east side of the road, a group of low, pale yellow buildings sprawled out just beyond a sign bearing their collective name.

"Sweet Briar," Dent said, and turned into the parking lot. He drew the car into an open space near the front door and killed the engine. "Doesn't look too bad," he said after a long moment. The shrubbery around the buildings was well tended, and the grass was clipped. A threat of rain hung in the overcast sky, but somehow, the surroundings weren't at all somber.

"You haven't been to see Kowalski before?"

"I've been putting it off." He rubbed the back of his neck. "I owe him a lot. He wasn't the kind of guy who tolerates drunks. But he put up with it. Kept the heat from the brass off me when he could. I'm trying to figure out a way to make amends in a quiet way. Can't let him know I'm back, of course, and he wouldn't believe it anyway. But it'd be nice to get his forgiveness."

Bree noticed Dent's hands were trembling. "How old is he now?"

"Ninety-two."

"We've got an excellent reason to see him. We're following up on Florida's visit. I read her interview notes.

She thought he was in pretty good shape. I know what I want to do. I want to ask him about that missing witness, and hope like heck he remembers. So we'll start with that. Have you got any ideas about how to bring the conversation around to what you want to do?"

Dent chewed his lower lip.

"I do. I've been thinking about it." Bree reached into her tote and pulled out an envelope. "Write him a note. Tell him your father was a Marine Corps buddy of Dent's who was asked to go through Dent's effects when he died, and he found this letter. Tell him when your father died a few months ago, he passed the note on to you."

Dent scowled. "He's not going to buy that. He's ninety-two, but he's a ninety-two-year-old cop. He's going to know I wrote the note."

"My grandmother kept a day journal most of her life. I took a blank page from the back. This paper is old." She shook it out of the envelope and smoothed it out on her knee. It was a heavy rag-content paper, with the soft, yellow patina that only comes with years. Dent picked it up and rubbed the worn surface with his thumb. "Franklin left all his effects to me when he died—including a fountain pen. If you use that, it will look old, too. It might work, Dent. Can't hurt to try. I'll go on ahead to reception and make sure that he can see us today. You think about that note." She dropped the fountain pen on the dashboard and went into the building.

The door was handicapped accessible, for which she was grateful. She tapped the red button for the automatic door and walked through into a quiet, carpeted space with a small reception center in the middle of the foyer. A neatly dressed, middle-aged woman looked up with a smile as Bree hopped in. "Can I give you a hand there?"

"I'm fine, thank you." Bree paused to take in her surroundings. Two hallways ran off the foyer, one to the right and one to the left. Small brass plaques set in the wall listed room numbers. The air was faintly scented with the odors of food, hospital disinfectant, and soiled linen. A small bureau set against the wall adjacent to the reception desk held a big bowl of silk flowers. Behind the reception desk, a set of glass doors gave into a large open space with a skylight. It was filled with plants, several televisions sets, and a lot of elderly people in wheelchairs.

"Are you a family member of one of our guests? Have you visited us before?" The receptionist was polite but wary. She had a name tag pinned to her white blazer: FLORENCE BAGLEY. She grinned, suddenly, at the crutches. "Unless you're checking in."

"Not yet, at any rate. I'm here to see Robert Kowalski." Bree dug a business card out of the side pocket of her tote and handed it over.

"Brianna Beaufort. Of course! That's where I saw you. You were on TV. Something to do with that rich guy that killed himself up in New York."

"Mr. O'Rourke. My fifteen minutes of fame. Now in the past, fortunately. I'm here with a . . ." She stumbled slightly. She was beginning to think the biggest problem she had with her Angelus Street cases was the number of times she had to fib to temporals. If there was a scale somewhere in the Sphere with her bad behavior piled up on it, it was tilted heavily to the downward side. "A client, who's tidying up his father's estate. His visit coincides with an older case I'm working on. I'm hoping Mr. Kowalski can help me with that, as well." She heard the front door open and close behind her. "This is Mr. William Dent, who is here on his father's behalf. Mr. Dent? This is Mrs. Bagley."

"We're here to see Bobby Lee," Dent said. Bree noticed the envelope with her grandmother's journal paper was tucked in his breast pocket. "My father had a message to pass on to him."

"He'll be glad of the company, I'm sure." Mrs. Bagley took a ring of keys from the desk drawer and headed down the hall labeled 115 TO 215. "Last visitor he had was a pretty young colored girl."

So how come you're not giving this woman heat about her language?

"Get out of my head, Dent."

Mrs. Bagley turned around. "Pardon?"

"Sorry. I'm still getting used to these crutches."

"Takes some of our residents that way. A lot never do get used to them. Anyway, he's in here. You came just in time. He likes to watch *Jeopardy* in the afternoon, and it's about over. She tapped on the swinging wood door as she pushed it open and said loudly, "Bobby Lee? You've got some company. A pretty lady and a friend of hers."

A very old man sat huddled in a leatherette armchair in front of a small TV set. He was bent like a fishhook.

His skin was spotted with age marks. He reminded Bree of a plant that needed a good soaking. The eyes in the incredibly wrinkled face were dark brown and alert. At Mrs. Bagley's greeting, he grabbed the cane resting against the side of the chair and got to his feet. "Who's this?" he demanded.

"Visitors!" Mrs. Bagley shouted.

"Keep your voice down, woman. I'm not deaf." He frowned at Bree. "You notice how that happens when you get on in years a bit? Everyone shouts at you."

Mrs. Bagley kept her voice pitched high and loud. "This is Miss Winston-Beaufort, Bobby Lee! And Mr. . . . ?"

"Dent. I'm William Dent." He cleared his throat. "It's . . . good to meet you, Bobby Lee." He took two steps forward and stood in front of the old man as if he were awaiting sentence.

Bobby Lee stood with both hands on his cane and craned his neck forward like a turtle. He squinted at Dent for a long moment. "Dent," Bobby Lee said finally. "I suppose it's nice to meet you, too, Mr. Dent. Although I won't know until you tell me what you came for."

"I'm Mr. Dent's attorney," Bree said. "We're here because Mr. Dent's father passed recently, and he had a small task he asked my client to perform."

"Dinner's at five o'clock," Bobby Lee said. "It's not going to run into that, is it?"

"I shouldn't think so."

"Good. Then you can scoot on out of here, Bagley." He waved one hand at her. "Shoo."

"I'll just be off, then," Mrs. Bagley said. "You ring that buzzer right there if you need me."

Bree nodded her thanks.

The room was spare but adequately furnished. There was a small table in one corner, with two utilitarian straight-back chairs. The TV sat on a chest of drawers. The hospital bed struck the only discordant note. It had a rolling rack for intravenous medicines next to it. A medical clipboard hung at the foot.

"Don't mind all that stuff," Bobby Lee said. "Once in a while I get dizzy-like, and they put an APB out on me. Go on. Have a seat at the table yonder." He looked around in a confused way. "Y'all want some coffee? Not much I can offer you in the way of hospitality."

"We're just fine, thank you." Bree settled herself in one of the chairs, regretting that she hadn't taken the time to bring the old fellow something.

"I brought you this," Dent said awkwardly. He groped in his sports-coat pocket and pulled out a fistful of candy bars.

"Bit-O-Honey!" Bobby Lee said. "My glory, I haven't seen those for years." He sat back in the armchair, the candy in his lap. "Thing about these candy bars, son, is that they aren't too good for the false teeth. Bet I can suck on 'em, though. Lord, the sugar in those things kept me good and awake when I was on the night shift."

"Yeah," Dent said. "Me, too."

Bobby Lee cocked his head to one side. "Sounds like maybe you were on the job, sonny?"

"Retired," Dent said. "Some time ago. Bobby Lee,

250

we're here about a couple of things. I've been looking into some cold cases for the department. We were wondering if you recall much about the Haydee Quinn case."

"That pretty girl with the funny name—Flurry, Flurry Smith was here about that a couple of months ago," Bobby Lee said. "Pulled her body out of the Savannah River this morning, according to the news." He looked sad. "Called her up this Sunday and talked to her as a matter of fact. Got something to give her that might help. I should have remembered it sooner, but I do tend to forget easy these days." He pulled at his lower lip. "It's like my memory's written in pencil and somebody's erasing it."

Bree felt the familiar thud of excitement. "There's a possibility the cases are related, Sergeant Kowalski. Now that Flurry's gone, we've taken up the banner, so to speak. We'd like to find out why she died."

Bobby Lee snorted. "Don't see how they could be. Ms. Smith passed on this morning. Haydee's been dead these sixty years, and whoever killed her is deader than a doornail, too."

"So you do recall the case?" Bree asked.

"You bet I remember. One of the biggest cases of my career. She asked me a bunch of questions, that girl did. You go right ahead and ask them, too."

"There was a witness who never actually came forward at the trial," Bree said. "It may have been someone who saw Haydee after Norris attacked her at the Tropicana Tide. Did you discuss that with Florida Smith?"

Bobby Lee leaned forward. "I sure did. Thing is,

the gal never showed up again after she gave Eddie the statement."

Bree didn't look in Dent's direction. "You're referring to Lieutenant O'Malley? Your partner on the force."

"You've done your homework, just like Ms. Smith. Pretty thing," he mused, "smart, too. Name of Charis Jefferson. Anyways, yes. Eddie and I had to canvass the area around the Tropi, see if anyone had a notion as to where Haydee had gone after Bagger Bill stuck her. Well, Eddie found her, all right. She danced, same as Haydee. Wanted to be another Lena Horne."

"Danced?" Bree said. "You mean she was a strip . . . in the show?"

"Chorus. In those days, it didn't do to have coloreds front and center, although she should have been, I suppose. Had a lot of talent. Now, that was a pretty girl, too. Not a beauty like Haydee, but a looker, all the same. Nice girl. Anyways, this girl Charis Jefferson was still backstage when Bagger Bill and Haydee started getting into it, so she hid somewhere's, a closet, I guess, or under a table. Haydee stumbled past her on her way out, bleeding from the front, the girl said, and the girl run after her. Got into a big old Buick that was parked at the back of the bar, Haydee did, and the car took off."

Dent's voice was husky. "Did she know the model? The make? The year?"

"All she told Eddie was that the car was a Buick, white."

"Do you remember anything else Charis told Eddie?" Bree asked.

Bobby Lee rubbed his scalp through his scant white hair. "No, I don't recollect more than that. Eddie, he could have told you. He had it all written down. He gave me the statement to put in the file."

"Sergeant Kowalski?" Bree spoke as gently as she could. "You were responsible for taking the case notes and filing them with the department, weren't you? That statement wasn't in the police records."

"No." Bobby Lee sighed. "No, it wasn't. I ditched it."

"This is an old case, and as you know, any statute of limitations has long run out." Bobby Lee didn't strike her as the kind of man who would have taken a bribe, but she had to ask. "Did someone ask you to ditch it?"

"Some crook, you mean? No. Thing is, you have to understand something about Eddie. He had a bad war. Spent time in a Jap concentration camp. Got himself a Bronze Star or two. When he got home, the cheap little gal who he was married to had up and run off with someone else. Plus, he was Irish. And you know what they say about the Irish."

Bree sighed. She was heartily glad attitudes had changed from 1952.

"He took to drink. He was hanging on to his job by the skin of his teeth. His old CO in the Marines was our commissioner. Creighton Oliver."

"Oliver?" Bree said. "His name was Oliver?"

"Yeah, his son went on to play a cop rather than be a cop." Bobby Lee laughed. "You might have seen the show, *Bristol Blues*. Good show, but they didn't get a thing right about being on the job. Anyhow, Commander

Oliver watched out for Eddie as best as he could, but our captain was a Methodist, and you know how they feel about booze of any kind, especially on the job. So Eddie was on thin ice."

Bobby Lee sighed. He unwrapped one of the Bit-O-Honeys, broke off a piece, and sucked on it. "Eddie used to bring me these. Picked 'em up at the Woolworth's down on Whitaker."

"You were telling us about the statement from the dancer, Charis Jefferson," Bree said gently.

"Yeah." He sagged in his chair. He was running through whatever reserves a ninety-two-year-old man had. "Thing is, Eddie had a few too many when the captain sent us out to canvass the blocks around the Tropi, and that statement was useless. It was hand wrote, and the writing was all over the place. You could tell Eddie wasn't exactly sober. We might a got away with that, but it wasn't signed, neither. Some smart defense lawyer got hold of that, it'd be tossed out on its ear. Me, I went back to the Tropi to get the girl to make another statement, but by then she'd run off. Scared, most likely. And then Bagger Bill confessed. So I didn't put it in the murder book, no sir. I gave it to the defense lawyers, and they said it was as useless as I knew it was. And they pitched it, I guess. I mean, we had our perp, so it would have just confused everybody."

Bobby Lee's eyes closed. His head fell forward on his chest. He was asleep.

"God," Dent said. It was both a plea and a prayer. "I don't remember a thing about it."

"We've got a lead. We need to jump on it." Bree hauled herself to her feet and laid her hand lightly on Bobby Lee's shoulder.

Bobby Lee mumbled in his doze. He lifted his head and blinked at them. "Who are you?" he demanded. "What are you doing in my room?"

"I'm Bree Beaufort, Sergeant Kowalski. Mr. Dent and I came by to talk with you." His eyes were confused. He looked exhausted. "We won't bide for very long. Would you like us to go? Are you tired of company?"

"You came to see me about that pretty young girl, Florida Smith."

"Yes," Bree said.

"I was sorry to see that she'd passed, and in such a way." He put his hands on his cane and struggled to his feet. "Got something I wanted to pass on to her." He looked suddenly shy. "Thing is, she was going to put me in her book. Took a picture of me and everything. I don't have much to pass on, but I do have this." He shuffled over to the bureau and pulled open the bottom drawer. He brought out a dented tin box and handed it to Bree. "Thought Ms. Smith might want a picture of these, maybe under the one of me in my uniform."

"A tea caddy," she said.

"Open it up."

The box had a collection of odds and ends. A few buttons. Some sealed plastic bags with flattened bullets, what looked like dirt, a bit of hair. A short link of nylon rope.

"Souvenirs from my cases," Bobby Lee said proudly.

He picked up the rope. "This one's from the poor old fellow who dragged Haydee's body out of the river. That bullet's from the Bishop Heights sniper."

Bree picked up the bag with the coil of hair. "And this?"

Bobby Lee put a trembling hand to his face and rubbed his chin. "Now that—that wasn't really a case. Least, not as far as the department. But me, I wasn't so sure. That's from the hand of Mrs. Consuelo Bulloch."

Bree stared at it.

"The one from the Haydee Quinn case, you know. I took this years later. She had a heart attack, the old lady did. Fell in the tub and near drowned. Lasted only a couple of days after they found her. Always thought she must have grabbed on to somebody while she was fallin', but the med tech thought she grabbed it off herself, while she was struggling." He shook his head sorrowfully. "Me, I thought it was murder. No proof, though." He shuffled back to the chair and half fell into it.

"Dinner's at five," he said into the silence. "You go on and take that tin. I don't need it anymore."

"Yes," Bree said. She was having trouble catching her breath. "Thank you."

"Nice to see you folks."

Bree breathed deeply and was finally able to answer. "Yes, and we'll be sure you won't miss dinner. There's just one more thing." She looked over at Dent. "Mr. Dent came into possession of a letter from Eddie O'Malley. He'd like to read it to you. Is that going to be all right?"

"Eddie." Bobby Lee looked up at Dent. "Eddie."

Dent fumbled the envelope from his pocket, unfolded the letter, and looked directly into his old friend's eyes. "Hey, Bobby Lee: Wanted to say so long. Wanted to tell you I screwed up while we were partnering together and I hope you forgive me for it. I never had a brother. But that's how I thought of you. I'm sorry, brother. If you can forgive me, I'd go down the road a better man. If you can't, well, that's okay, too." He laid the letter on Bobby Lee's knee.

"What the heck, Eddie," Bobby Lee said. "You did the best you could. Don't need to say a word more about it." He smoothed the yellowing paper out with a hand trembling with age, trembling with a shy delight. "Good to have this, though. Good."

"Thank you, partner."

"Hey. No sweat. See you soon, I think."

Bree stood still for a moment, absorbed in watching the old face drop off into sleep. She was happy and sad all at once. The light in the room seemed very like the light that surrounded her angels when she watched them unaware: the color of sunlight through new leaves.

"Well, then, Dent," she said, "we'd better go."

He didn't answer her. She knew he wouldn't.

Dent was gone.

Fifteen

Chance governs all.
—*Paradise Lost*, John Milton

"A happy result," Petru said. "Dent's rehabilitation."

"Except that Bree had to drive herself back to the office," Ron said. "I could have come and gotten you when you called, you know."

The three of them were back in the conference room at Angelus Street, staring at the whiteboard with the time line on it. Bree was beginning to think of it as the infernal time line. This case was maddeningly elusive. The plastic envelope with the coil of hair lay on the table in front of them all. She'd tried to raise Consuelo from it. It hadn't worked.

"I drove back on my own." She wriggled her leg. The bone-deep ache was gone. The knee was reduced to an occasional twinge. Even the itchiness was minor. "It feels a lot better. It's a relief to be able to drive myself. I did just fine." Her private opinion was that the light that had taken Dent on his journey home had a spillover effect on her leg, but she didn't bring it up. Her angels wouldn't have answered her anyway.

"We have a crack in the case," Petru announced.

"You managed to trace the registration of the Buick that picked Haydee up outside the Tropicana Tide, Petru," Bree said. "Good work! Who owned it?"

"I do not know that yet. I have set my search program on that particular issue. We should have an answer soon."

"Then you've located the 1952 employee tax records for the Tropicana?"

"T-cha! Yes."

"Was Charis Jefferson an employee there?"

"She was, yes."

"Do you know what happened to her?"

Petru shrugged.

"See if there's a death certificate. Right now."

Petru's fingers sped over the keys. "Not in the State of Georgia, no." He clicked on for a few minutes, then sat back. "And not in the United States. I cannot speak globally."

"Good. Now tell me what you wanted to tell me earlier."

"It is about Florida Smith's whereabouts on Sunday afternoon. It is Ron's work. He should be the one to tell you."

Bree turned to Ron and raised her eyebrows expectantly.

"You want it step-by-step? It's best to take it step-by-step. I talked to the folks at the Mulberry Inn, where she was registered. She asked how to get to a funeral home out in Belle Glade."

Bree looked at the time line. "The Ernest Cavanaugh Funeral Home, where Haydee's body was taken after she died at the hospital."

"Exactly. At the request of the Bullochs," Ron reminded them. "So I went down there, too, and talked to the current owner, Nathan Scotto. Flurry asked to see all the records from July 3, 1952, when Haydee's body was admitted." Ron pulled out his Blackberry. "I photographed the admissions sheet for you. The AP was Dr. Pythias Warren, which is consistent with the police report.

"Flurry then went to the county morgue, which is located at Montgomery. She asked to see the employee roster for July 5, the actual day that the autopsy was performed. Guess which private physician was present at the autopsy?"

"Dr. Warren?" Bree said.

"Dr. Warren."

Bree felt a stab of excitement. "Hm."

"Then she went back to the hotel and made two phone calls that evening. The police requisitioned the records as part of the current investigation into Florida's death, and the report's been filed, so the information was available."

Bree didn't ask how Ron actually got the report. It would be part of the public record when the case was either resolved or sent to the cold case division. The Company's rule was that any information available to the public was available to them; there weren't any rules about when.

"Who did she call, Ron?"

"Craig Oliver."

"Craig Oliver?" Bree sat back. She had a theory of the case. Finally. "Craig Oliver the actor. The one who's playing Dent in the movie."

"Eddie O'Malley," Petru reminded her.

"Whatever," Ron said impatiently. "We know who she means, Petru. Flurry called Oliver twice. The first phone call lasted about two minutes. The second one lasted almost an hour. The interval between the two calls was exactly twenty-two seconds."

"He hung up on her," Bree said. "And she called him back."

"Surmise," Petru said. "But a sensible surmise. Wait one moment please." He tapped his keyboard, read the screen, and looked up at them with a grim smile. "I asked for the search to cross-reference white Buicks registered in 1952 with all of the names in Florida Smith's database. Look at this." He spun the laptop around so that both Bree and Ron could see it.

"Creighton Oliver," Bree said. "Craig Oliver's father."

Petru whirled the laptop around to face him again, and spoke as his fingers flew over the computer keyboard. "The man is sixty-three years old. It is his father, surely. Aha! Aha! This is the break in the case! It is his father. More than that! He is at the time the commissar of the police!"

"The commissioner. Of the police. Dent's old CO."

"You seem to know this already." Petru grumbled under his breath as he read the screen. "If you know this, why am I working? If you know this, why did you not . . . Here I will print it out for you. And then we shall see."

It was all falling into place, with a suddenness that made Bree dizzy.

"Are you feeling quite well, my dear?" Petru asked.

"Is there any way you can check the morgue records for 1952 and find a Jane Doe, age early twenties? She would have died on the fourth of July. Probably African-American. Dr. Warren would have signed the death certificate. She would have been brought in by a policeman reporting directly to the commissioner."

"Of course. Would you like me to accomplish that now?"

"I would."

"Craig Oliver's still registered at the Mulberry Inn, isn't he?"

"As far as I know," Ron said. "The police might have gotten there before us."

"I'm not worried about the police."

It was dark outside, and cold. The Mulberry Inn was only two blocks from the Angelus office, and Bree decided to walk. She could walk on two legs now, after a fashion, and Petru had generously lent her his cane.

The room was a comfortable suite, right off the main entrance. Bree tapped at the door and waited. Craig Oliver's voice demanded to know who it was. When Bree told him, he opened up and stood there, a drink in his hand. It clearly wasn't his first of the evening.

"Is Justine in?" Bree stepped inside without waiting for an answer. Justine sat on the couch, a drinks tray on the coffee table in front of her. She was wearing an elaborate bathrobe—a tea gown, Justine's generation would call it. The peacock jewel was pinned to the collar. Florida Smith's manuscript, *Death of a Doxy: Who Killed Haydee Quinn?*, lay in her lap.

"Hello, Haydee," Bree said.

The old actress looked up at her, stone-faced.

"You wanted to break the contract with Norris because you were pregnant."

Justine smiled. Haydee's three-cornered smile. The one Bree had seen in the black-and-white pictures taken sixty years ago. "And wasn't it lucky that I was?" she said. She jerked her chin at Craig Oliver. "You want to know who killed Florida Smith? Ask him. Ask my baby boy."

Sixteen

Leave her to heaven,
And to those thorns that in her bosom lodge,
To prick and sting her.
—*Hamlet*, William Shakespeare

Antonia, Bree, and EB sat around the small table in the town house kitchen, eating boiled shrimp from Huey's. Sasha lay at Bree's feet. Hunter had arrested Craig Oliver for the murder of Florida Smith the night before. It was close to noon, and Bree hadn't been to bed yet.

"Craig Oliver is Justine Coville's son?" Antonia said. "And Justine Coville is really this B-Girl from 1952? Haydee Quinn?"

"Craig Oliver is Haydee's illegitimate son by that police commissioner," EB said. "That right, Bree?"

"That's right. Haydee promised to turn the child over to Creighton Oliver and his wife if Oliver helped her fake her own death."

Antonia shook her head. "Wow. Wow. How come the tabloids never picked up on that?"

"Police cover-up," EB said succinctly.

Antonia nodded. "Happens all the time."

Bree was tired and snappish. "It most certainly does not happen all the time. But it happened here. There wouldn't have been a cover-up if Haydee hadn't been pregnant. The child she bore five months after Norris attacked her was almost certainly Commissioner Oliver's. Craig Oliver seems to think so, anyway, since that was the man who raised him. Although unless somebody orders some paternity testing, no one will know for sure. Justine just shrugged when I asked her directly. And she's lied so much and so often I wouldn't trust it if she did say so. My guess is she's not sure who the father was, and doesn't care much."

"She must be a cold, cold woman." EB picked up a shrimp and set it down again. "So there was no murder at all, was there? All this fandango and Haydee Quinn's as alive as you or me."

Bree was grim and angry. "Murder was done, make no mistake about that. Three murders. Three innocents. Poor Flurry. Bagger Bill Norris, executed by the state for a crime that wasn't committed. And Charis Jefferson, whose dearest wish in life was to become a star like Lena Horne. It was her body that Alexander Bulloch burned that night by the banks of the Savannah River."

"Justine confessed to all this?" Antonia said. "How come she isn't in jail with poor Craig Oliver?"

"Don't waste any sympathy on Craig Oliver." Bree rubbed her eyes with the heels of both hands. "He admitted to having a role in Florida's death. Hunter may have to reduce the charge to manslaughter. I hope not. As to why Haydee isn't in jail . . . Hunter doesn't have any admissible evidence to charge her with a thing. Except complicity in the false reporting of a death, and the statute of limitations ran out on that years ago."

EB shoved the bowl of shrimp at her. "Eat something, child. You look like death warmed over."

"And then start from the beginning," Antonia said.

EB frowned. "She needs her sleep."

"You're not tired, are you, Bree?"

"I'm not tired, I'm mad as hell."

"She's not tired, EB. She said so herself. I can't believe this. *The* Craig Oliver arrested for murder. Are you sure he killed Florida Smith? Why did he do it?"

Bree ate a shrimp. Then another one. "I'm sure he did it. As to why he did it? I suppose he's the only one with the true answer, and Hunter says he's already lawyered up. So maybe we'll never know for sure. But I'll tell you this. I'm convinced that Haydee pressured Craig for the job on *Bitter Tide* so she could keep an eye on Flurry's research. She couldn't afford to have the truth come out after all these years—and Craig couldn't, either. Haydee didn't want to go to jail, and Craig's career wouldn't have survived the scandal."

Antonia ran her hands through her hair. "All that stuff Justine, I mean Haydee, told you about the sabotage?"

"Haydee herself. Mercury was right. She was trying her best to derail the shoot any way she could. Poor little Tyra was ripe for the suggestion that she was 'possessed' by Haydee's spirit. And it was easy for Haydee to flub her lines, trip and fall, mess up equipment. I almost feel sorry for Vincent White and Phillip Mercury. Almost."

"And when Flurry started getting too close to the truth?" EB asked.

Bree nodded. "Flurry had to go, too."

"Thing I can't get is a mamma turning in her own blood." EB looked grim. "Can't believe it."

"It started and ended with Haydee's ambition. Her ego. Her arrogance. She wanted to be a star. She grew up poor. Most important, she grew up poor in the '40s, Tonia, and neither one of us knows what it was like for smart, ambitious women then.

"For Haydee, with her looks, men were the only sure route to success. So that started early, and because Haydee wanted to get up and get out fast, it was often. She must have had some magic that I don't see now, with age and rampant selfishness having taken their toll on her face and personality, but men fell hard for her. Norris wasn't the first. Creighton Oliver and Alexander Bulloch weren't the last.

"Anyhow, she had a violent argument with Norris the night of July 3. She was pregnant. She wasn't going to be able to dance much longer. He wanted her to get rid of it. She wanted to use the baby for blackmail.

"Norris picked up the knife from the counter and slashed at her breasts. She still has the scars—they're faint, but they're there. Her blood was on the telephone at the bar, by the way, so we can confirm that she made a phone call. She called Oliver at home. Hunter can verify that with old records. I think Haydee demanded that

Oliver come and get her and help her get out of town. There's a witness statement from the dancer Charis Jefferson, now lost, that suggests Creighton arrived at the bar around one thirty and picked her up. Craig Oliver claims that Haydee told him his father refused to have anything to do with faking her death. I think that's true, and that initially, he refused.

"Did Haydee jump in the river in a fit of despair? Maybe. Justine is the only one who knows, and she's not talking. Did Creighton Oliver throw her in? I doubt it. She was pregnant with his child. My personal guess is that she slipped and fell. And the fisherman pulled her out.

"At the hospital she must have demanded to see Alexander Bulloch senior, and most important, Alex's mother, Consuelo. I think she told them the price of her leaving her son alone was to help fake her death. Haydee took it from there. She's nothing if not resourceful.

"I don't think the Bullochs were involved in the murder of Charis Jefferson. I think Haydee came up with that on her own, although they were certainly complicit in the disposal of the body. She appeared at young Alex's bedside, having provided a handy corpse, and Alex did what she asked. Whether he knew he was burning the body of an innocent victim or not, the whole affair tipped him into a breakdown."

"My Lord," EB said. "That poor Charis. How did Haydee get to her?"

"Haydee had a pretty decent setup. The Bullochs were well connected then. Their family physician was part owner of a funeral home. The physician, Dr. Warren, signed a death certificate, and there's hospital documents that show a body was transported to the funeral home the afternoon of July 3. Haydee agreed to turn the child she was carrying over to the Olivers after the baby was born, so Creighton Oliver ended up participating in a cover-up after all. Anyhow, Haydee had cash, and Haydee had a bus ticket. All she needed was a body to bury. She had a candidate—the one person who could have blown the whole story apart.

"I think once she had the Bullochs and Oliver on board, she called her best friend at the Tropicana Tide, Charis Jefferson, who had seen the white Buick pick up Haydee after the altercation with Norris. Haydee asked Charis to pack up her things for her and bring them to the funeral home.

"Craig Oliver says his mother planned to leave town on a bus to go north at this point, with money from Creighton Oliver. My guess is that she had a bunch of cash from the Bullochs, too. I don't have admissible proof that all this occurred, but we have supporting documents. Where it gets tricky is in the area of what happened next. Haydee knows. But Haydee isn't talking. I think Charis either asked Haydee for money or threatened to blow the whole thing apart. I'm as sure as anything that Haydee killed her, left her body in the funeral home, and showed up at Alexander Bulloch's bedside. I think she told him to burn the body. I also think she told him the baby was his, and that if he did this for her, they could run away together as they planned. So Alexander burned the body, Haydee skipped town without him, and the poor guy ended up spending a couple of years in what was euphemistically called a rest home."

"The police can't prove any of this?" Antonia demanded.

"They can probably prove everything up to who's responsible for Charis's murder," Bree said. "Haydee's lived too long and is too smart to confess to it now. But I'll tell you one thing: I'll go to my grave convinced that Haydee killed her. Haydee's medical records from the hospital and the autopsy report on Charis's body show nearly identical wound patterns. Who is most likely to have replicated that but Haydee herself?"

Antonia ran her hands through her hair again. It was beginning to look like a bird's nest. "Yeah, but Bree, was the autopsy report faked, too? You said Charis Jefferson was African-American. Haydee Quinn was white."

"Wouldn't have occurred to a coroner back then that a black woman and a white woman look the same inside," EB said. "Body was burned pretty good, from what they said."

Antonia pulled back. "You're kidding, of course."

EB smiled at Bree. "You ask your sister, Tonia. She knows."

Bree nodded. "You've never encountered old-style racism, Tonia. With a little discreet pressure from the commissioner's office to get the autopsy over and the body buried as fast as possible, you don't think that could have happened? I do. Charis was female, the same age as Haydee, and about the same height. A coroner who just wanted to get it over with wouldn't look much past that." Bree got up and stretched. She was beginning to feel the effects of her all-nighter. "I've got one more thing to do this afternoon. I'll see you all later."

"Hey!" Antonia rapped her knuckles on the table. "What about Craig Oliver killing Florida Smith?"

"Florida was getting too close to the truth. She was putting the pieces together, just the way we did. Flurry learned about the white Buick that picked up Haydee the night of the assault, traced the Buick to Creighton Oliver, and called Craig about it Saturday night. Craig called his mother. When Sammi-Rose Waterman whacked Flurry over the head on Monday, Justine—Haydee—grabbed the opportunity to confront Flurry in her trailer. Craig Oliver says Flurry ran out of the trailer clutching the manuscript and fell into the river. Me? I think Haydee pushed her and kept Craig from calling for help. Either way, they have the manuscript."

"Any water marks on it?" EB asked.

Bree's smile was tight. "Not a one." She'd left her tote bag on the floor near the kitchen table. She picked it up and slung it over her shoulder. "I have one last thing to do. I'll see y'all in a bit."

⸙

Most of the cemeteries in Savannah were serene, well-tended spaces. The Belle Glade cemetery wasn't one of them. It was small, the landscape ill tended, and the graves themselves neglected or forgotten. Bree stood outside the wrought iron gate for a long moment. Justine stood under a live oak, half hidden by a sweep of Spanish moss. She stared down at a small headstone.

Bree let herself in and followed the weedy gravel path on its winding way through the tombstones. She passed Haydee's angel weeping over the flat stone, and paused to run her hand over the angel's marble wing.

Justine looked up, startled at Bree's approach.

"You look surprised to see me," Bree said.

"What do you want?" Her voice was ugly.

"Did you think I was going to let things stand as they are?" Bree's hand went to the back of her head, where the hair was growing back too slowly. Maybe she could charge the woman with assault, if nothing else.

Justine fingered the peacock pin at her throat. "You can prove nothing," she said. Her voice was harsh.

"Maybe not in this life," Bree said pleasantly. "But surely in the next." She stood beside Justine and looked down at the headstone:

CONSUELO BULLOCH BELOVED MOTHER 1929 TO 1978

"Stuck-up bitch," Justine said.

Bree wasn't sure whether Justine was referring to her dead client or to her. It didn't really matter.

" 'Beloved Mother.' What a joke. Look at this place." She swept a contemptuous glare around the decrepit grounds.

Bree propped herself against a nearby tomb and slung her cane over one arm. "Dixie had a curious story to tell me."

"Another stuck-up bitch."

"She said you worked for Consuelo in the early '70s."

Justine raised her head. Her gaze was steady. A nasty smile curled her lips. "I had a bit of a dry spell in the thee-ay-ter. Movies, too. You might remember it. There were a couple of years when drama was moving from the grand old stories that I grew up on, to this modern stuff. For a while, nobody wanted me. So I was broke. Nothing new in that. I've been broke off and on most of my life. But Savannah had been good to me, one way or another. It was a place to get renewed." Her smile got nastier. "And to get myself a family lawyer."

Bree's gaze was just as steady. "You're lucky no one recognized you."

"Consuelo did."

And Franklin? Had Franklin known? Bree clenched her hands so tightly she could feel her nails sink into her palms.

Justine dropped her eyes to the ground. "The brats were too young, of course." Her fingertips brushed her cheeks. She ran her hands over her chin and nose. "And I'd had a little work done, right off. Wouldn't do to have the world recognize me as Haydee Quinn, would it? So Haydee had to go. Justine took her place."

The triumph in her voice chilled Bree to the bone. "So you came back and blackmailed Consuelo Bulloch into a job."

Justine wrinkled her nose in distaste. "Blackmail. Blackmail. Ugly word. But you see the world in an ugly way, Miss Fancy Lawyer Beaufort. The way I saw it.

The way I see it now, that woman owed me. I didn't have a whole lot to lose right then. Didn't matter to me if the whole town knew about the trick I'd pulled off. Consuelo Bulloch feared scandal more than anything. Stuck-up bitch." The smile got uglier. "You know I met her for the first time that night. After Billy pitched a fit in the Tropi and tried to mess me up. She was just like I thought she'd be. Nose in the air. Jealous. All in a hoorah over her precious baby boy. You know she had the nerve to tell Alex we could get married after all?" Justine lifted her chin, flung out her arms, and for an eerie moment, Bree saw what Consuelo must have looked like in life. Her voice took on a soft Southern drawl. "Now that I see how it is with you, Alex, I won't stand in your way. Go ahead. Marry her!" Justine let her arms drop with a contemptuous snort. "What does that little slut Tyra say? 'As if!' That's it. As if she really would have let baby Alex marry! As if I wanted to stick around this backwater town when I could go to New York City."

"It might have been true," Bree said quietly. "That she dropped her objections to your marriage."

"She didn't want to give me any money," Justine said. "That's what that was all about. She didn't want to fork it over then, or when I came back almost twenty years later."

"Which was when you thought you might tempt Alexander back into your life." This was a guess. Bree saw immediately that it'd hit home. "But that didn't work. Creighton Oliver didn't want to have anything to do with you, either."

"Most men do and did," Justine said reflectively. "Alexander? He was weak and crazy to boot. Creighton, he was different. Took me a little time to get him to come around with a proper amount of money to set me back up in Hollywood. But when he saw I meant to stick around at the Bullochs' . . ." She raised her hands, palms up, and clenched them. "He paid up. Didn't want to mess up that nice life he had with his wife and my son. But, don't worry, I'd find my baby boy again when he became a star," Justine said. "And you know the damn Bullochs were near broke themselves? Couldn't believe it. All that money gone. All that holier-than-thou attitude. And they didn't have a dime."

"Consuelo paid in a different way, didn't she?" Bree said. "So did Charis Jefferson. Do you come to gloat over her grave, too?"

"I haven't the faintest idea of what you're talking about."

"'Buried right next to each other.' Isn't that what you told me that first day in my office? Efficient, if nothing else, having two of your victims next to one another in death."

Justine's expression didn't change, but she hissed like a snake. "You can't prove a thing."

"You know how sophisticated forensic science is. Your work on *Bristol Blues* should have given you a pretty good idea of what a determined pathologist can do."

"Don't be absurd." She shifted impatiently. "What is it you want, Miss Beaufort?"

"Of course, it depends on how you killed her. She had a weak heart, the family said. She became dizzy. Slipped and fell in the bathtub. Struck her head. And she eventually died of it. Because somebody held her under. Just like Florida Smith." Bree took the tin box out of her pocket and opened it up. "Do you know what's in here? Bobby Lee Kowalski keeps mementos of his unsolved cases. Consuelo Bulloch had a fistful of hair in her hands when she fell in that tub. I wonder if Charis does, too." She held up the sealed evidence packet. The coil of hair inside was as black as a crow's wing. As black as a starless night. "Look familiar?"

"Damn you to hell," Justine said. "Get out of here. Get out!"

—∞—

"So I got out," Bree said into the cell phone. She was sitting in her car, outside the cemetery. Her first thought had been to call Hunter. "Left her standing alone in the cemetery, by the graves of two of her victims. I suppose Bagger Bill Norris is in a pauper's grave somewhere. Or the equivalent. Anyhow, she's gone now. A cab drew up a little while ago and picked her up."

"It'll be a tricky case to prove," Hunter said.

"Impossible, I should think. But she knows I know, Hunter. That's something, isn't it? And I made her turn over that peacock pin." The pin lay next to her, in the passenger seat. It seemed to her that the bird's ruby eye looked reproachful.

"We'll look into it. To tell you the truth, I don't think

the county would have held on to evidence from a sixty-year-old murder case. We'll see."

"It's like hunting old Nazis."

"Come again?"

Bree sighed. "Once in a while, even now, there'll be a news story about how somebody's identified a ninety-year-old guy who was a guard at Bergen-Belsen or some other awful place. Justice demands accountability. But there again, there's this ninety-year-old guy, frail, sick, *old*. So the state puts him through a trial, and he can barely sit upright on the witness stand." Bree rubbed her forehead with her free hand. "I don't know what to do."

"Leave it to me. It's not your problem anymore. I'm not sure why you made it your problem in the first place. You need to come home. You've been pushing yourself too hard. It's late. I'm a little worried about you. I'm going to pick up something for us to eat, and I'll meet you at the town house. That okay with you?"

Suddenly, she wanted nothing more on earth than Hunter's arms around her. "That sounds more than okay. That sounds wonderful. But could we make it tomorrow? I've got pleadings to write tonight and a court appearance in the morning."

"Tomorrow, then. Will Antonia be at the theater?"

She could hear both the smile and the hope in his voice. "Every day and every night for the rest of the week."

"Just wanted to know how much food to bring."

"Till then." Bree clicked off.

She had a Celestial Court case in the morning. Finally, she had a defense.

It was getting dark. She picked up the jeweled peacock and slipped out of the car. Without the sun, the air was cold. The wind picked up, bringing the scent of rain. Bree held the brooch in the palm of her hand and said firmly, "Mrs. Bulloch? Consuelo?"

At first, Bree was sure she wasn't going to get through. Then, Consuelo's shadow stirred and shifted, wrapping her hand in a dark swirl of something that Bree could only think of as Not. Not human, not earthly, not real, as she knew reality. She didn't have words to describe it. She had no reference point.

Miss Winston-Beaufort?

"Yes," Bree said. "It's me. I discovered how you died, Mrs. Bulloch. I'm extremely sorry."

Treachery.

"Yes. The worst kind. Mrs. Bulloch, I'm going to schedule your appeal. I want to let you know what I'm going to say in your defense."

My treachery. I regret . . . I'm so sorry . . .

"Genuine penitence is a very good thing for the court to hear, Mrs. Bulloch. So that will help. There's something else, though." Bree hesitated. "You hated Haydee Quinn."

Bad for my boy.

"Yes, she probably was. Haydee claims you would have allowed them to marry, the night she came to you for help after Bill Norris stabbed her. Is that so?"

Bad for my boy. Worse for my boy without her.

Bree nodded. "You loved your son Alexander. That's really clear. And it seems to have been unselfish. I just wanted you to know that I'll do my best for you."

The wraith faded in her hands to nothing.

Bree went home to prepare her case.

Epilogue

"You've lost weight since Lavinia made this for you." Ron shook out the supple red velvet robe that was mandated for counsel appearing before the angelic justices. Bree slipped into it. The hem and lapels were intricately worked with gold embroidery. The two of them were on the seventh floor of the Chatham County Courthouse. It was Wednesday morning, three weeks since Justine Coville had walked into the Bay Street office and made a claim on Bree's time and pity.

"I'll gain it back once I get this bloody cast off."

Ron rolled his eyes. "That makes no sense at all. What does the cast have to do with it? It happened to Leah, too, you know. She slimmed right down. Like a greyhound." He bent forward and looked into her face. "Something wrong?"

"There's a price to pay for the work I'm doing, Ron. I'm not sure I'm willing to pay it."

"I see." His tone was noncommittal. The silence stretched on until Bree couldn't stand it anymore. "Ron," she said urgently, "can I quit? Can I?"

"Of course you can." He smoothed the gown over her shoulders with a gentle hand. "There's a process for it, like there is for everything else. If you do quit, you won't remember us. You won't remember any of this. It will be as if it never happened. But otherwise?" He stepped back. He smiled at her. "No penalty."

Bree adjusted the high, stiff collar with one hand. She'd bundled her hair into a bun at the back of her neck, to hide the spot where they'd shaved her skull in the hospital. It was growing back, but not fast enough. Her leg was doing fine, though. She whacked the floor with her cane. "I think I can leave this outside the courtroom."

"There's that big escalator to negotiate. Better carry it just in case. Besides, the justices are supposed to be totally impartial—but I personally think the Brave But Injured Warrior is a great attitude. Keep the cane."

Bree grinned. "Maybe you're right." She sighed. "Okay. I'm ready."

"We've got a few minutes. Mind if we stop and see Goldstein? He wants a word."

"Sure."

Bree followed Ron down the hallway and into the great vaulted space. As the heavy oak door shut silently behind, she heard Goldstein shout, "Ha! Aha!" Several of the monks looked up in mild surprise. One waved his quill pen jauntily at her. A few of them clapped. Goldstein rustled down the flagstone aisle, his sandals slapping merrily on the stone. "My dear, my dear!" He enfolded her in a hug. He smelled like paper and damp wool, with a slight whiff of incense. A bit of feather from his wing got up Bree's nose, and she sneezed.

"Three pending judgments closed at once! I believe it to be a record! Thank you for dropping in, my dear. I know you're due in court in a few moments, but I just had to offer my congratulations."

"You could have sent an e-card," Ron said. "If you were online, that is. They've got some great ones at thankyoulord.com. Choirs of cherubim singing away. The whole bit."

"What? And miss the embarrassed-but-pleased expression on her face?" Goldstein let her go and clasped his hands. "Norris—first circle in Hell, not bad considering his checkered past. Alexander Bulloch, first circle in Heaven, not bad, either, considering the charge of abusing a corpse. Poor Charis Jefferson—she wasn't pending, but I know she's as pleased as Punch. As for Consuelo herself . . . well, we shall see. Are you ready to argue, my dear?"

"It's a bit of a change of pace," Bree said. "I'm not filing an appeal; I'm filing for a summary judgment. So I adjusted the language in the pleadings."

"The very best of luck," Goldstein beamed. "The very best."

Minutes later, Bree descended the long silver escalator to the floor of the courtroom. On either side, the high walls held moving murals of Consuelo's life. She saw Alexander as a small child in his mother's lap. Consuelo at her wedding, stiff with pride and joy.

Consuelo and Haydee, backs arched like spitting cats.

Caldecott and Beazley lounged behind the solid oak table for the defense. Bree took her place on the opposite side of the aisle, set her briefcase down, and stacked her pleadings in order. The massive bench loomed in front of them, carved with readings from the Koran, the Bible, and the Torah.

The room reverberated with the sound of a mellow gong. All the lawyers rose. An immense golden sphere took shape behind the bench. The winged scales of justice appeared on the thick marble slab that covered the dais.

The golden light behind the dais paused and seemed to regard the cane Bree leaned upon in a kindly way.

Then the great Voice rang out, "Proceed."

"Your Honor," Bree said. "I am representing Consuelo Bingham Bulloch, a woman who loved her son completely and unselfishly. We are here to ask for mercy."

<hr/>

"That went pretty well, I think." Bree shrugged herself out of her robe and folded it carefully before handing it to Ron. Ron punched the Down button for the elevator. "Good thing you took the cane. Helped with the sympathy vote. Caldecott had a couple of zingers up his sleeve. Might have gone the other way."

"Purgatory," Bree said. "I asked for the first circle of Heaven."

"I think you should be thankful we got what we did."

"You're right. The woman was a complete bigot in some ways." Bree sighed. "A product of her time, I suppose. Which is no excuse."

The doors whisked open, and they stepped in. Bree fell into abstraction, only rousing herself as they came to a stop on the first floor. The case was over. Justine's fate was in hands other than her own. Consuelo's case had been heard, for good or for ill. Florida Smith's murder case would wind its way through the temporal courts. Bree sincerely hoped Justine would be held to account for her role in that. And she would drop in, now and again, on the brave and honorable Bobby Lee Kowalski.

The case was over.

"The thing is," she said to Ron, "I really want to know what happened to Dent."

"Excuse me?"

Bree looked up. She'd seen the young lawyer in the elevator before. At Huey's maybe or the gym. The woman smiled at her. "You were asking about a dent?" Ron was right next to her, so close, in fact, that Bree knew he wasn't visible.

"Sorry. Just thinking aloud."

"No problem," the woman stepped aside so that Bree could precede her out the door. "You're Bree Beaufort, aren't you?"

"Yes, I am." Bree hooked her cane over her arm and held out her hand.

"Margery Slack. Heard you took quite a thwack on the head a couple of weeks ago."

———∞∞∞———

"Which is just fine," Bree said bitterly as she and Ron walked back through the fresh morning to the Angelus office. "I'll bet Margery's already on Facebook with forty of her closest friends letting them know I talk to myself in elevators."

"You accomplished a lot with this case. Goldstein's not what you'd call an indiscriminate praiser. He hasn't let out a 'Hosanna!' since before the Flood."

"Very funny," Bree grumbled. They stopped at the iron gate in front of the house at 666 Angelus Street. The sun was out. The spheres worked into the wrought iron fence seemed to spin the clear and sunny air.

The cemetery was as dank and gloomy as ever.

Bree opened the gate and let herself in. Ron followed her. They stopped at the newest grave. It hadn't been there when they'd left for the Court that morning.

The marker read:

HAYDEE QUINN
b.1930————————————d.
The Evil Men Do Lives After Them

Mary Stanton is at work on the fifth Beaufort & Company novel, *Angel Condemned*. As Claudia Bishop, she is the author of twenty mystery novels, including the popular Hemlock Falls Mysteries. She is the senior editor of four successful mystery anthologies, including *A Merry Band of Murderers*. Stanton divides her time between a working farm in upstate New York and a small house in West Palm Beach, Florida. She loves to hear from readers and can be reached at www.marystanton .com or www.claudiabishop.com.

Edited by **#1 *New York Times* Bestselling Author**

CHARLAINE HARRIS
and
TONI L. P. KELNER

Death's Excellent Vacation

New York Times bestselling authors Charlaine Harris, Katie MacAlister, and Jeaniene Frost—plus Lilith Saintcrow, Jeff Abbott, and more—send postcards from the edge of the paranormal world.

With an all-new Sookie Stackhouse story and twelve other original tales, editors Charlaine Harris and Toni L. P. Kelner bring together a stellar collection of tour guides who offer vacations that are frightening, funny, and touching for the fanged, the furry, the demonic, and the grotesque. Learn why it really can be an endless summer—for immortals.

penguin.com

M723T0610

NEW FROM NATIONAL BESTSELLING AUTHOR
Madelyn Alt

Home for a Spell

Indiana's newest witch, Maggie O'Neill, needs a
new apartment. But when she finally discovers a
chic abode, Maggie's dream of new digs turns into
a nightmare: The apartment manager is found dead
before she can even sign the lease. And Maggie finds
herself not only searching for a new home—but for
a frightfully clever killer.

penguin.com